For Papa, who taught me to love books
I hope there's Kindle in Heaven :)

PROLOGUE

"**G**ot everything?"

Rosalie Underwood answered Clyde's question with an enthused smile. They met each other halfway, kissing under the rising Louisiana sun. Next to them on the sidewalk, Rosalie's single suitcase tipped over onto its side. She had spent the better half of last night stuffing it with as many belongings as possible. She needed to be packed and ready to go come dawn.

Clyde hadn't given a time, and she didn't want to leave him waiting outside.

Worse, she didn't want to alert Ma. It would only lead to another heated confrontation. Their fourth in less than a week. The most recent one had shoved Rosalie over the edge. She reached her breaking point and snapped. She made a decision she had threatened in the past, but never gone through with: she was running away with Clyde.

"Get in," he said in his deep baritone. He clicked the tiny remote on his key chain and walked around to the car's driver side. "If we roll out now we'll be halfway there by tonight."

Rosalie paused for a quick second to release a tremor of excitement. She had never crossed the Louisiana state border, let alone traveled to a big city like Baltimore. For the seventeen years she had been on this earth, she had been stuck in St. Aster. She assumed she would be for the rest of her life. Just like her ma and her grandma before her.

But now everything was changing. Within the next two days, she would be starting her life over again with Clyde.

"My wallet," said Rosalie. She glanced in her crossbody bag and found only her lip gloss and cell phone. She looked over her shoulder at the narrow shotgun house Ma was proud to own. The house was silent and the curtains were drawn. If she snuck inside really fast, the chances of being heard were slim to none…

"I'll be back."

Clyde shook his head but said nothing. He didn't need to in order to express his opinion of Ma. He hated her. And she hated him. The relationship between her boyfriend and Ma was contentious at best. Downright hostile at worst. Ma hated the rebellious streak Clyde brought out of her. Clyde hated the rules and boundaries Ma set. Ma thought Rosalie had no business running the streets with a guy six years her senior. Clyde thought Ma was a hypocritical, mean-spirited nag.

Rosalie agreed with Clyde. Ma's primary goal was to keep them apart. She refused to give in to the dictatorial rule. She was a grown woman—sort of. In another four months she would turn eighteen. That was close enough.

She squared her shoulders, stepped forward toward Ma's house, and didn't look back. Her key twisted in the lock and the door clicked open. Her petite body slipped between the thin crack and she hesitated for a second longer. The living room and hallway were both empty. She slunk toward the staircase, moving lightly on her feet like a dancer.

Every other step she stopped and listened. No sound. Ma was either asleep or in the bathroom. She continued onto the second floor landing, tiptoeing by Ma's room. In her own bedroom, she found her wallet under her bed and stuffed it into her purse. She crawled to the window and peered onto the street below. Clyde waited in his car, bobbing his head to his music. She smiled watching him.

"You're really leaving with him."

Rosalie froze on her knees by the windowsill. The smile dropped from her face and she avoided turning around. The stern but syrupy voice contradicted itself, but then again, so did Ma.

"You'd be stupid to go," she continued with a bluntness that cut deep. "If you leave with him, you're going to regret it."

"It's too late. I'm going." Rosalie zipped her crossbody purse and rose to her feet. The teenage fear inside of her held her back from facing Ma, but after a few tentative seconds passed, she broke free from it. She spun around and glared. "I packed my stuff. He's outside."

"I know he is. I have windows. And if you go, you're a fool."

"I'm a fool anyway," Rosalie replied. "Isn't that what you always say? I'm a fool for being with him?"

Ma's lips pinched into a smile. "You don't have to believe me now. But you'll see. You'll come back to me crying and begging."

"I'm done," Rosalie said coldly. She scanned her bedroom for any last belongings. Tension zinged through her entire body, shooting up her toes to her brain. She ignored the strain on her temples and stiffness in her neck. "You're not gonna see me again 'cause I'm not coming back."

Ma sneered and Rosalie's anger surged in a hot flash that left her flesh warm and clammy. She rushed for the door, but Ma blocked its width.

"You can't go," she said. "You're only seventeen. I'll call the police."

"Go ahead," challenged Rosalie. "You can't stop me."

She shoulder checked Ma on her way out. The insolence was unlike her, but it was too late. Her temper had already soared beyond rational reach. She stormed down the hall and skipped steps on the staircase. Halfway down she heard the pad of Ma's steps scurrying after her. She didn't turn and look. She shot for the front door.

"Rosalie!" Ma called in a tone that broke. She stopped on the last stair and drew a shuddery breath. "You're not welcomed back! I don't care what foolishness he puts you through."

Rosalie wrenched the door open, the summer warmth a rush that blew onto her cheeks. Clyde's car idled by the curb waiting on her to hop in. Behind her, Ma put her foot down and gave her an ultimatum. She hovered between two different futures, building the resolve to choose one and never look back.

She hesitated long enough to scan the family pictures on the wall. The one hanging by the door was from over ten years ago. In the photo, she sat in Ma's lap and beamed at the camera with missing front teeth. It was back when everybody called her Ma's mini-me. When she was proud of the nickname. Skin as smooth and brown, and hair as thick and coarse, a time she couldn't wait to grow up and be just like Ma.

Then she remembered *who* snapped the photo and any nostalgia soured. Ma's boyfriend at the time, Terrance, had pulled out his Polaroid camera and asked them to pose for a picture. She hadn't known it as he snapped away, but in a matter of weeks, he would wreak havoc on their lives. He and the other men in and out of their home over the years. The men Ma had invited inside…

Her choice was clearer than ever.

"Bye, Ma," she said, crossing the threshold outside. Her walk toward Clyde's car was stilted and unnatural, like a little girl walking in her mother's heels for the first time. She slid into the passenger seat and stared straight ahead. Though she said nothing, her silence communicated enough. She was ready to go.

Clyde shifted gears and pressed on the gas. The car shot forward and Ma's house began to sink out of view. Rosalie closed her eyes and inhaled a fresh breath. Her earlier excitement slowly trickled in and her mouth spread into a triumphant smile.

"What's that look for?" Clyde snuck her a glance, his heavily hooded eyes sparking with an amusement of his own. "She give you any problems?"

"It doesn't matter anymore. Nothing she says matters anymore," Rosalie boasted. The realization sunk in and she released a girlish laugh. "Now we can do whatever we want."

"Uh-huh, *whatever* we want."

Rosalie rolled her eyes, but her smile lingered on her lips. She couldn't wait until they arrived in Baltimore to start their new life together. She couldn't wait to be his wife. Things would probably be rocky in the beginning as they scrimped and saved. Clyde was going to take on a job at his cousin's auto shop and she was going to start classes at the community college.

But it was going to be worth it. Her heart fluttered in confirmation.

"Tell me about Bmore," she requested. She leaned forward so the AC would blow in her face. Air sputtered from the vents and cooled her skin, breezing through her fluffy, tightly coiled curls in equal measure. "You said your cousin's place isn't far from the auto shop?"

"Couple blocks. One stop on the subway."

"I've never been on a subway before."

"It's a'ight. Nothing special."

The eager lilt in Rosalie's tone revealed her age. The immaturity she often tried to hide from Clyde. Once she saw him shrug off the subway, she cleared her throat and tapered her excitement. If he didn't think it was anything special, she probably shouldn't either. He knew what he was talking about.

Clyde must've sensed her sudden shift in mood. He cut her a sideways glance, giving her a once over. His hand found hers in her lap. She stared at his thicker fingers curling around hers, and almost smiled.

"You've gotta chill, Ros. You'll see when we get there."

"I know. I can't wait."

"Just sit back. We'll be there tomorrow. And you'll be Mrs. Mackie."

"Rosalie Mackie sounds good."

"Uh-huh. Better than Underwood."

"Way better than Underwood," Rosalie agreed, staring off outside the window. The surrounding green of the marshland was invisible to her as instead she disappeared in her head and imagined their small, intimate courtroom ceremony. They didn't need anybody else there. It was their lives becoming one, no one else's. Besides, eloping was romantic—an endearing story she could tell their children someday.

Clyde dialed up the music, the speakers so loud they caused a vibration in the car. They continued down the road leading out of St. Aster, whizzing by the termite-bitten town sign at the border. For a second time that warm summer morning, Rosalie said goodbye. She twisted in her seat to look at her past shrinking behind her, and she smirked, certain she would never be back again.

CHAPTER ONE

Seven years later…

Five dollars and sixty-two cents. The dismal number stared up at Rosalie from the light of her phone screen. She labored a breath and pressed the "make a transfer" button on the banking app. The quick transfer between her savings account to her checking account took less than a minute, but it didn't make it any less demoralizing. She couldn't borrow from her savings forever.

For a while now, she had been robbing Peter to pay Paul. Cancelling a cell phone service to afford an electric bill. Asking for an extension on a school loan payment to keep from losing the car. Whatever it took to feed and clothe Remi. Her brief study in college as a finance major helped her stretch pennies as long as possible. Though she struggled, she knew she would figure it out eventually. In the meantime, she needed to keep her head on her shoulders and put on a brave face.

She smiled at the five-year-old in the car's rearview mirror, offering motherly reassurance. Remi stared back, dark brown eyes blank and little mouth curved into a frown. Since their lives disintegrated into ruins, she hadn't bothered to hide her unhappiness; she was too much of a precocious child to do so.

Rosalie couldn't blame her. Things had been bad for a couple years now, even before Clyde abandoned them…

"Mommy, I'm hungry."

"I know, baby. We're almost there. Grandmommy Lacie said she'd cook us dinner."

"But I'm hungry *now*."

Rosalie staved off a sigh as she reached for the cheap polka-dotted tote bag perched in the front passenger seat. She called it her mommy bag, a wealth of lifesavers when on the go with Remi. It had moist towelettes for sticky situations, juice boxes and water bottles, coloring books and crayons, and miniature baggies carefully portioned with snacks like pretzels and apple slices.

"Here you go."

"I don't want raisins."

Remi turned her cheek to the offering, stuck in the car seat or else she'd likely skip off. She liked to do that these days in a show of defiance, protesting Clyde being gone and Rosalie being broke. Rosalie understood *why* she behaved this way, even if it drove her stress levels through the roof.

At age five, she'd caused Ma the same type of headaches. If anything, Remi was karma. Despite her best efforts, she'd wound up in the exact same predicament as Ma after all. She was an Underwood at heart.

"It's raisins or cheese crackers, Remi. That's all we have left 'til we reach Grandmommy's," Rosalie said, starting the engine. They sat parked beside gas pump number three, off the shoulder of the highway at another random truck stop. After a while, they blurred together, no different from any others. "Another hour, and we'll be there."

"There's food in the store." Remi pointed toward the window, where through the glass, she could see the gas station convenience store some twenty feet away.

"Remi, do you remember what we talked about the other day?"

She stubbornly shook her head side to side, her braided ponytails swinging at her ears.

"*Remi.*"

"Uh-huh. We don't have any money for stores."

"Bingo," Rosalie confirmed. She stared at her in the rearview mirror again, observing her puckered pout. "But we will soon, okay? In our new home, I'm going to work really hard, and we're going to go back to how things were."

"But with no Daddy?"

Rosalie's breath stalled, clogged in her throat. "Daddy's not around right now. We'll be okay anyway. Me and you."

"And Grandmommy Lacie."

"Right, and Grandmommy Lacie," repeated Rosalie. Nerves swarmed her stomach at any mention of Ma, buzzing in a frenzy crazier than bees to honey. It had been years since they'd seen each other, and up until a couple weeks ago, just as long since they'd even said a word. She hated to come crawling back.

Now she was a failure just like the other women in the family. The first phone call she made to Ma was full of awkward silences, where she closed her eyes, gave up her pride, and cringed through admitting fault. Ma relished in her failure. While she didn't directly say the words, Rosalie knew better than to believe some part of Ma wasn't pleased; however small, a kernel of satisfaction silently gloated, "I told you so."

On the passenger seat, next to her mommy bag, her phone pinged its text message notification. In a speak-of-the-devil moment, Rosalie reached for the phone and swiped to read the message from Ma.

Are y'all almost here? How far out?

Rosalie glanced at the GPS mounted on her dash and texted a short reply. Ma responded instantly, her phone pinging again in her hand.

It would be nice if you kept me informed...

"Is that Grandmommy Lacie?" Remi asked.

"Yes."

"Tell her I said hi and I am hungry."

"Sure, baby." Rosalie swallowed against the constricted feel in her throat, voice now tight. Remi had no idea any tension existed between them, and Rosalie preferred to keep it that way. She didn't need to know her mommy and grandmommy struggled to remain amicable, much less loving. She quickly typed another reply, but at the last second, deleted the words. Instead she left Ma on read. The obvious slight gave her petty satisfaction and the grip on her airway loosened.

For the rest of the drive, reentering the highway lined by dense trees, she turned up the Elmo sing-along music to distract Remi, and she focused on clearing her head. She didn't want to think about Ma anymore, or about Clyde and their disastrous marriage. She just wanted to finish the long three-day drive and make it to St. Aster.

⁀∞⁀

It came as no surprise that in seven years little about St. Aster had changed. The town still operated off of a few stoplights, its downtown area two streets of antique buildings built over a century ago. Rosalie drove by the elementary school she once spent hours at, rocking on the swings and skipping through games of hopscotch. The screeching bell that rang whenever school let out was a sound fresh in her ears even after so many years. Remi pointed out a dog walking down the sidewalk with its owner. Rosalie glanced and recognized Mr. Porter, the town plumber who had lived his entire life in St. Aster.

Just like everyone else. And now she was like them too. Another relic in the nowhere town, doomed to stay there for decades. Even when she tried to escape, St. Aster reeled her back in. The curse was inevitable, hardly worth a fight. Her best bet was to find a job anywhere doing anything, save up every red cent she earned, and focus on giving Remi stability. At least they were far away from the awful memories Bmore brought them; on their old block, every corner they turned presented fresh pain from the bad times they endured. In St. Aster, Remi wouldn't be reminded of 1:00 a.m. screaming matches.

Her phone pinged with another batch of text notifications. More texts from Ma asking for their whereabouts and making passive aggressive remarks about their stay. Rosalie ignored them as she'd been doing since their last gas station stop. The pings had begun to stir more nerves out of her already roiling stomach. Earlier, she had looked at the dozens of miles left until they reached their destination and blew a steadying breath that she wouldn't need to see Ma just yet.

Those miles wound down to nothing. Her house was a couple blocks away. Their tense reunion a couple of minutes from happening. The failure would be realer than ever. She could no longer put off the reality, or savor the time left before its acknowledgment. The next chapter was here. No more excuses. No more delays. Just failure.

Rosalie rattled a breath and tightened her grip on the steering wheel. The traffic light up ahead required she hook a left onto Lawson Street. Another block down before she reached Ma's. Rather than make the left, Rosalie braked at the first open street parking. The snap decision bought her more time. She turned off the engine and sat there staring out the window at Main Street.

"I don't see Grandmommy's house," Remi mumbled.

"It's nearby, baby."

"Why did we stop?"

"Are you still hungry?"

Remi nodded, small fingers picking at her favorite stuffed animal's fur. During the last leg of their road trip, she had resorted to nibbling on crackers, but the snack wasn't filling enough. Rosalie unclicked her seat belt and got out of the car.

"We're going to eat a quick bite at this restaurant."

"But, Mommy, you said—"

"I know what I said, Remi baby. It turns out this is a special exception. Okay?"

"Okay."

Rosalie lifted Remi from the car seat and set her safely on the sidewalk. She hadn't checked what restaurant they were about to walk into. The Lawson Street sign had loomed near and panic struck her as she slammed on the brakes. She happened to pull over in front of Ady's Creole Café.

In its heyday, Ady's was a St. Aster gem. The bright green building stood out among the drab red brick on Main Street. The restaurant sign had as much personality; hanging off the eave by chain, a cartoon crawfish wore a chef's hat and a smile. Day in and day out, the small and squat restaurant drew dozens in town. It wasn't out of the ordinary to see a line forming down the block.

None of that was the case anymore. Rosalie surveyed the chipped paint on the building's worn-down wooden slats and then tipped her head upward to stare at the faded cartoon crawfish. Even the chain had rusted. The windows, once a crystal clear view of customers crowded at tables, were foggy and smudged. The fragrant scents of garlic and pepper were no more, replaced by a less appetizing fishy smell. What had happened to Ady's in the last seven years?

"Mommy, what's that smell?" Remi pinched her nose and shuddered in disgust. "It smells like fishies."

"I'm guessing it's the restaurant, baby."

"I don't want to eat there. It's gross."

Rosalie spotted the crooked Help Wanted sign in the window. What started as an impromptu stop outside Ady's began to transform into a visit that was potentially productive. She was killing two birds with one stone. Not only was she buying herself more time before reaching Ma's house, she was job hunting. The lunch was worth a shot.

Her hand tightened on Remi's. "I'm sure the food's delicious. I've eaten here before when I was a girl."

That was the truth. She had eaten at Ady's time or two during childhood. Ma hated the establishment, but even she couldn't help when it was chosen as the venue for different celebrations. From birthday parties to formal dinners, it was the restaurant most in town chose. Even if it now looked run-down, the food still had to be amazing.

Walking into Ady's, Rosalie discovered how wrong she was. The door swung shut behind her and Remi, chasing away any natural light. The once bright and familial tone was gone. The restaurant was dark, sparsely lit by melted candles on mantels. The tables were empty from front to back. She glanced at the unmanned hostess podium and noticed a sheet of dust atop the stacked menus.

But it was what hung above the podium that stunned her most. Rosalie gasped at the portrait memorial of Adeline Fontaine. Her kind smile looked down on the room, crow's-feet bracketing her pale green eyes. Beneath her picture it read: In Loving Memory, 1966–2017.

"Can I help you?"

The normally helpful question was asked in the curtest tone possible. Rosalie tore her eyes off the portrait in time to watch the lone waitress on shift walk up. Her straight-from-the-box fire-engine red hair swung in sync with her steps.

"Hi, table for two," answered Rosalie. "Do you have a booster seat for my daughter?"

"I can prolly grab a box or something. Take your pick where you wanna sit. It's open seating."

That was no understatement. Rosalie surveyed the dining area again. The two dozen empty tables were a pitiful sight. At Remi's request, she chose one by the window. The waitress disappeared into the back and emerged with what looked like a plastic carton for Remi to sit on.

"Best I can do," she said, setting up the carton on Remi's side of the booth. It wasn't a traditional booster seat by any means, but it gave Remi the height she needed to sit comfortably at the table. "I'm Zoe, by the way. Never seen y'all before, so I'm guessing you need a sec to look at the menu."

"We do, thanks. But mind if I ask, Adeline Fontaine—the Ady who owns this café—is she no longer with us?"

Zoe's deadpan expression morphed into a somber look for a brief second. "She passed a year back. Right outta nowhere. Some sorta aneurysm or something."

"Oh."

Rosalie wasn't sure why that information left her speechless. She hadn't known Ady personally. Her childhood visits to the café had been few and far between. The extent of her interactions with the woman were quick and simple. Things like Ady calling her an adorable doll or complimenting her on how well-behaved she was. She knew little else about the woman other than she was considered the best chef in town, ran her own restaurant, and had a son.

Across the table, Remi had taken to snapping and unsnapping her pink crossbody purse. The purse was a gift from Grandmommy Erma, Clyde's mother. Because it was pink and sparkly, two of Remi's favorite things, she insisted on carrying it everywhere.

"When do I see Grandmommy Lacie?"

Rosalie watched Remi fiddle with the strap of the purse. "Soon, baby. We're going to eat first. Then Grandmommy Lacie's."

"Is she nice like Grandmommy Erma?"

"She will be to you."

"I miss Grandmommy Erma."

"How about we call her tonight?"

"Okay."

When Zoe returned to take their orders, Rosalie carefully selected the most affordable items. She ordered the day's special for herself—a cup of gumbo—and a grilled cheese sandwich and chocolate milk for Remi. Before Zoe could walk off again, she asked the next question that had been on her mind since pulling up in front of Ady's.

"I saw the hiring sign in the window. Can I have an application?"

For the first time, Zoe cracked a smile. It wasn't warm or friendly, but it was a start. "We don't got any applications. You've gotta talk to Nick. He's running things now."

"When can I speak with him?"

"Gotta catch him when you can. Now might be your best bet. Pretty sure he's holed up in the back office."

"We'll eat first. Thanks."

Remi waited for the waitress to disappear as if she understood what was going on. No longer interested in her purse, she wrinkled her nose from across the table. "Mommy, are you gonna work here?"

"Maybe. If they'll hire me."

"If they do, Mommy, you can get rid of the fishy smell."

Rosalie couldn't suppress her smile. "How'd you know that's the first thing I'd do?"

The rest of lunch was uneventful. By its end, Rosalie eyeballed the $14.21 ticket and hesitantly handed over her debit card. Zoe directed her to head to the back and knock on the door next to the utility closet if she wanted to talk to Nick. Rosalie followed directions, bringing Remi along for the job inquiry.

She vaguely remembered Nicholas Fontaine. The image in her head was one of a boy a year or two older than she was. If she remembered correctly, he inherited Ady's pale green eyes and loosely waved hair. The similarities ended there; the rest of him was his father, bronze in skin tone with features square and masculine. She knew nothing else about him other than the

Fontaines divorced when she was a teenager, and his father soon left town.

She held her fist up and knocked twice. Beyond the door, the office was silent. Was Zoe mistaken claiming he was inside?

Rosalie knocked again, expecting more silence in answer.

Instead, a male's drowsy croak answered her. "Come in."

CHAPTER TWO

Nick Fontaine assumed the rapping at his door was his imagination. Vivid dreams were no stranger to him. He had once dreamt about a giant talking crawfish. As real as it'd seemed at the time, it turned out to be fake.

He stayed where he was, seated at the desk in the room, surrounded by stacks of papers. None of them fazed him, though. How could they? His eyes were closed. Not that he didn't ignore them when they were open too. Over the last year since Ady's had become his, he had gotten pretty damn good at it.

The knocking persisted. Whoever it was wasn't going away. He suppressed the urge to keep napping. Sitting up, a single white sheet of paper stuck to his cheek, he mumbled for the mystery person to enter. He wiped his mouth free of any possible drool, using his rolled-up shirtsleeve, and he tried his best to at least *appear* busy. If he sat up as straight as an arrow and shuffled a thick sheaf of paper, he'd seem swamped. He did just that as the knob turned and the door opened.

He expected his ever-snappy waitress Zoe or his bumbling cook, Jefferson. Possibly Que, the mediocre busboy. Nobody else came to visit him except…

Nick's blood pressure spiked thinking about the others. Everybody else. The folks in town who felt it was their place to stop him, any time, any place, and offer their pitying condolences for losing Mom. He always thanked them in quick, rehearsed gratitude. Then he changed the subject using his natural Fontaine charm. That was his best asset.

But, as the door opened and Nick fixed a dimpled grin onto his face, the person who entered was a surprise—or should he say people? It was a woman clutching the hand of a small girl who must've been around his daughter Maxie's age. The mother and daughter looked like twins in a way, a reflection of past and present. Skin a deep sienna brown and hair tight and thick in texture, they stared at him with matching catlike eyes. The woman's mouth opened to speak, lips distracting in their heart shape and prominent Cupid's bow.

He was listening.

"Afternoon, Mr. Fontaine, are you busy right now?"

"Uh, no. Not at all. Come in." He shuffled more papers for dramatic effect. He watched as the two crossed the room and stopped in front of his desk. The more he stared at the woman, surveying the beauty mark on her left cheekbone and the delicate curve of her jawline, the more familiar she looked. He'd seen this woman before. Somewhere. He cleared his throat and let his dimples and grin do the talking. "What can I do for you? Is this about the food? Jefferson's in the kitchen. He has his off days. Mistakes basil for parsley all the time."

"The cooking was, um, fine."

"I had a grilled cheese sandwich," the little girl piped up. Her hair was styled in four ponytails thicker than rope, one beside each ear and another two in the back. She wore a cotton swing dress girlier than Maxie would ever tolerate, tiny bows patterned across the fabric. And she was clean. Cleaner than Maxie an hour into the day.

"Grilled cheese sammich, eh? Safe choice. Smart girl."

The girl skipped the compliment, scrunching her nose. "Why do you say it like that?"

"Say what like what?"

"Sammich."

"*Remi*," the woman sighed. "Remember when we agreed not to interrupt grown-ups?"

"It's alright. I've got a daughter her age. I think. How old are you, Remi?"

"Five."

"Maxie's five."

"Is Maxie here to play?"

"Anyway, Mr. Fontaine," the woman cut in. "Sorry to bother, but my name's Rosalie Underwood. I'm new to town and saw the hiring sign in the window. What position are you filling?"

"Underwood." He knew that name. In a small town like St. Aster, he knew just about everyone's. The Underwoods were a family who lived a couple yards off the bayou. Was she related?

In a sweep of sudden memory, he finally placed her face. *Rosalie Underwood.* Daughter of Lacie Underwood, she had lived in St. Aster for years. What did she mean by new to town?

"You're nobody new," he said, chuckling. His fingers found his loose waves, sifting through them out of habit. "You're Ms. Lacie's daughter, right? How's she and Henry doing?"

"I've been away long enough to be new again."

"Is that how it works?"

The delicacy in her jaw wavered, clenching up. "Yeah, it is. About the job, though. What position is it?"

"What d'you have experience with?"

Nick could tell his cavalier responses dug under her skin. She let go of Remi's hand and her posture went rebar straight. She wasn't up for his frivolous questions. Anything outside of job talk she deemed a waste. Ms. Lacie was the same way, straight to business, no chaser.

"I've waitressed before."

"Then I'm looking for a waitress."

Remi glanced between the two of them, brows squished together. "Mommy, you can be the waitress."

"What a coincidence. I'm guessing the job pays off tips?"

"I pay a flat rate of three bucks an hour. Everything else earned is through tips."

"How soon do you need this waitress to start?"

"When are you available to start?" Nick reclined in the office chair, arms folded behind his head.

"How about tomorrow?"

"Tomorrow works."

Rosalie quirked her right brow. "Just like that? I'm hired?"

"Yeah, sure…why not? If you're interested in the job, I'm interested in hiring you."

"Err, okay. What time should I be here?"

"Ask Zoe when she starts. She'll be training you."

Nick picked up a red inked pen and started clicking it, pretending to focus on the stacks of paperwork. For as many questions as he had about Rosalie Underwood and her sudden reappearance, he wanted his alone time more. If he reverted back to looking busy, she'd get the hint…

"Mommy, can I have a pen like that?" Remi tugged on the hem of Rosalie's blouse and pointed.

"I'll give you my extra pen in my purse."

Nick clicked the red inked pen one last time and then slid it across the desk. "How about you take this one? I've got plenty."

"I've never had a red pen before."

"Now it's yours."

"Say thank you, Remi."

Remi beamed, clicking the pen like him. "Thanks, mister…"

"Nick."

"Mr. Nick," Remi said with another click of the pen.

"We better get going. It was nice meeting you. I'll be here tomorrow at whatever time Zoe comes in. I really appreciate you hiring me."

"Hey, don't sweat it. No big deal."

Rosalie stood there a second longer, hands gently placed on either of Remi's shoulders. If he didn't know better, it seemed like more words dangled on the cusp of her tongue, a mental back-and-forth going on as she debated to say whatever it was. She decided against it, and cut him a small, appreciative smile.

"See you tomorrow."

Nick flashed a thumbs-up before shuffling more papers. Remi returned the gesture and then clutched Rosalie's hand the rest of the walk out of the office. The door thudded to a close and Nick let the papers slide freely from his hands.

The clock on the wall read 4:26 p.m.

Too late in the afternoon to go back to sleep. He scrubbed a hand over his face and resigned himself to a fate of tedious responsibility for the rest of the day. His reward? Coming home to Maxie.

⌒⤫⤬⤩

"Papa!"

"Kiddo!"

Nick opened his arms wide to catch a dashing Maxie. Today's tomboy fashions, chosen with help from the babysitter, Ellie, was a pair of corduroy overalls and a baseball T-shirt. Her hair, loose, wavy, and golden-brown like his, bounced in a knotted mess. He caught her in his arms and slid a tangled strand between his fingertips.

"Kiddo, were you shipwrecked on an island again? What's up with the hair?"

Maxie giggled, perched in his arms. "Ellie and me played hide-and-seek."

"And did you hide in the wilderness?"

"No!"

"Could've fooled me." He tickled her between the base of her neck and shoulder. She erupted into more giggles and writhed in his grasp.

"Her hair didn't start out that way, Mr. Fontaine. Promise." Ellie was a freshman college student, nervous all of the time, but a kind teenager who Maxie enjoyed. She fidgeted beside Nick on their walk down the hallway. "Originally I put it in two mini buns, but…uh, that didn't last long."

"No kidding. But I'm not surprised. This one plays hard."

"I caught a frog!" Maxie boasted.

Nick turned her free, putting her down onto her feet again. She burst into energy and hurdled up the stairs. He rushed to the bottom step to call after her.

"Careful, kiddo! No running up the stairs."

"Yes, Papa!"

"She never gets tired. She has energy for days."

"Tell me about it. How much do I owe you this time?" Nick freed his wallet from his back pocket and split the leather pouch open for his cash.

Twenty minutes later, Maxie thrashed around upstairs playing Godzilla. She cleverly mixed in Barbies with action figures and stuffed animals, terrorizing them all as she stomped through the make-believe city. Nick half listened from the kitchen. Even if he now spent his days holed up in the office, in the evenings he got to cook for Maxie. Cooking eased the taut strain in his muscles. His Adam's apple ceased its lumpy bob on each swallow. He no longer had to put on a grin and fake charm.

Not when he was cooking.

Mom used to say cooking was its own labor of love. Whether for others or yourself, it didn't matter.

Nick agreed. He created entire feasts with his bare hands, toiling from scratch. He got to watch the joy unfold on the faces of others as they took their first bite. In turn, he rode the wave of pride until the wheels fell off. That high was the reason Mom opened the café so many years ago.

Culinary artistry was in his *blood*. The Fontaine family had a reputation for mind-blowing creole cuisine. For generations as far back as the late nineteenth century, his family was known for its cookouts about town. Mom claimed they were some of the first settlers in St. Aster, eager to cultivate a community for people who looked like them. The in-betweens that didn't quite fit anywhere else.

But his love for cooking changed when Mom passed. Before, he spent his days following in Mom's footsteps, running the kitchen at Ady's. It was a role he excelled in, feeding the thousands who visited their restaurant over the years. After she passed away, he couldn't bring himself to bear the restaurant's kitchen anymore. He could no longer cook for Ady's as if things were like they used to be. They never would be again.

Now he could cook only in private. In his own home as he mused on Mom and the life passion he had inherited from her.

Nick opened the cabinets and removed the pots and pans needed for tonight's dinner. Maxie was a picky eater, so he often remixed the few ingredients she liked. Tonight he was whipping up sausage and cheese rolls. He preheated the oven and prepped the sausage. The pastry dough he rolled flush across the counter. After placing sausage chunks and sprinkled cheese on top, he would deftly fold the pastry and cut them into slices. Some butter for light coating, minutes in the oven to bake, and time to cool off, and dinner would be ready.

Mom would ask him, *where are the veggies?*

He had that covered as he would've smirked and told her.

From the pantry, Nick retrieved ripe tomatoes, dried basil, and olive oil among other ingredients. The concoction was going to become the dipping sauce. Blender full of sliced and diced ingredients, Nick snuck in a bundle of spinach leaves at the last second. Maxie wouldn't be able to tell. He could practically *hear* Mom's shriek of laughter. She'd done the same to him growing up.

"Papa, is it dinnertime yet?"

He peeked over his shoulder at Maxie. She had dirtied her overalls yet again, now with what looked like smeared crayons. He abandoned the blender to meet her in the doorway. She was a spitting image of her mother, with soft little features, from her puckered pink mouth to the nub of a nose, wild gold hair framing her face. He crouched low to her eye level.

"Wanna help me set the table?"

Maxie vigorously nodded.

"You wash your hands yet?"

This time she shook her head side to side.

"What are you waiting for, kiddo? C'mere." Nick hoisted her off her feet, carrying her the entire way to the kitchen sink. He turned on the faucet and held her up as she created a sudsy mess washing her hands. For the first few seconds, the sound of streaming water seemed enough for her. Then she plucked up the courage to surprise him with innocent grief.

"I miss when you cooked with Grandmama."

The strings of Nick's heart tugged sharp and hard. "I know, kiddo. Me too."

"But she's not ever coming back."

"No…she's not."

Maxie said nothing as Nick lowered her back to her feet. Her sadness emanated off her in a haze. He wanted desperately to clear it for her, but how could he when he couldn't clear his own?

Together, he and Maxie moved on to setting the table. Maxie wasn't up for speaking. He wasn't much either. His thoughts were already on tomorrow and the exhausting day at the restaurant awaiting him. The headache-inducing accounting and budgeting that needed to get done. The piles of bills stacking up by the day. He couldn't avoid them forever, even if he tried to napping away at his desk. And now he had a new hire in the mix—Rosalie Underwood was a wildcard.

He hoped, like the others she'd know better and stay out of his way. He was doing just fine sabotaging the restaurant on his own; the last thing he needed was a new hire sticking her nose where it didn't belong.

CHAPTER THREE

It was minutes after five o'clock by the time Rosalie and Remi turned up. A man Rosalie assumed was Ma's boyfriend, Henry, lazed on the porch. He sprawled across the two-seater swing and held a beer bottle in hand. He sat up as Rosalie shut off the car engine.

Rosalie had never met him, but she already knew she didn't like him. He was more of the same. From the time she was a young girl, a half-dozen boyfriends walked in and out of Ma's life. Different faces. Different names. Deep down, though, the same man. Each and every one a slacker, a liar, a brute, and a man who couldn't keep his dick in his pants. Henry had all the markings of these men, from his shifty gaze and wrinkled, ill-fitting clothes. He *was* them.

"Is this Grandmommy Lacie's house?"

"Yep. Like it?"

"It smells funny."

"That's brine from the bayou."

"What's brine?" Remi asked, unable to help her innate curiosity.

Rosalie shut the car door with her hip, one arm holding Remi and the other her mommy bag. She cautioned the five-year-old about running off before she set her down. The burly cypress trees with their hunched branches were the last barrier from the bayou. A quick stroll beyond, and you reached the murky green water banks in no time. Even someone with as pint-sized footsteps as Remi.

"How's it going?" Rosalie asked, meeting Henry on the porch steps.

He had gotten up, wiped beer off his mouth, and jutted his chin in acknowledgment. His once-over drank them in, assessing their belongings and moving on to their car.

The muscles in Rosalie's stomach contracted. "Is my mother home?"

"She's cooking."

"Grandmommy Lacie!"

"Remi!"

Rosalie yelled after Remi, but it was too late. Remi scuttled past them, crossing the porch and yanking open the screen door. If nothing else had changed about Ma's house, it was that no running was allowed. Certainly not in shoes from outside. Those were to be left beside the door and coat closet.

Their suitcases were forgotten on the porch as Rosalie sped to catch her. Remi reached the midpoint of the hall when she snatched her up. She hardly ever spanked Remi, but she would be lying if she said it wasn't a temptation in that moment. The urge spread as an itch across her palm. She suppressed it by inhaling a deep breath and casting Remi a stern look.

"Sorry," said Remi, bottom lip plumped.

"Remember the house rules we talked about? No running inside, baby. Grandmommy Lacie doesn't like it."

A simpered laugh sounded from behind them. Both turned around to discover Ma standing in the hallway. Hair tucked into curlers and apron draped over her slender frame, Ma hadn't changed much. Except for a wrinkle here and there, she reminded Rosalie where she had gotten her features from. Her toothless smile, lips pinched together, stretched wide across her face. She was staring at Remi.

"Who says I don't want my grandbaby running in my house? My grandbaby can do whatever she wants. C'mere for a hug!"

Remi abandoned Rosalie to hug Ma. The two embraced in a bear hug that left Remi's feet dangling off the floor. Rosalie's ribs squeezed tight as her teeth found her tongue. She gnawed on the fleshy organ, literally biting down to keep from speaking.

"You hungry, sweetie?"

"Not anymore. I had a grilled cheese!"

Ma shot Rosalie a scolding glance. "Didn't I tell y'all I'd be cooking? How about some cake? You think you got any room for a slice?"

"Uh-huh, I do!"

"Let's cut you one then."

Ma led Remi to the kitchen, leaving Rosalie in the dust. Standing there as the bad guy in the situation, Rosalie had no choice but to return to their toppled luggage on the porch. She carried the pieces inside and double-checked she locked the car. Henry strolled in steps behind her.

"You're worried about nothing. Nobody's finna take the car."

"It's a habit." Rosalie shrugged.

"That's Bmore. You're back in St. Aster now."

Rosalie watched Henry disappear down the hall. He joined Ma and Remi in the kitchen. She hung back alone to collect herself. Five minutes in and she was already struggling. Already she was an outsider. Seven years later, nothing had changed.

Ma's house was exactly the same. The dull prism wallpaper still peeled off the walls. Ma disguised the tears with brass picture frames older than Rosalie's twenty-four years. If she studied the carpet beneath her feet hard enough, she could see the stain from that time she spilled grape juice when she was eight. The furniture was no better, the wood finishing worn down and chipped over time.

More importantly, the tension between her and Ma was as thick. If not thicker. The quick glance she shot her spoke volumes. Ma wanted to speak with her once alone. The talk was going to be a grating lecture about what a massive mistake Rosalie made running off with Clyde. As if Rosalie hadn't beat herself up about it enough over the years…

By the time she walked into the kitchen, strawberry frosting smudged Remi's lips. Henry was on another beer. Ma hovered by the sink, washing dishes. She peeked over her shoulder and murmured something about leftovers in the fridge. Rosalie wasn't hungry, pulling out a chair beside Remi.

"Mommy, try some cake. It's really good." Remi held up her fork, the spongy chocolate moist even at a glance.

Rosalie humored Remi and accepted the forkful. "Mmm. Delicious."

"Grandmommy Lacie baked it all by herself."

"Did she?"

"She did," interjected Ma, turning off the faucet. She wiped her pruned hands on her apron. "You know all the Underwood women love baking."

"Not Mommy," said Remi, innocently confused.

"Your mommy's the exception. Like always."

Rosalie resisted the urge to gnaw on her tongue again. "Remi, it's getting late and it's been a long day. How about we get you in the bath and then your pj's?"

Ma hurried to cut in. "I'd like it if you joined me for tea before bed. I've been drinking this lavender flavored one that relaxes the muscles."

Rosalie agreed with a curt, silent nod. It took about thirty minutes to haul the luggage upstairs, get halfway unpacked, and help Remi into the bath. Due to the limited space in the house, they were sharing a room. She preferred it that way, and Remi was used to it by now. Anything was a step up from crashing in the living room of Clyde's family.

Remi emerged from the bathroom squeaky clean and changed into her purple Disney Princess sleep shirt. Her eyes lit up when she spotted the toys unpacked from her suitcase. Embroiled in a game of dress Barbie for her date with Ken, Remi noticed nothing when Rosalie left the room.

As expected, Ma waited at the breakfast table. The soft, soothing notes of lavender filled the kitchen, doing anything but relax Rosalie. Instead, her heart beat rigidly against her chest. Her eyes lasered onto Ma without blinking. It was strange how she suddenly felt like an unruly teenager again, coming home for her tongue lashing.

"How was the drive?"

Rosalie lowered herself into a chair. "Long, but we made it. That's all that matters."

"Tea?"

"No thanks."

Ma nudged the second mug toward her anyway, steam wafting into the air. "I'm glad y'all are here, safe and sound."

"Me too. Thanks for having us. It...it should only be a few weeks. A month or two at most. I just need to recover money-wise."

"Of course you do. He left you with nothing but a name."

"The name's not mine anymore either."

"You've done one thing right," Ma said, exasperated. She sipped on her tea. "You've given me a precious grandbaby. She'll like it here—St. Aster's perfect for children."

"Right," Rosalie replied. She ignored the glaring fact that it had been far from perfect for her. Often anything but. "I'm gonna be starting work tomorrow. I got a job at Ady's Café."

"Ady's? Doing what? *Waitressing?*"

"Yes. Ady's son hired me. The pay will add up eventually."

"And what about what we talked about?" Ma's sparse brows arched.

"The real estate thing?"

"You study those books hard. You take the test in a few weeks. You hopefully pass and earn your license," explained Ma. Though she looked great at age forty-two, laugh line wrinkles bracketed her mouth as she scowled. "How d'you think I afford the mortgage? It's good pay. Better than wiping down some tables for two dollars an hour. It's not like Ady's is what it used to be."

Rosalie refused to argue Ma's point. Objectively, she was right. Waitressing paid pennies and Ady's business had steadily declined. But that didn't change the fact that she held little interest in becoming a real estate agent. She had yet to divulge that truth, though. It was too soon and she was too in need of a roof over her and Remi's heads. For now, pacifying Ma worked best.

"I'll start studying the books on my first day off," she fibbed. Her yawn followed, feigned for the purpose of escape. Rising to her feet, Rosalie stretched. "I'm gonna head up. Thanks again for letting us stay."

"Of course." Ma's tight, pinched smile spread.

"Night." Rosalie was at the threshold of the kitchen door when Ma spoke one last time.

"Oh, and Rosalie?"

"Yes, Ma?"

"No running in the house."

The next day, Rosalie stood outside Ady's Creole Café at ten o'clock sharp. Earlier in the morning she had taken Remi to register at the elementary school. Ma agreed to watch her for the rest of the day. Her heart ached being apart from Remi, even if it was for work, but luckily, she had taken to her Grandmommy. How could she not? Ma lavished Remi with a level of adoration Rosalie didn't remember experiencing as a girl.

The late September wind blustered through Rosalie's tight curls at a careless speed. She shielded herself by hiding behind the worn-down restaurant building. Her best cold weather gear was Clyde's old denim jacket around her shoulders and the ankle boots on her feet. Everything else was lost in the old storage locker she and Clyde dumped their belongings into. At one point in time she used to have a drawer of hats and scarves perfect for windy days like this.

That was back when she was still in school, working part-time as a waitress while also pregnant with Remi. Their marriage was in its honeymoon phase, which was a period spent in a rose-gold tint. Her love for Clyde trumped everything. His love for her solved any problem. Though cracks were already well-formed, she ignored them for the blissful ignorance within her fingertips.

It backfired on her more horribly than her early-twenty-something brain ever conceived. Clyde stepped out on her. She forgave him. He came back and then months later, he was doing it again. And again. And *again*. After a while, she lost track. Her heart shriveled up, unable to process the depth of his betrayals anymore. The money troubles soon arrived. Remi was a small and expensive bundle of joy. Her student loans piled up. Clyde lost his job. They lost their apartment and their things weren't far behind in their repossessed storage locker. Before her eyes, her entire life had gone up in flames.

So here she was, standing outside Ady's Creole Café in her hometown, St. Aster, Louisiana; the one place she vowed she would never allow herself to return to. She was waiting to start her first day of work, told to be here at ten o'clock for training. Yet, she checked her phone and the time glowed 10:16 a.m. back at her.

Her jaw tightened into a clench. She looked up at the empty parking lot.

Not one soul was in sight. Stepping out from around the building, she peered down both sides of Main Street. Other townspeople wandered the sidewalks, battling the wind with their beanies and coats, chins tucked into their chests. The shops were open for business, lights on to invite customers inside.

But no one from Ady's was anywhere in the vicinity.

Had they decided to take a *Monday* off?

Rosalie nibbled on her lip, swiping on her phone screen to bring up her internet browser window. She wasn't sure what she was searching for, but her fingers decided for her. They typed "number for Ady's Creole Café" into the search engine and tapped "go." It was a long shot that Nick Fontaine's personal number would be listed. She scrolled through the search results anyway.

All things considered, she had nothing but time. She clicked on a St. Aster business page that had the restaurant's details listed. Tires crunched over gravel louder than the wind and its incessant blowing. The tires belonged to a bronze pick-up truck similar in color to its owner's complexion.

Nick Fontaine swung into one of the many empty parking spots. The truck's rumbling engine died and his driver's-side door popped open. He hopped out, sticking the landing with effortless swagger. He whistled on his approach, sunglasses obscuring his pale green eyes from view, coffee cup clutched in hand. By appearance alone, he had zero cares in the world.

The tense clench in Rosalie's jaw only increased. She had been standing out in the uncharacteristic Louisiana winds for what was now twenty minutes. He was about town grabbing a coffee and whistling the tune to what sounded like Otis Redding's "Sitting on the Dock of the Bay." The disconnection was glaring.

Nick took one glance at her, key ring looped on his finger, and said, "You're early."

"I'm on time. She said ten. You're late."

"*I'm* not late. Zoe's late. Where is she?"

"I don't know. She wasn't here to meet me."

"So you've been standing out here all this time?" If Nick meant to sound sympathetic, he failed. Rather, his smooth timbre was blasé at best. He unlocked the door to the café and held it open for Rosalie, shooting her a dimpled smile as if he was the definition of gentlemanly.

Rosalie thanked him and hastened inside. The wind wrecked the twist-out style of her coiled hair and she didn't want to know how many knots had been caused. As far as she was concerned, she would be happy if she never encountered another gust. Her hand found her curls and she began gently combing through with her fingers.

Nick had returned to his whistling, headed for the back office. Rosalie called out to him.

"So will Zoe be here to train me?"

"Don't know. She's probably called out."

"If she's not here, who will take her place?"

Nick stopped but didn't turn around. His shoulders braced into a rigid posture that she could tell was unnatural to him. He thought on it another second and then peered at her from over his shoulder.

"Hmm. Guess it'll have to be me."

CHAPTER FOUR

Nick hated Mondays. Mondays were bothersome and soul depleting. His least favorite day of the week. Turning up at Ady's that Monday morning, his favorite latte from Ms. Maple's in hand, he hoped to spend much of the day locked away in the office taking it easy. He even planned to hit Main Street for Maxie's birthday presents. His two-hour lunch would be squeezed in between.

Coming to Ady's, he had little intention of running into Rosalie Underwood stranded outside. Less than that, he had no intention of sticking around to train the new waitress. It wasn't that he was unfamiliar with waiting at Mom's restaurant; in fact, for a long time during Ady's peak, *he* had been the star waiter, holding down the dining area for the crowds of customers coming and going.

The strained silence of a skeptic met his offer. Rosalie fought off any trace on her face. He knew better, spotting tell-tale signs in how she held her mouth and inhaled a puff of air. She was *not* happy with his suggestion. For whatever reason, she didn't want him to train her. Perfectly cool with him since he wasn't keen on the idea either.

"Look, I get it. You had your heart set on Zoe." He shrugged his shoulders while he reached up to rub the back of his neck. "I'm not Zoe. But...but I *am* the owner now. Guess that means it falls on me."

Nick wanted to kick himself. How unsure could he possibly sound?

He hated when his easygoing veneer slipped. He needed for everyone around him, Rosalie Underwood included, to believe he was as cool as a cucumber. His antics normally more than made up for any flubs. The lax stride, the whistling and grinning, the constant unconcerned replies that rolled off his tongue. They were all by design. At least that was what he told himself. He could do better if he wanted, yet somehow as of late, he never chose to…

"Okay, what do we do first when opening?" Rosalie crammed down the skepticism once oozing from her pores and stepped forward with renewed interest. She might not've realized it, but she looked damn cute standing there like that. The heavy denim jacket drowned her small frame, her cattish brown eyes blinking at him, face framed by those jet-black, zig-zag curls of hers; right now they were wild thanks to the wind outside, blown askew in a natural way he could only think of as bedhead sexy.

Nick's cheeks warmed and he hurriedly cleared his throat. Those thoughts he banished. Not only were they strange and out of nowhere but they were inappropriate. Rosalie was his *employee*. Sure any idiot with eyes could see she was an attractive woman. Alluring brown eyes, rich brown skin, pitch-black curls, and nice full lips shaped like a heart. The woman was worth more than a double take on the busiest city street.

But he was her boss. She was his employee.

Any thoughts about her outside of work-related matters was wrong. No ifs, ands, or buts about it.

Nick squashed his innate and sudden attraction then and there. Another clear of his throat later, he rushed to give her the tour of the place. She dutifully shadowed him, curiously surveying anything he pointed out. He stopped in the kitchen and handed her a half apron. His own he tied about his waist.

"We'll get you a T-shirt and name tag soon," he said. "When Zoe gets back in, I'll have her order 'em for you. 'Til then a white or black shirt is fine."

Rosalie had tugged off her denim jacket to reveal a navy V-neck shirt. She glanced down her front and back up at him. He rushed to clarify, heat still warming his cheeks. If anything, it had begun to fan out across his skin, down his back. Why the hell was it so hot in the kitchen when no stoves, ovens, or burners were going?

"Blue is fine too. Uh, anyway…your focus is the dining room. You've waited tables before, right?"

"Right," answered Rosalie, now in step with him. "I'm guessing opener takes down the chairs and preps the dining ware?"

"Sounds like you're gonna be a fast learner."

They started unstacking the chairs off the tables, dividing the room down the middle. Muffled voices sounded outside belonging to males he assumed must've been Jefferson and Que. The men were half an hour late, but it wasn't like he could be pissed at them. His failure as a boss wasn't their fault. If he expected them to be on time, he should've held them accountable as soon as it became a problem.

Zoe too.

Now he had a roster of employees doing whatever they wanted. Zoe skipped out on shifts. Jefferson and Que showed up late. His other part-timers came and went on even worse whims, quitting with no notice. No wonder newcomers like Rosalie thought it strange that Ady's was deserted while the other businesses in town thrived.

His fingers enclosed on the uneven legs of another chair, but he froze in place. His attention was on the café's front window, where through the pitted glass he could distinguish the outlines of two men. Not only were Jefferson and Que late, they hung around outside for an impromptu smoke break.

Shouldn't he say something? Nick hovered by the dining table, chair in hand, debating.

The weight of Rosalie's stare bogged him down. He glanced over and realized she was watching him watch the window. Though she was silent, he heard her judgments loud and clear. She thought he was spineless. He couldn't argue that she was wrong.

"Excuse me," he said. He broke away from the dining area and beelined for the door.

A haze of smoke enveloped him as he approached Jefferson and Que on the sidewalk outside. The cook and busboy greeted him without hesitation. They saw no error in their tardy, slacker behavior. If it had been a few days ago, Nick couldn't lie and pretend like he would either.

Yet, here he was. Preoccupied with what his new waitress thought of him as a boss.

"You guys gonna get started on kitchen prep?"

Jefferson inhaled a drag of his cigarette, pale skin tinted pink from the wind. "We'll get around to it."

"Man, me and Zoe went out last night and she had me doing shots," Que said. His red and bleary eyes revealed the extent of the damage done. So did the unshaven patches on his face. "Zoe make it in?"

"No, she didn't show up."

"I don't blame her."

Jefferson sneered at Que and flicked his cigarette onto the ground. Nick cut to the chase, squaring his chin and firming up his tone.

"Fellas, I'm gonna need you to get to work."

"After our smoke break—"

"Now," Nick said louder.

On their walk to the kitchen, he overheard Jefferson and Que grumble. They exchanged disgruntled complaints about him. He snagged only a word or two of the muttered conversation, but he picked up the words *blowhard* and *asshole*. He rejoined Rosalie, who was now rolling forks, spoons, and knives into napkins.

"They finally decide to show up for work?" she asked him.

She was teasing. His heart skipped its next beat. He cracked a smile.

"If I had anyone else play hooky, it'd be just me and you."

"I don't know. I think we could handle it."

"That's what you say now. Then when the crowd comes rolling in…" His arms flourished open, gesturing toward the empty dining room.

Rosalie merely shook her head in an incorrigible sort of way. Still like he was hopeless, but amusingly so. Nick decided it was an improvement.

It opened up the possibility that maybe he could improve in other ways. For months after Mom's death, he had been swimming in a pool of grief. He temporarily came up for air for one thing only—Maxie. She was his oxygen. The breath in his life that kept him going. As a result, he fumbled managing the restaurant. He took shortcuts and half-assed things. The restaurant suffered for it. He grinned through the spreading failure and acted like everything was fine.

Everything was not fine.

If asked to pinpoint what was wrong, Nick couldn't put his finger on it. He just knew he was down on his luck. That when alone, exhaustion crashed down on him and he sunk to his chair. His face dropped into his folded arms and his eyes closed. Sleep was life's great fixer. It shut out the paralyzing fear that he was failing more and more each day.

The restaurant crumbled around him. They were running on fumes, on the cusp of falling behind on the mortgage. He told himself it was going to be okay. Somehow.

Maybe it could be different now.

Nick shot a furtive glance in Rosalie's direction as she attentively wrapped the cutlery in napkins. Judging by how meticulous she was with each one, she prided herself in her work at the café. As owner, son of Ady himself, shouldn't he?

꧁∞꧂

That day saw four customers. All four of them regular. Nick supervised Rosalie's waitressing, but it was difficult with business slow. He could no sooner tell if she could handle a packed house now than when their workday began. Then he strained his memory for the last time Ady's had been full and he came up with a fuzzy time not long after Mom passed…

Nick eventually heard from Zoe. She called him yawning and explained about her night out at the bar in town. She and Que stayed until closing hours and she wound up oversleeping. Nick hung up the phone on her empty promises of returning tomorrow.

He and Rosalie were doing fine on their own. Jefferson's cooking needed some work, but that was no surprise. The food had been suffering for months now. Mom's recipes were no longer prepared passionately, cooked fresh for their diners. In order to make up for the declining business—and those monthly mortgage payments—he had had to sacrifice quality.

The more he thought about it, working alongside Rosalie as they cleaned up a table, the more he wondered if he should sit down and crunch some numbers. He could find a different workaround. Another way to save money so that he could reinvest in food quality like Mom always had.

His usual lackadaisical demeanor subsided. Determination replaced it, spiking like adrenaline in his veins. He was going to do something unlike him. He was going to stay an hour later to devise a plan. He headed for the back office to call Ellie, the babysitter, and let her know he would be late.

Rosalie called out to him. "Is it okay if I take my lunch break?"

"Go ahead. Knock yourself out."

Nick shut the door to the office and dug his cell phone out of his pocket. Ellie answered on the second ring, sounding as skittish as he expected.

"Mr. Fontaine?"

"Hey, Ellie. Something came up last minute at work. I'm gonna be an hour late. Are you able to look after Maxie? It'll be double pay for that last hour."

"Oh, sure. I've got a paper to write anyway."

"And why don't you pick up something from Ms. Maple's for Maxie and you? It's on me. Get extra sprinkles and fudge or whatever you guys like."

"Really? Wow, thanks! Maxie's gonna love that. I'm leaving in a few minutes to pick her up."

"Text me how it goes. I'll have my phone on me. See you later, Ellie."

Nick visited the kitchen to see how Jefferson and Que fared. Both were shooting the shit. Despite their fifteen-year age difference, they had found common ground in their crass sense of humor. Any other day, the guys would've kept yucking it up and guffawing when Nick entered. Today, after his earlier severity, they fell mute as soon as he walked into the kitchen.

His newfound determination gave him the nudge he needed to lecture them. "Fellas, I'm gonna need you to get to work. If nobody's dining in then we can always find other things, right? How about you organize and relabel the pantry…"

For a second time, he overheard Jefferson and Que grousing. So long as they did what he asked, he didn't give a damn. He plucked a full trash bag from its bin and hauled it to the backside exit. His intention was only to throw out the trash. After he would head back inside and see what else needed to be done.

What he came upon was the last possible situation he wanted. On a day where he had finally mustered up enough gumption to make changes around Ady's, he walked in on a phone conversation Rosalie was having. She was behind the slatted building, phone pressed into her ear, braving the windy autumn weather again. Like earlier, it messed up her curls, but she didn't seem to care. She was arguing.

He figured out instantly it was Ms. Lacie, her mother. His foot stuck to the asphalt and wouldn't move when he overheard his name.

"Nick hired me so it doesn't matter," Rosalie snapped. "What else am I supposed to do? I need to work. Even if it's a place like this. Even if it's a crap job for some guy who can't be bothered to care about his restaurant. The place is *awful*—a dusty old pigsty. But it's a paycheck. That's what matters."

The buzz of adrenaline fizzled. Nick blinked, face slack, body still. He tuned out the rest of her conversation, which grew terser by the word. He was too busy replaying Rosalie's words in his head.

Crap job. Some guy who couldn't be bothered. Awful place. Dusty old pigsty.

Nick backed away from the dumpster after tossing the trash bag. He slipped inside and retreated to his office. The lock clicked on the doorknob and his fingers raked through his cropped golden-brown waves. He blindly found his desk chair and sat down.

Crap job. He really thought he had made great strides in the last few hours.

Some guy who couldn't be bothered. He spent his day proving his waitstaff skills were like riding a bike.

Awful place. The café had dated furniture and dim lighting, but that was part of its charm.

Dusty old pigsty. He couldn't deny the cobwebs and dust cloaked over every corner of the restaurant. Some spring cleaning and that could be fixed. Was Ady's really that bad?

Deep down he knew the answer.

Nick slumped in the chair and blew a cold breath. He was a fool to think he could change much. He had spent months—a full year to be exact—being cavalier, turning the other cheek to any responsibility beyond his duty as a father. Did he really believe one morning chastising some employees and serving some customers was going to change anything?

The naïveté astounded him. For hours into the day he believed it possible. He owed Rosalie Underwood a thank-you. She was only speaking the truth. The blunt words he was too chickenshit to hear. To look in the mirror and confess. Over and over again he kept telling himself he decided not to sell the restaurant in order to keep Mom's dream alive.

But what if he had already failed? What if it was too late? What if it was already dead?

CHAPTER FIVE

Over the course of the next week, Rosalie slipped into a routine. She was grateful for it. After four months of tumultuous couch-surfing, routine was a blessing. Remi started kindergarten at the elementary school. Ma lent Rosalie an armful of books needed in order to study for her real estate license. Henry spent his days asleep on the couch in the living room.

Rosalie spent hers settling into her waitress role at Ady's Creole Café. Her first shift was no fluke; the employees at Ady's, including Nick Fontaine himself, were content half-assing their work. Their lack of concern for the dwindling business baffled Rosalie. She tried to bite her tongue on the matter, but each shift proved harder. The breaking point came at the beginning of week two.

Mrs. Marie Kettles thrust her arm into the air, snapping her fingers. Zoe rolled her eyes without discretion and puffed out a sigh. Her feet scuffed the floor on her sluggish walk toward the retired schoolteacher's table. In apprentice mode, Rosalie shadowed her, curious as to how the situation would be handled.

"This onion soup is too cold and thick," Mrs. Kettles said. She spooled soup into the spoon, the syrupy consistency dribbling like a string of molasses. "How recently did the kitchen cook this?"

Rosalie checked Zoe's reaction. Her drawn-in eyebrows arched and she stared at Mrs. Kettles from under lids weighed down by her false lashes. "I'm not sure. I can bring you another batch if you'd like."

"No need. Bring me the check."

"Believe me, it'll be my pleasure." Zoe's snark seeped into her tone. She snatched the bowl off the table and pivoted for the kitchen. Her dye-job red hair swayed side to side. Rosalie caught up, throwing another glance in Mrs. Kettle's direction.

"How'd Jefferson screw up the soup?"

"Prolly has something to do with it being two days old."

Rosalie braked in the middle of the room. "Two days old? It's not cooked fresh?"

Zoe's answer was a snort. "You kidding? Almost nothing's cooked fresh anymore."

"Why not?"

"Dunno. Ask Nick," Zoe said, indifferent. She slid the uneaten bowl of soup across the kitchen window's ledge and dusted off her hands. "Jefferson's not the best cook. Ain't it obvious?"

"Did the old cook quit when Ady passed?"

"Something like that."

"Maybe we can get him to come back," pondered Rosalie, frowning. She hated meddling, but the deserted dining room was pathetic. She needed this job to provide for Remi. "If we can convince him to cook for Ady's again—"

"Ask Nick," Zoe repeated. She gave Rosalie her back at the register, totaling up Mrs. Kettles's order. The hint was crystal clear. Don't speak on the situation again.

Rosalie drew a breath and then turned to face the office door. She would address the issue when he stopped loafing around and bothered to show up to work.

⁓∞⁓

"We need to talk."

"A little busy. Later good?"

"I'd rather it be sooner than later."

Nick breezed through the front door of Ady's at half past noon. He wore his shades indoors, clutching a coffee from Ms. Maple's. He didn't spare a glance at the empty dining room.

The startling reality dawned on Rosalie. For Nick and the rest of the staff at Ady's, a day with only a handful of patrons was the norm. They were used to standing around, going through the motions for a paycheck. Nobody cared about the declining business.

Nick tore off his sunglasses and noticed Rosalie in his shadow as he unlocked the office door. Surprise flickered in his eyes and he almost laughed as if she'd told a ridiculous joke. "You're serious. You mean *right now*?"

"If you don't mind." Rosalie quirked her brow. They both knew he wasn't busy.

Nick pushed the door open and brandished an arm to welcome her inside. "Ladies first."

Rosalie strode up to his desk, claiming the seat opposite him. Since her last visit, the room had grown messier. Crinkled papers stuck out from closed drawers. Days-old Styrofoam cups sat perched atop a filing cabinet. The trash overflowed, producing a mutant odor of rotten vegetables and aged cheese. Her nose wrinkled on a single whiff alone. Nick's cheeks colored a faint pink and he rushed to collect the overloaded bag and tie it up.

"Forgot to take the trash out last night. So, uh, what's that urgent thing you wanted to talk about?"

"It's lunchtime and we've had two customers in the last hour."

"Two, huh? I'm guessing Mrs. Kettles was one. Ever since she retired, she comes by every day."

"I don't think she'll be doing that much longer. Today her soup was thicker than molasses."

Nick plopped into his chair with limbs draped like spaghetti noodles. "She's not going anywhere."

"What makes you so sure?"

"She would've stopped a while ago like the rest."

Rosalie paused, choosing her words carefully. As the new girl on the scene, she understood how the others might think she overstepped boundaries. In theory, she should've been happy to have a job in the first place. The reality was too hard to ignore, though. No business could go on forever with such low patronship. She was thinking about the future. The others weren't.

"I think we're in trouble."

"Trouble—what d'you mean?" Nick sipped his coffee in between words.

"I don't want to butt in, but it seems like we're underperforming. We average around ten customers a day."

"We get more than ten. *Sometimes…*"

"I just can't imagine we're on target profit-wise. What happens when our few regulars stop coming? We can't rely on them when we can't even cook them fresh food."

"Back to the soup, huh?"

"Mr. Fontaine—"

"Nick."

"*Nick,*" she corrected, teeth grinding, "we could probably improve our reputation if the food was better. Don't you think?"

"Jefferson's doing the best he can." Nick drained the last of his coffee and leaned back into his leather chair.

"Zoe mentioned an old cook that used to work here. I was thinking if he's still around, maybe we can reach out to him."

"He's not willing."

"Oh, I didn't know you already asked him." Rosalie's hope fell with the volume in her voice.

"No need to ask him. He's not interested."

She didn't understand. "How do you know?"

"Because I'm him."

Of course it was Nick. She didn't see how she hadn't figured that out on her own. He was Ady's son after all. It made sense that she would show her son the ropes in the kitchen. That she would eventually hire him as her head chef.

The revelation soon led to more questions. If he was the chef Zoe had mentioned, why had he stepped down? Why was he no longer involved in overseeing the kitchen and the dishes being prepared? Did it have something to do with Ady's passing?

When seconds went by and she said nothing, Nick flashed a dimpled grin. "Did that throw you off? You know my mom was Ady, right?"

His tease jolted Rosalie out of her thoughts. "Obviously I knew. I just didn't put two and two together."

"I'm joking, Rosalie. Anyway, that was before I became the new owner. Things are different now."

"But why?"

"Why they're different? Now *you've* gotta be the one joking," said Nick, staring at her in furrowed-brow disbelief. "My mom passed away."

Rosalie's teeth caught her bottom lip. She hadn't meant for it to sound like that. She didn't want to seem insensitive to the grim situation. Ady's passing clearly changed the dynamics, not just in the restaurant but of Nick's life.

"I'm sorry," she apologized. "It's not my business why. Please forget I said that. I was just trying to figure out why the restaurant's the way it is now."

"I won't lie, I don't wanna talk about me being the old chef. As far as I'm concerned, that's all in the past. But if you wanna know why the restaurant's the way it is, I'll tell you."

"What do you mean?"

"You said you wanna know," he said, sitting up in his chair. He fixed her with an intent gaze that most women in St. Aster would've swooned over. "My mom's gone. It's not—and it's never gonna be—the real Ady's again."

"I think it's the opposite. It's still Ady's if it's your family restaurant, right?" Rosalie asked, stubborn. "It might not be the exact same as the past, but I think the place has potential."

Nick studied her for a long second. He looked stuck between confusion and amusement, as if he couldn't decide if he wanted to laugh or frown. He settled on a half grin that read as skeptical. For whatever reason, he didn't believe her and she couldn't figure out why.

"You're being serious. You think this place has potential?"

"Why shouldn't I? I remember how Ady's used to be. I don't see why we can't get there again. It's going to take some work, but it's doable."

"Most employees would be fine with no customers. The work's easier that way."

"For how long?" she asked smartly. "I don't know anything about your profit margin, but I'm guessing it's not much. If we don't turn this around soon, we're all going to be out of a job. I don't know about you, but I need this job, *Nick*."

Her emphasis on his first name broke through his hold on his amusement. He released a short laugh and leaned forward on his desk.

"I've gotta admit, you make a convincing argument."

"I was a finance major in college. Maybe I can help you with accounting. We can come up with some ways to keep costs low, but fix up the place. Call it Project Fixer-Upper."

"I don't think Ady's needs fixing."

Rosalie arched a brow and gestured to the mess around the office. "You don't think a little spring cleaning would help out?"

"It's October."

"Something tells me you skipped out last spring."

"Point taken. Okay, if we do some spring cleaning, what's it involve?"

"We need to get rid of all the dust and clutter around here."

"Fair."

"And scrub down the bathrooms. And clear out the pantry."

"Doable."

Rosalie sensed his interest increasing and played into the back-and-forth with a small smirk. "And do something about our thirty-year-old furniture."

"Not happening," Nick said right away. "We can't do anything about the furniture. We can't afford anything new."

"I didn't say buy *new* furniture. I said do something about the stuff we have," explained Rosalie. "We could fix the uneven legs. Paint the wood with a fresh finish. Patch up some of the cushions for the chairs. And maybe we can hit up the town thrift store. The used stuff in there is cheap. What do you think?"

Nick clenched shut his eyes and sighed. He took his time giving her an answer, in clear deliberation over her proposal. The little smirk she wore slid off as the seconds went on and she realized it was going to be a no. He wasn't willing to make changes around Ady's, because he was content letting the business flounder. Soon she'd be back at square one: broke and jobless.

"Alright, you've convinced me," Nick said suddenly. He opened his eyes and offered up a handshake. "If you can help me figure out a small spend plan that makes sense then alright. Let's give it a shot."

Rosalie accepted his handshake, surprised by his firm grip. Her gaze met his and she didn't hide the determination in her own. He needed to know she was serious. She was going to help him make this happen. Being a waitress at Ady's was considered a basic minimum-wage job, but she took pride in the idea of turning the restaurant around.

"One condition," Nick added as their handshake ended.

"I'm almost afraid to ask. What's the catch?"

Nick's cheeks spread as his dimpled grin crept onto his face. "*You're* in charge."

CHAPTER SIX

Project Fixer-Upper caught Nick by surprise. He hadn't expected Rosalie to breeze into his office and propose the plan. She had no idea he overheard her phone conversation, but it was difficult for him to forget. She hated working at Ady's and considered the place a pigsty. He assumed she would never want to waste her time trying to fix what was a lost cause.

But she was right. Ady's could only survive for so long on their current trajectory. He was struggling with the mortgage payments as it was. If business declined any lower, he wouldn't be able to pay without dipping into his own personal savings. That was no solution. Something needed to be done.

When he shook Rosalie's hand and agreed to Project Fixer-Upper, he looked her straight in the eye. He saw how determined she was based on her taut expression alone. She meant every word she said; she wanted to help transform Ady's into what it had once been. He held her hand in his and his stomach flipped. His mind began to wander…

Maybe he had misunderstood her over the phone. Maybe she didn't think so lowly of Ady's. Maybe she didn't think so lowly of *him* after all. For as new as she was at Ady's, her opinion inexplicably mattered.

For the rest of the afternoon, he hid out in the office, but he refrained from his usual nap. He chose to think about the last year. Before Mom passed away, his life had been simple. Even as a single dad, times around the restaurant and the Fontaine home were good. He hadn't understood how quickly things could change. How tragedy could strike in the blink of an eye and spin his entire world upside down.

One day Mom had been there. The next she was gone. He was left with exhaustive grief and the keys to the restaurant. Instead of stepping up and accepting the responsibility like a man, he had done the opposite. He had turned a blind eye and avoided his new role as owner of Ady's. The whole town knew he was a slacker. He was a loser who failed to do Mom's memory justice and pick up the reins in her absence.

Nick rose from his chair and grabbed the stack of weeks-old mail. If he was going to try to make a change, he could handle the small things he had avoided. The mail seemed like a good place to start. He sorted through tedious bills like those from the electric and water companies and tossed the junk mail into the trash. The last envelope he hesitated on, frowning at the sender's address.

He had never heard of Yum Corp. He tore open the envelope and scanned the letter. At the top was the company's logo—a smiley face with a spoon hanging out the side of its mouth. He read only a couple sentences into the letter before he snorted and crushed the paper into a ball within his fist.

Whoever Yum Corp was, he didn't trust them for a second. Their offer was a scam. No one in their right mind would be interested in buying Ady's, even a corporation as lucrative as they claimed to be in their letter.

Nick put the strange mail in the back of his mind and checked the time on his phone. Maxie's kindergarten class let out in thirty minutes. He grabbed his car keys and headed for the office door. The dining area was as vacant as earlier. Zoe sat at one of the tables scrolling through her phone and there was no telling where the guys were. He cared more about where Rosalie was; she was nowhere to be found.

"Rosalie on break?"

Zoe spared him a glance from her phone. "She left five minutes ago. Had to go pick up her daughter."

"I forgot. That's where I'm headed."

"It'd be funny if her girl and Maxie are buddies."

Nick merely smiled on his way out. "Doubt it. Not just any kid can keep up with Maxie."

At the school, a parental crowd gathered outside the chain-link fence of the kindergarteners' playground. The two kindergarten teachers, Ms. Gumbel and Mrs. Richards, stood at the entrance matching little ones with their parents. Nick parked half a block down and joined the back of the crowd.

Ms. Gumbel spotted him once the group diminished to a handful. She smiled and pointed out Maxie on the playground. "Mr. Fontaine, I hope you don't mind. Maxie made a special friend today and wanted a few extra minutes of playtime. The other girl's mother didn't seem to mind. I figured it was harmless considering how hard of a time Maxie had in preschool making friends."

"I don't mind at all. She was going to play outside again once we got home anyway."

"Good. You can go introduce yourself to Remi's mother if you like."

Nick didn't bother mentioning that he already knew Remi's mother. He excused himself from the small sidebar conversation with Ms. Gumbel and ventured onto the playground. Rosalie sat on a bench outside of the playground while the girls took turns on the slide. Maxie's face lit up the second she spotted him. She whizzed down the slide belly facing down and landed in a flip on the sand.

"Papa!" she screeched. She shook the tiny grains of sand from her hair and hopped to her feet.

"Hey, kiddo! Be careful. Go down the slides right side up."

Maxie heard nothing. She dashed toward him and jumped into his arms. He caught her and hugged her close. It took him a while to notice Rosalie had gotten off the bench and walked over alongside a breathless Remi. He set Maxie back onto her feet.

"I hope you don't mind the extra playtime. I figured why not since my shift was done," said Rosalie.

"No, sounds like a good idea to me. Who would've guessed they'd be friends?"

"It's definitely a coincidence."

Maxie and Remi grew bored of their adult talk and skipped off toward the playground. Nick considered calling after Maxie, but thought better of it. A few more minutes couldn't hurt.

"Remi told me Maxie is her bestest friend in the world."

"Bestest friend, huh?"

"After a week."

"Looks like they might be onto something. They've forgotten about us already." Nick pointed to the playground where Maxie and Remi had hopped onto the swings. They were too far out of reach to eavesdrop on what they were saying, but the five-year-olds' mouths moved, chatting away. Both he and Rosalie smiled at the sight.

Maxie had struggled to make friends. Her tomboyish, sometimes bossy antics put off the other girls her age. They wanted to be make-believe princesses and play house. Maxie wanted to frog leap and catch fireflies. The differences left Maxie, already an only child, stuck playing by herself more often than she liked. He and Ellie, among other family, tried to backfill the open positions that belonged to childhood friendship, but they were never enough. They weren't the real thing.

A girl like Remi, though? She was. She giggled along with Maxie as the two raced higher on the swings.

Nick glanced to Rosalie, who also stood watching the girls. Her face glowed with satisfaction, the autumn sun highlighting the dew on her brown skin. She was lost in similar thoughts. Could it be possible she felt the same way about Remi finding a friend in Maxie?

"Do you think we should sit down? Looks like they're gonna be a while."

"That's a good idea. This is a first for Remi. She usually struggles to make friends," Rosalie confessed.

"That sounds like Maxie."

"Remi can be a bit…bossy."

"So can Maxie."

To his surprise, Rosalie laughed. It was an airy note soon carried away by the wind, but nevertheless it caught his attention. She too seemed aware of how the urge arrived on a whim. Her full lips spread, the dip of her Cupid's bow more defined. She was going with it. Whatever *it* was.

"I don't know how that's going to work—two bossy little girls."

"Guess we'll find out. Should we?" Nick's shifting gaze suggested they move to the metal bench overseeing the playground. Rosalie agreed by stepping forward with him, the crisp leaves crunching underneath their boots. They sat side by side, leaving a space between them for the invisible man.

Nick was usually calm and collected with women, but in this instance—any instance around Rosalie—he preferred the space. In a matter of a few days he had unearthed an attraction for her that was wholly inappropriate, and he needed to keep his head. The space on the bench helped accomplish this, though the wind conspired against him; it blew the scent of her perfume in his direction.

He intentionally refused to breathe. He skipped an inhale, sensing touches of sweet vanilla and fresh cotton fragrant in the air. He concentrated on Maxie and Remi playing. They pumped their legs, rocking high on the swing set, fingers bunched around the chains.

Say something. He racked his brain.

"Maxie's birthday is in a few weeks. You and Remi should come."

"Remi would love that."

"I'll make sure to get you an invitation. Maxie told me she doesn't want to hand 'em out in class. She's sorta afraid the other kids will laugh at her."

"Kids can be like that sometimes."

Nick leaned against the bone-straight backing of the bench and sighed. "It's been hard for Maxie. Her mom's never been around and mine is gone. This'll be her first birthday since her passing."

"I'm sorry about your loss," Rosalie said, frowning. "I'm sure it's not easy losing a parent—or grandparent."

"No…it's not. But what can you do? It's a part of life."

"I remember your mom from when I was a kid. She was always so nice. She had one of those personalities that's instantly likable."

Nick grinned, reminiscing. "That's what everybody says about her. People used to drive across state lines to come see her and eat her cooking."

"They will again soon."

"You mean Project Fixer-Upper?"

"I can tell by your tone you don't think it's going to happen," said Rosalie.

Her mouth curved into a scant smile. "Just remember I'm going to gloat when it does."

"Knowing you I don't doubt that for a second."

"It's only because I'm grateful to have a steady income again. Thanks for the job."

"Huh?"

"You didn't have to hire me."

Nick shared in her growing smile. He knew sincerity when he heard it. She really was grateful. The thank-you was real. "If Project Fixer-Upper works, it's more like I should be thanking you."

Ms. Gumbel cleared her throat and interrupted them. The kindergarten teacher had seen off the last of her afternoon class and now needed to lock up the playground. They got the hint loud and clear, rising off the bench.

"Guess it's time to head out." Nick stuck two fingers in his mouth and whistled for the girls' attention. They dashed over puffing for breath. Nick held out his large palm for Maxie to take. "Ready to go home, kiddo?"

"Papa, can Remi and her mama have dinner with us?"

"What? Uh, no, kiddo—"

"Please, Mommy!" Remi chimed in, tugging on Rosalie's shirt. The girls developed a synced routine, bouncing on their feet in an impromptu dance.

Two adorable little girls begging for something. One of whom was his daughter. His kryptonite.

Nick deferred to Rosalie. She was softening much like him, at first staunch and then wavering once they broke out in chorus. Her eyes met his. Neither wanted to be the first parent to cave.

"Doughboy's Pizzeria is a block away…" Nick trailed off.

"Doughboy's! Doughboy's!" Maxie and Remi cheered as one.

Rosalie checked the time on her phone, teeth chewing on her bottom lip. "Doughboy's for pizza. I don't think—"

"My treat." Nick blurted the offer to more cheers from the girls. He didn't think about it beforehand, the words just tumbled out when he saw Rosalie's hesitation.

His suggestion coupled with the girls' cheerleading convinced Rosalie. She waved her white flag and gave in.

"Doughboy's it is."

❧

Doughboy's Pizzeria was one of two pizza parlors in St. Aster. There was debate around town about which joint baked the better pizza. Nick thought it was Mikey's. Maxie preferred Doughboy's. The foursome arrived to a parlor full of other dining families. The waitress on staff—Allison Porter, the plumber's daughter—seated them in a booth by the front window. She produced miniature coloring books for the girls.

As she walked off, the nerves in Nick's neck pinched out of agitation. Allison Porter was the same age as his babysitter, Ellie, but she behaved with half the maturity. The girl loved gossip. Considering he was thought to be one of St. Aster's biggest bachelors, he understood what being sighted about town with Rosalie Underwood meant. He expected a flurry of rumors come tomorrow.

Just great.

"Papa, can I have the double cheesy pizza sticks?" Maxie asked.

Remi's eyes widened. "Oooh, me too! Please!"

Nick clapped his hands, rubbing them together. "Double cheesy pizza sticks sound good to me."

"Remi, we're going to have the special. It's $2.99 for a slice and a soda," Rosalie said firmly. Her gaze avoided his as she spoke in that sharper tone again. The same one she used when launching into bossy busybody mode at the café. "Do you want cheese or pepperoni?"

"I want double cheesy pizza sticks!" Remi squeaked back, nostrils flaring.

Nick saw the brewing tantrum. He cut in. "It's okay, Rosalie. I'm paying."

"The pizza sticks are double the price."

"Rosalie," he said, matching her earlier firmness. He reached across the booth table and lowered her menu so that she had no other choice but to look at him. "It's okay. I don't mind. Go ahead and order whatever you want."

Even as Rosalie agreed and Allison returned for their order, he could tell how uncomfortable it made her. For whatever reason, she didn't like the idea he was treating them to dinner. The ease in her body language from their short time at the school playground had long since vanished.

The girls were in a world of their own in the same booth, seated by the window, coloring and giggling. He and Rosalie sat across from each other in an uncertain silence. She found distraction first in reading the regular menu and then reading the drink menu posted on the side of the table. He couldn't resist a low laugh.

"You don't like accepting things from people, do you?"

"What was that?" Rosalie continued her act of distraction.

"You feel weird when people do stuff for you."

Rosalie blanched. "Is it that obvious?"

"It's extremely obvious. But it's okay," he added swiftly. "Everybody's got quirks."

The food arrived with its tantalizing aromas of melted cheese and garlic marinara. Maxie and Remi dug in while Nick's window for conversation with Rosalie opened wider.

"I'm still recovering from a bad divorce. The way our relationship was set up, he was always in the driver's seat. I was younger and I didn't know any better. He gave me things, but he took away things too. Then he left us. I don't like relying on people."

Nick considered himself a great listener, but he sucked at advice. Not only had he never been married, his most serious relationship had been with Desiree, Maxie's mom. That fiasco was an on-again, off-again nightmare lasting for an entire year. What right did he have to say anything about Rosalie's marriage?

"That sounds rough," he mumbled. What else *was* there to say?

Like a book, Rosalie snapped closed as promptly as she had opened. "Forget it. Sorry to make it awkward. I shouldn't have mentioned it."

"No, it's alright. I don't mind you talking about it. I just...I wish I had something better to say. I've never been married."

"You're not missing out on anything."

"But I *am* a father, and..." Nick glanced to Maxie and Remi coloring with carefree abandon. "And I don't get how any man worth his salt could ever leave his child behind."

"I don't understand it either."

The residual hurt spasmed across Rosalie's features. Her teeth raked over her lips. Her jaw clenched. Her lashes lowered as her eyes did, gaze cast on her relatively untouched pizza slice. The immediate urge to bring a smile to her pretty face surfed through his now feverish pulse.

He wanted to cheer her up.

No.

He *needed* to cheer her up.

"Whoever he is, you're better off without him," Nick said adamantly. "Anybody that'll leave you like that isn't worth it."

The utmost corners of Rosalie's lips twitched. "Thanks for the pick-me-up. I'll call you next time I'm stuck on the past."

"Who said bosses can't be therapists?"

He meant it as a joke. Rosalie laughed it off. She finally took a bite out of her pizza. The girls kept coloring, crayon in one hand and a double cheesy pizza stick in the other. Everybody was clueless as to the fast speed of Nick's pulse. The slow churn in his stomach. The realization that he didn't think he could deny a second longer.

So maybe he had a crush on Rosalie Underwood. His employee. It was inappropriate. It was unexpected. It was wrong.

But it was harmless.

It had to be.

CHAPTER SEVEN

Rosalie came home to a stack of real estate books on her bed. The books were the most obvious hint yet from Ma. Since she arrived in St. Aster, she had largely avoided her company. Her schedule thankfully gave her the excuse she needed.

The books felt like bleak invaders. Remi kicked off her buckled Mary-Jane shoes and bounced around the room, hyper from their dinner with Nick and Maxie. She had no clue the hundred-page books on Rosalie's twin bed were like coming across a burglar in their home—if a small guest bedroom could be considered a home anyway. Rosalie inhaled for a good breath, but came up short.

She supposed the real estate books bothered her because it was a sign their room was *not* safe. It was under Ma's roof, a ten-by-thirteen-foot space she had unlimited access to. She had spent her first week in St. Aster thinking she could stall about the real estate license. Even though she understood it was likely her best option. Any time she thought about alternatives her mind blanked.

Her choices were waitressing at Ady's Creole Café or following in Ma's footsteps and earning her real estate credentials.

Ma said she could get her a job. Show her the ropes. Teach her what she knew. Rosalie ignored the fact that their past track record was a poor one. She was eight when Ma tried to teach her her times tables. That was a failure. Fourteen when Ma tried to show her how to apply eyeliner and mascara. Another attempt that bombed. Sixteen when Ma gave her driving lessons.

The instruction ended in a hostile mother-daughter fight. They weren't *good* together, defective as mother and daughter no matter their age.

Rosalie pushed that miserable truth from her mind. She had to think beyond her strained relationship with Ma. She had to think about Remi and the stability she needed. Stability required funds. Funds weren't earned at a café on the brink of going out of business. Long-term-wise funds were earned from solid careers. Ma's real estate job was just that.

Besides, the last time she disobeyed Ma's advice, she ran into the arms of Clyde. Obviously her own judgment was lackluster. Ma knew what was best. She never did, which was why she was back at square one. Back in St. Aster as the cursed failure she had proved herself to be.

Remi bathed and changed into her jammies. She played with her dolls for another hour. Rosalie sat by the window and peeled open the first book off the stack. The text was small, arranged in paragraphs of run-on sentences that produced yawns out of her. She managed three pages before she tapped out for the evening. She wasn't the only one yawning. Remi's head started to fall forward, nodding off.

"Time for bed, baby."

She tucked in the five-year-old and flicked off the light. Left no choice but to leave the room so that Remi could sleep, Rosalie gathered her toiletries and headed into the hallway. She didn't want to go downstairs. Ma and Henry were down there. She could drag out her shower and nightly bed routine for the next hour. If she went to bed any sooner, she would be up at the crack of dawn.

"Did you see the books?"

Rosalie stopped in her tracks. Ma materialized out of thin air, rounding a corner so fast Rosalie hadn't first noticed. She hugged her sweats, loofah, toothbrush, and toothpaste closer to her chest, and gave a mechanical nod. Ma eased closer, mouth stretched in a pinched smile.

"I spoke to Mr. Hebert at my agency. He says we can get you in for the pre-licensure course in six weeks."

"That seems so…soon."

"A month and a half away? It's not soon enough," Ma said, patting her on the back. Her hand prodded Rosalie forward so that they fell into step side by side. "You don't have time to waste at that café. You said it yourself—it's a pigsty going out of business."

"I was being dramatic." Rosalie's guilt poured in as a roiling sensation in her stomach. She had forgotten what she'd said about Ady's Café. Her slip of the tongue was just that; brief frustration she mistakenly expressed over the phone to the wrong person. She and Ma stopped outside the hallway bathroom. "It's not the worst job. Besides, tomorrow we're going to start revamping the café."

Ma's brows arched and she said, "Did Nick Fontaine finally get tired of doing squat?"

"It's a project. We're going to make the place look better." Rosalie's vague answer was her cue to exit. She flashed a smile and retreated into the bathroom. On the other side of the door, the soft pad of Ma's footsteps died out.

Rosalie breathed for the first time since encountering Ma. She had forgotten about what she said on her first day working at Ady's. The phone conversation was nothing more than boiled over frustration. She had been venting. Nothing more. Unfortunately, she failed to think about how that would shape Ma's perception.

It had done nothing but goad her further. As far as Ma was concerned, the only acceptable way for her to get back onto her feet was by earning her real estate license. Rosalie wasn't so sure. Her job at Ady's wasn't perfect, but following in Ma's footsteps didn't feel right either. She couldn't articulate why.

Just that it wasn't for her.

Project Fixer-Upper was starting. It was going to require a large chunk of her time. She had already begun mapping out the details. She couldn't—and didn't want to—put that on hold for the real estate licensure. Renovating Ady's felt like something she could do right. These days that list was getting shorter and shorter.

Instinct told her to focus on Project Fixer-Upper. Ma would have to understand.

On day one of Project Fixer-Upper, Nick agreed to meet her at Ady's at 9:00 a.m. Since punctuality wasn't one of his strong suits, she assumed he would be late and dragged her feet showing up. She still wound up early, parking her Honda Civic on Main Street. For the next few minutes she would have to sit and wait.

From her purse she dug out a pamphlet for the upcoming Autumn Festival. Yesterday she had picked it up from the community center at town hall. She had read the pamphlet cover to cover, paying special attention to page three. The page dedicated to the annual town restaurant competition spelled out the guidelines. As far as she could tell, Ady's qualified.

It was a matter of convincing Nick to enter.

Rosalie stuffed the pamphlet back into her bag and glanced around Main Street. The other shops were open for business and cars lined the sidewalks nearby. Then she spotted the familiar glint of bronze behind Ady's. She hurried onto the sidewalk, turning the corner around the building. Sure enough, Nick's truck sat parked behind the restaurant. Her jaw dropped. How long had he been here?

"I didn't expect you to be here," she called out upon walking through the door.

The dining area was empty, untouched since closing shift, but the dry dust scent was gone. The aroma replacing it was heavenly. The savory scent could only be from one place. Rosalie left her denim jacket on the hostess podium and headed for the kitchen.

The light from under the door spilled onto the floor of the otherwise dark restaurant. Rosalie pushed the door open and paused in the doorway. Nick's back was to the door as he stood tinkering over the stove. He whistled as he reached for an egg from the carton on the counter. He cracked the egg, splitting it open for the yolk to fall and sizzle on the pan. He had no clue she was there.

She debated on watching him some more. By the looks of it, he was enjoying himself. His whistle was theatrical and his demeanor was effortless. Unlike his clumsy attempts of managing the restaurant, he looked to be in his element in the kitchen. He added a pinch of salt to the frying egg and moved on to the next pan where andouille sausage was browning. If the women who thirsted after eligible bachelor Nicholas Fontaine could see him now, in his natural habitat, they'd swoon…

Her own cheeks warmed at what started out as an objective thought, but tumbled into another category altogether. Nick not only looked like a pro in the kitchen, he looked *good* in it. His tall, broad-shouldered frame moved fluidly around the stove. His large hands delicately handled the food he cooked. The contrasts were jarring and worse, undeniably affecting.

Rosalie squashed those thoughts and cleared her throat to interrupt.

"You're early," he answered without turning around. He dialed down the heat on the pan with the sausage and wiped his hands on a towel hanging off the wall. "I thought I'd have the place to myself for another ten to fifteen minutes."

"I would've been here even earlier, but I assumed you'd be late."

"Ouch."

"I mean, not that I don't think you can be on time. Just that…you're usually not."

"Flattery's not your thing, is it, Rosalie?" Nick sidestepped to the rack of clean plates and grabbed two off the top. "Hungry? I'm making some breakfast."

"I thought you didn't cook anymore?"

"I never said I don't cook anymore. I said I'm not the chef anymore. There's a difference."

"So, what, you sneak into Ady's each morning and cook yourself breakfast?" Rosalie asked, folding her arms. She walked deeper into the room and leaned against the counter across from him. His deft ease with which he flipped the egg in the pan looked right out of a culinary show on TV. She gave an impressed nod from behind his back. "Looks like you could probably teach Jefferson a thing or two."

"I'm making breakfast. It's a simple meal."

"You haven't spent much time with Jefferson in the kitchen, have you? He fumbles over the toaster."

Though Nick was still facing the stove, she saw the hint of a grin curve his lips. "He gets the job done. It might not be done well. But not everybody's a natural like my mom."

Rosalie wanted to point out that it seemed like *he* was. She bit her tongue and refrained, deciding to mind her own business. Nick had his reasons for stepping back from the kitchen work at Ady's. Reasons that were none of her concern. What *was* her concern was fixing up the restaurant in order to keep her job, rebuild her savings, and provide for Remi.

Nick handed her a plate loaded with well-seasoned eggs, colorful peppers, browned sausage, and pan-fried hash. Her confusion was plain on her face, eyes dropping to the plate in her hand and back up to him. He laughed and leaned against the counter opposite her.

"It'd be pretty rude to eat while you're standing here," he explained, digging in with his fork. "What's the matter? Not a big breakfast person?"

"No, it's not that. Just that…this looks delicious."

"It's a family favorite. We call it creole hash. Maxie loves it."

"You might have to share the recipe. I'm pretty sure Remi would too."

"Thanks for joining us for dinner last night," he said between bites. "You didn't have to humor the kiddo. I know you had other things going on."

"Remi wanted that dinner at Doughboy's just as much as Maxie—maybe more. She's been begging to eat anything other than PB&J's."

His brows lifted and dimples dented his cheeks. "PB&J's? As in peanut butter and jelly?"

"You said it yourself—not everybody's gifted in the kitchen. I'm one of those people. Luckily, my mom cooks fresh meals every night at dinner. Remi's made sure I know all about how Grandmommy Lacie is the better cook."

"Kids and their filters."

"Or lack thereof."

Rosalie took her first bite of the dish Nick called creole hash. The flavor hit her taste buds with robust flair. She paused chewing on the mouthful with widening eyes that met Nick's. He was back to looking amused, as if he knew exactly what her reaction would be.

"You look like you've got something to say."

"What's in these eggs?"

"Not a fan?"

"They're...they're delicious. The best eggs I've ever tasted. This whole hash is."

"It's just breakfast," he dismissed. "So about our plan for Project Fixer-Upper. Today's the day. Lead the charge."

Rosalie's taste buds were still reeling from the flavorful punch of her first bite. If anything else he cooked was even one-fourth as delicious as the hash, there was hope for Ady's yet. Her mind shot to the Autumn Festival's food competition, its pamphlet lying in wait in her bag, and she slowly smirked.

"Okay, fine. Let's get started."

CHAPTER EIGHT

That day, they got to work on Project Fixer-Upper. Jefferson and Que handled the pantry; the shelves of food needed to be sorted and relabeled. Zoe was in charge of the dining area, chasing away dust bunnies big and small. Nick and Rosalie tackled the rest of the café, scrubbing floors and clearing out the janitor's closet. They organized the office, shredding old papers and devising a filing plan. The office began to transform before his eyes, roomier and tidier than it had been in years.

Rosalie shoved apart the curtains and stood back, smiling at the natural light pouring in. The ceiling lights, artificial and filtered yellow, paled in comparison. The sunlight fell into the office room as a bright white hue, loosening the muscles in Nick's chest. He breathed easier, eyes on the powder-blue sky and scattered clouds. He had never realized how nice the view from his office was.

It overlooked Lawson Street, the back road off of Main Street, but beyond that was endless green. The wildly grown grass and cypress trees lined the area. The leaves dangled from the branches like feathered sleeves, so thick it was impossible to see through them. He already knew, though. After the patch of cypress trees was more wet marshland, stretching for miles around St. Aster as its own fencing.

He liked standing there at the window, looking outside and thinking. He had to do this more often. Fewer catnaps at his desk. More standing at the window in reflection. It sounded like an improvement to him.

Rosalie was waiting for his input. She had angled her body sideways, the window ledge digging into her waist, but it allowed her to face him and await his official stamp of approval. He lowered his gaze the eight inches needed in order to look at her, finding the spark of humor kindling in her eyes.

"Better?" She teased him a tiny smile.

"A whole lot better."

As he stared into her eyes, his stomach started doing funny flips. But he couldn't bring himself to stop. He couldn't control a thing about them, or the inappropriate thoughts tiptoeing into his head. His attraction to her was the elephant in the room. With little to no distance between them, it was damn near impossible to ignore.

Her soft scent, the vanilla cotton notes, lingered in the air. He could stand there and inhale that scent for another hour if possible, but he squashed the thought. He left the window and returned to the paper shredder.

Inside he cursed himself for yet again tumbling down the rabbit hole. He couldn't repeat the same mistake. Rosalie Underwood was his employee and he was her boss. Even if he enjoyed spending time in her company he had to keep it professional. That's what real bosses were supposed to do. He needed an excuse to put space between them.

"You should probably go help Zoe in the dining room."

Rosalie shrugged, glancing around the office. "There's still a lot of stuff in here. Remember, we didn't finish reorganizing the filing cabinets."

"I got it. You go ahead out there."

"I thought we were going to head down to the thrift store."

Shit. He had forgotten about that. Earlier when Rosalie broke down her plan for Project Fixer-Upper, she had mentioned a trip to the town thrift store to check out their bargains. It was a good, frugal idea for their renovation project, but what he hadn't considered was that he'd be in close proximity with her for the rest of the afternoon.

Organizing the office was difficult enough. Now they were headed for a one-on-one outing; he only prayed he could keep his cool that long. When she showed up that morning, she had taken him by surprise. He had tried to play it off, but wasn't sure it worked. Did she see right through his cool, laidback veneer? Had she picked up on his showboating in the kitchen? How he snagged every chance to show off his cooking skills?

"I forgot about the thrift store," Nick admitted. He busied himself with fixing the jam in the shredder machine. "How about you and Zoe go together? I'll take care of everything here."

Though he didn't look up, he felt the suspicion in Rosalie's gaze.

"Are you sure? Don't you want to have a say in what we get for Ady's?"

"It's not really my thing. Go ahead without me."

"Oh, okay. I guess I'll let you know how it goes."

He continued digging out the clumps of paper stuck in the feeder, pretending he didn't hear the disappointment in her voice. Her usual creamy tone had deflated even if slightly. She had thought he was going to come with her; she had assumed he wanted to go. Project Fixer-Upper was their *thing*, after all.

His stomach sank. He hated disappointing her. He cared what she thought of him. He wanted to impress her. He couldn't let her down on day one of Ady's renovation.

"Hold up," Nick blurted out before she could reach the door. "You're right. I should go. Let me grab my keys."

⌘

"Are you sure you're okay driving?"

Nick spun his ring of keys around his finger and grinned. "What d'you think?"

They buckled up, seat belts clicking into place. The back parking lot to Ady's was empty except for the cars belonging to Jefferson and their current customer dining in. He reversed and cruised down Main Street. The rest of town hung up Halloween decorations. Papier-mâché ghosts floated in shop windows and the carved mouths of jack-o'-lanterns glowed flames. Ms. Maple's Coffee Shop and Bakery played campy, up-tempo Halloween classics like "Monster Mash."

"I'm surprised Remi hasn't asked me about her costume yet," Rosalie said, eyes on the passenger-side window.

"Maxie knew what she wanted to be last November 1st."

"Pirate?"

"Nope."

"Wicked witch?"

"Too boring," he answered, steering them onto Lawson. "Werewolf. Guess who she wants to be one with her?"

Rosalie snorted back a laugh. "She has you hook, line, and sinker. You're a goner."

"Yeah, I know. The kiddo has me whipped. What can I say? It's hard to say no to her. But I already told her, plastic mask only for me."

"We'll see if you stick to it."

Nick braked outside the thrift store. The store had been around for as long as Nick could remember, always at the end of the small shopping mall strip. Hedges blocked the old sale signs plastered in the window, but nobody paid them any attention. The store was a cluttered, scavenger-hunt type of mess.

The decades' worth of vintage clothes and cheap upholstery created its own musty perfume. The stench was powerful at first, barely tolerable to inhale. In minutes, their noses adjusted, and soon recognized it as the new normal.

They perused the overcrowded aisles as a team. Shelves upon shelves of knickknacks crammed together with little sense as to how they were organized. On any given shelf, a baby monitor sat next to a stack of picture frames. Water-stained board games occupied the space between copper cookware and VHS tapes. Nick plucked a *Rambo* VHS and glazed over the summary on the back of the box. Rosalie folded her arms, eyebrows high on her forehead.

"Really? *Rambo*? I forgot we're here to rent a movie."

"Hey, I'd be *buying* it."

They moved on to what looked like the furniture section. The open space featured a collection of sunken sofas, a mismatched dining table set, and office pieces like a heavy oak desk and bookcase. Rosalie walked up to admire the dining table set. He wandered between the furniture, noting the price points dangling off the tags.

"What do you think if we went for a less traditional look?" she asked suddenly.

Confusion scribbled across his features, resulting in a blank stare. She took pity on him and launched into an explanation about her vision. Standing by the mismatched dining table set, she talked about going for a less dated, more eccentric style. Her eyes glinted passionately and the breathless lilt in her voice endeared him.

"We could make it work, give Ady's a cozier, homier feel. Paint the furniture different colors. Arrange things mismatched to make it quirkier. I noticed diners like Clementine Browning order stuff like coffee and dessert. What if we had a small dessert section? Just some armchairs and coffee tables so she can read her book, eat her banana pudding, and chill by the window," Rosalie explained. She moved on to the tufted armchair she had in mind, its fabric colored a berry wine. "Obviously, it might take a while. We haven't streamlined your budget yet—"

"This armchair is thirty bucks. I don't think that's gonna break the bank."

Sort of. His reply was the truth if he meant the modest inheritance he received from Mom. On the other hand, if he meant the profit from Ady's, he was lying. Ady's hadn't turned a profit for months now. Most months they barely scrapped by, breaking even. Once or twice less than that.

"Pick out what pieces you like and we'll add it to the list," he said, burying his hands in his pockets. "Maybe later we can sit down and map out what you think should go where."

Once they were done window shopping, they hopped back in his truck and started for Ady's. He could tell by the sideways glances Rosalie was casting that there was something else on her mind. Whatever it was, it wasn't about their trip to the thrift store, but he sensed it did have to do with Ady's renovation.

"You look like you've got something to say," he said, keeping his eyes on the road ahead.

He expected Rosalie to dismiss his observation, but to his surprise, she laughed.

"Was I that obvious?"

"The sideways glances might've been a clue."

"There's a part of Project Fixer-Upper I didn't mention."

"What do you mean?" Nick asked as he turned onto Main Street.

"The Autumn Festival is coming up next month."

The subject seemed random, but he had to admit he was curious. He snuck a glance at her and said, "I didn't think that festival would be your kinda thing."

"It's not. But then I saw the restaurant competition they're having."

"Rosalie—"

"Hear me out," she interrupted stubbornly. She had dug in her purse and retrieved what looked like a pamphlet on the festival. "It's for local restaurants in town. There's a cash prize, but you realize what first place means, right?"

"Some plastic trophy bought at the Save Mart?"

"I'm being serious. Think about it. First place gets news coverage town-wide for their restaurant. That's free advertising. What better way for Ady's to make a new debut than for us to compete at the festival and take first place?"

He didn't answer her. Her rationale was sound, but he had no intention of entering any competition. Project Fixer-Upper was enough of a major change for him. Adding an entire competition felt like too much pressure.

For years, Mom had dominated that same competition. Ady's was undefeated back then, its reputation flawless. He could never re-create that success. He could never begin to compare.

"Nick, we've got a shot. Don't you think?"

"I don't cook for Ady's anymore."

"We'll have Jefferson prepare the menu."

Nick shot her a sideways grin. "I remember somebody saying Jefferson fumbles toast."

"What other choice is there? He's the only other person who knows the menu."

"Or you," he said in jest. "You can enter and represent Ady's."

Rosalie snorted. "I already told you I'm not a big cook. I barely make spaghetti."

"Spaghetti, huh? Maxie could probably cook spaghetti. She's five."

"Go ahead and drag me for it. I can't even act like I'm bothered. Did I mention I use the spaghetti sauce from the jar?"

Nick groaned out of culinary umbrage. "Out of the jar? Really? You know that stuff isn't made fresh?"

"Neither are half the dishes at Ady's," she shot back.

"That's a low blow."

"You insulted my spaghetti first."

"Fair enough," he admitted. He pulled into the parking lot behind Ady's and nabbed the first spot open. Turning off the truck engine, he twisted in his seat for a straight look at her. "Tell you what. I've got an idea. You want Ady's to compete in the Autumn Festival's restaurant competition? I'll teach you the menu."

Rosalie stared back at him, lost at the proposal. "And you think that's a better plan than you cooking it yourself?"

"Already told you. I'm not interested in competing. But what's the difference who it is if it's the same recipe?"

"I can't cook, Nick. I'm not playing when I say that."

"Anybody can cook. It's not about who the person is. It's about the skill they have. Are you up for it?"

She sighed and slowly conceded his point with a nod. "If you say so. We've got a deal."

CHAPTER NINE

"**H**ow you liking St. Aster?"

Henry turned up in the kitchen, much to Rosalie's vexation. She went through great lengths to avoid him. Most of the time she managed. The only challenge was that he was *always* home.

Jobless, useless, and broke, he had nowhere else to go during the day. She couldn't look him in the eye. He didn't know it, but he was the men of the past. Difference in appearance aside, he was exactly like the others. She looked at him and saw Terrance from when she was seven years old. By the next blink, he was Chris, the man who lived in their home during her high school years. His lethargic murmur sounded startlingly like Andre's low drawl, another man from Ma's gallery of rogues.

She gathered a breath, shoulders braced, and stuck to basic pleasantries. "St. Aster's good. No complaints here."

"Heard you're having a rough time at Ady's?"

"That's what my mom thinks and she doesn't know what she's talking about, so…"

"She's worrying you're wasting time. I keep telling her to chill. You'll figure things out. Everything's temporary," he mumbled, propping open the fridge for a deep dive inside. "She thinks you needa be in real estate like her. You know how it is—if it ain't her way, it ain't no way."

Rosalie laughed it off; a hollow sound that warbled uncomfortably in her throat. She couldn't think of anything else to do. She collected the handful of PB&J sandwiches and dropped them into her mommy bag. Henry was too busy digging in the fridge to notice her exit.

Being Saturday, she had promised Remi a mini picnic and trip to the bayou. Beyond the brush surrounding their home, the wetland was a short fifteen-minute walk away. Rosalie explicitly forbade Remi to venture there alone, but that further intensified her curiosity. Every morning since they arrived in St. Aster, she pressed her nose to their second-story bedroom window and exclaimed she could see what she called, "the grassy pool."

They began their stroll hand in hand. Remi insisted on stopping for ladybugs. The little red-and-black insects were her favorite. She stooped low enough to allow the ladybug to crawl onto her hand, giggling in delight as her invitation was accepted.

"Look, the ladybug wants to come!"

"There's room for one more. Tell her she's welcome."

"What if it's a boy? Can ladybugs be boys, Mommy?"

"I don't see why not."

"Should I name it? He can come home with us!"

Remi jumped upward, cupping the ladybug in her palms. For the next few minutes she gushed about how the boy ladybug was her new pet and how he was going to live with them forever. Rosalie hung on each word as if the possibility was plausible. She didn't dare dash Remi's spirits. Ma had done enough of that to her growing up…

"What's Daddy doing today?"

Rosalie choked on air, sputtering out a cough. "Daddy? Remi baby, we've talked about that already, remember?"

"But…but he's not gone forever?"

"Daddy's on a break."

The vague answer didn't satisfy Remi. Her brows bunched close, long lashes fluttering with her fast blinks. She was trying to make sense of what that meant. Truthfully, Rosalie was too. She didn't know what his break entailed or how long it would last. Just that he had vanished out of their lives indefinitely.

No number. No email. No social media. No updates from his family. Nothing, as if he never existed. As if they never married, spending seven years together, bringing a daughter into the world. None of that mattered to Clyde in the end. He was done with her, which translated to being done with Remi, as well.

It was harder to put into words than she anticipated. How to explain to a child that the man who was supposed to love and protect her unconditionally was no longer in the picture—that he likely would never be in the picture again. As a grown woman recently divorced from him, the man she thought was the love of her life, she struggled with the heartbreak. The sting of his rejection hurt to the bone. How could she possibly expect Remi to handle it?

The bayou emerged among the towering cypress trees. Rosalie welcomed the distraction as Remi gasped and tugged her hand free. She trundled forward, mouth agape. The thick reeds parted for them, scratching their shins. Twenty feet ahead, the green water rippled from the late morning wind. The duckweed floating atop its surface whirled into different patterns. A lone frog hopped along, carefully leaping his way to the gnarled branches bent over the water.

Remi's fascination rendered her speechless. She wasn't one for nature, but the bayou was the rare exception. Rosalie understood why. A sense of calm swayed in the air as gentle as the breeze. The bayou's seclusion shut out their troubles. Frenzied thoughts fell by the wayside, quieted by the lull of the water stream and distant coo of birds.

"Mommy, it's like *The Princess and the Frog*."

Rosalie's smile was warm. "Yes, baby. Just like the movie."

"There's a frog too!"

They settled on a bench off the bayou, situated next to an old cabin long since abandoned. The last owners of the home had also left their rowboat, oars propped up on its sides. Something Remi pointed out as they munched on their sandwiches.

"Can we live in the cabin? We'll be by the grassy pool!"

"It's called a bayou, Remi."

"Bayou sounds funny."

Rosalie shared a small giggle with Remi. The wrinkle in her nose was like looking in a mirror. Clyde had often said how much Remi resembled her; it disappointed him that she hadn't come out looking like him. Though Rosalie suspected Remi would be on the taller side thanks to his genes. She was already taller than Rosalie was at her age.

They made quick work of their PB&J's and the juice boxes she brought along. Remi was telling Rosalie how excited she was to see Maxie on Monday when she caught on to noises that weren't the bayou. They were distant voices growing louder by the second. She figured out who they belonged to only as the owners appeared.

Nick and Maxie nudged their way past the leafy brush. In Maxie's hand was a knotted broken-off tree branch that she swung like a sword. Nick laughed watching her duel an invisible enemy. He gave her the space needed for her swashbuckling fight, at ease with one hand in his pocket.

The appropriate thing to do would've been to look away. The father and daughter deserved privacy on their afternoon outing. Besides, she wasn't one to stare. She was on her own outing with Remi. They needed the alone time to bond. She assumed it was the same for Nick and Maxie.

Yet, she couldn't bring herself to pretend. Once she saw them, she saw them. She saw Nicholas Fontaine, who husked out a laugh as carefree as his twirling, sword-wielding daughter. He was in his natural form like this, in Maxie's presence, being the attentive father he was at his core. There was something inherently attractive about that.

When she tried to swallow, gulping down more air, the block in her throat wouldn't allow it. She was left to flounder for a breath, sitting beside Remi and acting like deep down she wasn't overcome with…*something*.

Nick stopped in his tracks. It took Maxie a second longer to follow. Their matching sets of pale green eyes gleamed and their mouths fell open in a laugh of shocked delight. They broke out into an instant trot, cutting the distance down to a foot.

Remi leapt off the bench to meet Maxie halfway. The girls clung to each other in their customary bestest friends hug. Rosalie was much slower. She rose with palpable caution off the bench, barely able to grapple the breathless feeling inside of her. Nick's grin was lopsided, showing his perfectly straight teeth.

"We can't seem to stay away from each other."

"What are you two doing here?" Rosalie's voice was more of a croak than the frog on the bayou.

"It's Saturday. Maxie, what are Saturdays for?"

Remi and Maxie had let go of each other, excitedly chatting. Maxie interrupted herself to answer Nick's question. "Saturdays are for papas and kiddos!"

"That's right. Saturdays are papa-kiddo days," he said brightly. He fixed Rosalie with his gaze, winking at her. "Maxie and I always come out here. She likes to try to catch the frogs."

"Remi wanted to see the bayou."

"You guys live nearby, right? Same house after all these years."

"My mother's in real estate. She snatched up that house and she's not giving it up," Rosalie answered. She hated how her palms moistened, feeling clammy to the touch. There was no excuse for it; the day was light and breezy. "What about Maxie and you? It's a far walk if you don't live in the area."

"Not far at all. We're on the other side." Nick jutted his chin out southbound.

"That's a…a coincidence."

"Sure is. How about we do something?"

"Do something?"

"The girls are going to be glued at the hip for another couple of hours. I'm here. You're here. It's Saturday afternoon."

Nick explained the situation so effortlessly it was hard not to be convinced. Rosalie caught her bottom lip with her teeth, looking up at him with momentary deliberation. Inside, nervous energy fluttered faster than butterflies.

It had to be Nick's relentless stare, expression lax and eyes honest. He never looked handsomer. Her fingers curled and uncurled, the temptation to reach up and run them through his golden strands rising high. The slight kink in his hair pattern amused her. Compared to her tighter, coiled, jet-black curls, the contrast was obvious. She wanted to finger a strand and twirl it long enough to define a *real* curl. He needed it badly.

Her lips spread. "What did you have it mind?"

∾

Nick suggested dessert at his house. The girls ran around outside while Nick and Rosalie sipped coffee in the kitchen. The last slice of banana bread pudding awaited them in the center of the table. Earlier, the girls wolfed down their child-sized portions. Rosalie and her sweet tooth devoured her larger slice, and Nick's was gone in two or three bites too. Now the debate wore on over who got the last piece.

"I'm the guest," Rosalie pointed out.

Nick leaned forward on the table. "I'm the one who slaved away for hours."

"Banana pudding? Really? It's that hard to make?"

"You think it's as easy as popping the lid off the jar of your spaghetti sauce?"

His tease heated up her cheeks. She rolled her eyes despite herself. His sense of humor was difficult to resist. She couldn't deny that. The longer she sat underneath his playful gaze, eyebrows wiggling and cheeks dimpled, the easier it became to stop fighting it. She gave in with a crack of laughter.

"How about we split it? That's fair."

"Leave it to you to bring logic into it."

Her nose wrinkled. "Is that a bad thing?"

"When I'm trying to have a whole 'nother slice of banana bread pudding to myself, it is," he joked boldly. He picked up the cutting knife and handed it over. "Alright, go on and do it. Cut it in half. Fair is fair."

"You sound like you're giving up your most prized possession."

"Did you taste this bread pudding? It's amazing—another recipe from my mom."

"Okay, it *is* pretty damn delicious," she admitted, laughing. "How often do you bake it?"

"I try to bake something for Maxie on the weekends. Mom used to—"

Nick stopped there, inhaling a sharp breath. His discomfort was clear. His posture stiffened and the vein in the side of his neck protruded. He was literally jamming down the emotion talking about his mother brought him. She wanted to offer sympathy, some brilliant words of condolence, but her tongue fumbled. Her eyes diverted to the glass dish with the banana pudding.

"You should have the last slice. It's special to you."

"Rosalie, cut the slice in half. I'll bake more." He drew another breath and shook it off. The morose lines faded from his brow. "It's hard sometimes talking about her. Especially if it's her cooking. It meant a lot to her."

"I'm sure it's hard when her recipes are probably another reminder."

"Don't feel bad for me. It's my own issue dealing with her being gone." Nick noticed her immobile hand hovering over the glass dish. His hand brushed hers, easing the knife out of her grasp. The little hairs on the nape of her neck prickled. Eyes on hers, he smiled. "I was joking earlier. We'll share it."

Now mute, Rosalie nodded shallowly. She let him cut the last slice in half and serve her. Her heart had faltered when his hand touched hers, skipping a beat. It soon recovered, but the surprise washing over her went nowhere. She couldn't think straight or else she would've tried to decipher what was wrong with her.

The feelings springing up were perplexing. The last type of emotion she expected. After years of struggling with Clyde, recent months of heartbreak and financial worry, these new feelings were a welcomed change of pace. They were light and sprightful, inflated like a balloon in her chest. She smiled back at him and brought her fork to her mouth for her next bite.

"Listen, I know we said we'd sit down for our budget on Monday, but it's gonna have to wait 'til Tuesday. I'm gonna be out of town most of the day."

"Oh, I didn't know you were going anywhere."

"If we're gonna start these cooking lessons to get you in shape for the festival, we've gotta have the right stuff."

Rosalie eyed him skeptically. "The right stuff as in…?"

"The right ingredients. We used to drive an hour to Coffy's every week for groceries," Nick answered, collecting the last morsel of banana pudding with his fork. "My mom refused to go anywhere else for certain things. She wanted to handpick everything herself."

"Coffy's. Isn't that the creole grocer in New Orleans?"

"Best in the state. It's expensive but worth it. We've downgraded to the Save Mart and our food hasn't been the same."

"Maybe I should go with you." She caught on to how that sounded last second, and added, "It'll help me learn the ropes. I don't know anything about what ingredients to use."

"You're really dedicated to this festival thing, aren't you?"

"I've already told you why. I need this job, Nick. I need Ady's to succeed, which I think means winning that competition. What time are you leaving on Monday?"

Her stern answer earned a low chuckle out of him. She didn't know if it was the natural light from the screen door or a light from within shining, but his eyes brightened. He rose from the table and gathered their plates to drop them off at the sink.

"How's nine o'clock sound?"

Two hours later, she and Remi waved Nick and Maxie goodbye. He had driven them to Ma's house and dropped them off by the porch. Remi bounced on her feet and begged for another playdate next weekend. Rosalie was on the verge of caving in. The buzz in her pocket interrupted her. She dug her phone out of her back pocket, but she was a split second too late. The call went to voice mail and she brought up the call history. Her brows knitted close.

The number was unknown. The voice message ten seconds long.

Rosalie pressed play. The smooth baritone that she had memorized from the time she was fifteen spoke on the other end, and her heart crashed against her rib cage in frantic beats.

It was Clyde.

CHAPTER TEN

Monday morning, Nick met Rosalie outside of Ady's. She skipped the usual Ady's uniform of plain white shirt and black pants, and wore a maroon sweater dress that must've hung loosely, because she cinched it at the waist with a belt. She paired the dress with boots and tights. Her thick curls she left free to flounce with the wind. He started smiling without realizing it. She looked beautiful.

"Excuse me, miss, but I heard you were looking to go to New Orleans today."

She turned around and smiled hello at him. "You're one minute late."

"I was stuck in traffic."

"Because St. Aster is known for its crazy traffic."

"Can't you tell?" he asked, gesturing to Main Street. A lone mail truck cruised by.

They broke into a quick laugh and she rolled her eyes, breezing past him. He unlocked the truck and they got in. He had spent last night thinking about today. His brain and his heart were at war. His brain reminded him how he was her boss. Their relationship needed to be professional and nothing more. His heart disagreed; it called for more time in Rosalie's presence. It had him out of breath and sensitive to the slightest reaction from her.

Every smile. Every laugh. Every *eye roll*.

Nick wondered if he was imagining things. The chemistry he felt between them. Their small, playful moments that seemed to happen no matter how much he told himself he should pull back. Was he alone, or did she pick up on them too?

"How was your Sunday?" he asked as they hit the road.

Rosalie hesitated for a second. "I had a lot on my mind."

"Anything you wanna share with the class?"

"It's probably best if I don't. I'm trying not to think about it," she said cryptically. "I've realized that I need to stay focused on what matters. I need to get back on my feet so I can be what Remi needs."

"You're already what she needs. She's your mini-me."

"Everyone says that. But what I mean is, I need to bring stability back into her life. This past year's been rough."

"You just got to town. You'll get there."

"I'm hoping you're right. I need some good luck after all this bad."

"How about today we pretend like it doesn't exist? All the stuff we don't wanna think about or that's bringing us down. Focus on having a good day," he proposed. "I haven't been to NOLA in months. It feels good to get out of St. Aster."

Rosalie smiled brightly and nodded her agreement. "That sounds like just what I need."

⌒∞⌒

The drive into New Orleans was a straight shot on the highway. Nick and Rosalie preoccupied themselves with random chatter. Rosalie told him about the first time she visited Ady's as a child. He told her about the disastrous first time he tried to cook a meal in the restaurant kitchen.

"You're exaggerating," said Rosalie.

"I wish I was. But that's the sad part. It's all facts."

"You expect me to believe you singed your eyebrows?"

Nick kept his eyes on the road as he grinned. "You don't believe me? Soon as we get to NOLA, I'm pulling over and showing you some throwback pics."

"A fifteen-year-old Nick Fontaine without eyebrows. I'm sure that was a popular look with the girls."

"Do you remember a kid named Iggy? Think his last name was Jameson? He double dared me to shave my head."

"To match the brows?" Rosalie's fingers crept over her face and muffled her gasp. "Why do I already know how this turns out? You shaved it, didn't you?"

"For the fifty bucks he offered? That same afternoon."

The two erupted into laughs as outside the truck windows they passed by the giant sign welcoming them to New Orleans. Nick noticed Rosalie's face glued to the window as she observed the enchanting city from afar, and he debated on driving the long way to give her a closer view.

"Coffy's is in the middle of nowhere," he explained. "It's in NOLA but not in NOLA."

"Oh, I know. It's backwoods," she said with an easy laugh. "It's just been years since I've been to New Orleans."

"Before you left St. Aster?"

Rosalie nodded. "I want to say I was sixteen. Clyde drove us…"

She trailed off there, and he sensed she wanted no further discussion of the memory. They retreated into silence for the rest of the drive to the specialty grocery store, with Nick wondering if he should say anything to lessen the awkward air.

Coffy's was located far off any main roads, surrounded by the thick brush of cypress trees. Nick hung a right off the back road and onto the gravely parking lot. In the many years since the parking lot had last been repaired, the white lines dividing the spaces had faded. Nick invented his own spot right up at the front, shifting gears into park.

At a glance, the shoebox-sized grocery store was lopsided. It leaned to the right, the wooden pillars that held it up exhausted after decades. Nick expected no less; he remembered being a kid and it looking the same exact way. Tourists might have considered the weathered building an eyesore, but everybody who mattered knew it was a NOLA staple.

Out front on its rickety porch was an out-of-service soda machine. Old sales posters peeling off the window advertised a sale on ghee that they were eight years too late for. On the doormat lounged a snoring Saint Bernard. Nick eased the door open so not to disturb him, but even his considerate effort was not enough. The Saint Bernard snorted his disgruntlement, lifting a single lid to eyeball them.

"He was a puppy last time I was here," Nick joked in a whisper to Rosalie. Her snicker was stifled by a low clear of her throat.

Footsteps inside, the aisles crowded over them. He could hardly move an inch without bumping into a shelf or a rack of merchandise. They started down the aisles in lockstep due to the narrow width. Along the way he pointed out the products Ady's used for their dishes. Rosalie rose on tiptoe to see over his shoulder as if studying for an exam.

"See these?" he asked. "Best red beans you'll ever taste."

"Unlike the ones we've been using from the Save Mart."

He paused midway down aisle four to twist around and look at her. His broad shoulders knocked into the top shelf and he fumbled to catch the glass jar that tipped over its edge. Rosalie jumped back out of the line of fire. He breathed a sigh of relief as his fingers gripped the jar before it smashed to the floor.

"Tight space in here," he said.

"No kidding." Rosalie looked stuck on a swallow, shaking her head in residual alarm.

"Nicholas Fontaine? Is that your big ol' broad self I see?"

Both he and Rosalie froze on the spot. The heavily twanged voice called out to them from the back of the teeny store. Rosalie expressed her confusion by frowning, but he recognized who it was. He beckoned her to follow him down the rest of the aisle and to the back wall of built-in coolers.

Francine Coffy waited for them. Like the store itself, she was as he remembered her. Her hair was a frizzy mess stuffed into a low ponytail and her pinkish skin was speckled with sunspots that were years premature, but her kind smile stood out more than anything else. She stretched her arms open for a hug as soon as he was within reach.

"I'm sorry about your mama," she said, patting him on the back. "Damn tragedy, but that's life sometimes. How're you holding up?"

"As good as I can be."

"And who's this?" Francine peeked around Nick and eyed Rosalie with interest.

Rosalie shuffled uncertainly on the spot before she stepped forward and held out her hand for a shake. Francine chortled loudly like it was the funniest thing she'd seen all day.

"She's cute," she said to Nick. "Girlfriend?"

"Waitress," Nick answered. "Which brings me to why we're here. Ady's is looking to return to before."

"You mean before you ditched us for the Save Mart?" Francine said derisively with hands on her slim hips. "You know you ain't shit for that, Nicholas Fontaine. Your mama was our biggest business here for years."

"I know, I know. It's just things have been…uh, difficult," he said with an awkward scratch of his scalp.

"Well, promise me one thing—even if y'all don't return to Coffy's, at least keep your mama's place going. Ady loved the hell outta that restaurant. It was like a child of hers."

Nick knew all too well. He had watched from the time he was a boy as Mom built Ady's from the ground up. Rather than cry over her divorce with Dad, she decided to turn her passion into her profession. She opened Ady's on a hope and a prayer and wished for the best.

He grew up in that restaurant. He spent afternoons in the dining area doing his homework and evenings in the kitchen shadowing Mom by the stove. He learned the value of a dollar as a pimply-faced teen bussing tables and hauling bags of trash to the dumpster. He saw the pride gleam in Mom's eyes each year as the love for Ady's grew in the hearts of diners everywhere.

"I wouldn't ever give up on Ady's," he promised Francine with a reassuring smile. He noticed Rosalie was watching him closely from the sidelines. He wasn't sure what to think of her interest in the exchange, but he decided to change the subject, motioning to the seafood selection next to Francine. "I see you've got them catfish we like."

Francine beamed. "We sure do. Ain't ever stopped selling 'em! Follow me and I'll cut you a deal."

Once done shopping inside Coffy's, Nick and Rosalie hauled the bags to the truck. He had purchased enough groceries to last them a week's worth of cooking lessons. He had also placed an advanced order for next week, picking up Mom's old grocery habit.

They left Coffy's behind with the initial attempt of getting back on the highway, but then their stomachs grumbled. They shared a glance. Nick figured he'd be the one to speak it into existence.

"Wanna grab lunch? If I turn onto this main road, the French Quarter's not too far away."

"But the groceries—"

"They should be fine for an hour or two," he answered.

"I'm not going to argue with you when my stomach's started growling."

"Is *that* what that noise is?" he joked.

Rosalie's answer was a laugh, and he grinned, loving how she could take a joke as good as she could give them.

The neighborhoods they drove through were old but colorful. Yellow houses and blue doors, clunker cars parked on overgrown lawns. Mardi Gras beads from previous years dangled off of power lines. The farther they drove, the louder music blared, welcoming them into the heart of NOLA.

They parked far off, deciding it was their best bet to walk the blocks into the crowded area.

On foot they ventured into the French Quarter. Soon the excitement on the block enveloped them. Every which way they looked, there was a sight to behold. A small parade of costumed street performers danced in celebration of the Halloween season. The band responsible for the blaring tunes was a quartet of men in fedoras. The foursome stood at the next street corner, playing their instruments with such ferocity they turned themselves red in the face.

People flocked from all directions and joined the impromptu party. Nick and Rosalie were no different. The mood in the air was too infectious to ignore. They found themselves cheering alongside the others, swaying to the snazzy beats come to life.

The crowd rolled like an ocean wave and swept them up toward the frontlines. Before they knew it they were falling off the sidewalk's edge and onto the grand stage that the street had become. The dancers were grabbing them, pulling them along as if now part of their live performance. Nick laughed and went with the flow, but Rosalie resisted, mouth open in mortified shock.

Nick caught her gaze, and he winked. He expected an eye roll, or at worst, for her to about-face and scurry back into the crowd. Instead, she burst into a laugh and surrendered to the dancers, goading her on. Now the focus of the parade, the two lost themselves to the moment.

He wasn't much of a dancer, and he never pretended to be, but what he lacked in skill, he made up for in enthusiasm. He reached for Rosalie and grabbed her hand. Together they shimmied and side-stepped and spun in clumsy circles. They panted as they tried to keep up with the other dancers, matching the band's jazzy beat that seemed to blare louder and faster by the second.

Any hesitancy of Rosalie's was abandoned. She let go of her inhibition and danced alongside him—sometimes out of step—but always with overflowing fervor that had them both feeling like they were floating in a dreamlike state.

The moment began to feel surreal. One of the first times in a while that Nick stopped feeling weighted down by grief, or hiding from it. He wasn't an actor and he wasn't pretending. He was himself again, only without the dark cloud that had been hanging over him the past year.

He looked at Rosalie, and a warmth hit his heart. She was a beautiful sight, dancing and laughing as if she wanted to savor the most of the unexpected celebration.

Her wild zig-zagged curls danced with her, bouncing with the beat, and falling into her face. He imagined they were buttery soft to the touch. What would it be like to spool one around his finger?

She looked at him as if reading his thoughts and smiled. He smiled back with a breathless laugh that was drowned by the loud music and cheers.

When the song ended, they held on to each other's hand and fled the parade. They were sweaty and tired—the good kind of tired—searching for a reprieve out of the spotlight. Back on the sidewalk outside a tearoom, they exploded into disbelief.

"That was unexpected!" Rosalie exclaimed.

"But a good time," Nick added, wiping his brow.

She gave a nod and stared up at him with a shine in her eyes. "We definitely worked up a sweat."

"Looks like we're in front of a good place to check out."

Nick gestured to the tearoom. He pulled the door open for Rosalie to enter, the fresh scent of mint the first smell to reach them. Harriet's was a quaint tearoom that, like every other shop and restaurant in the French Quarter, boasted a NOLA flair. The little room was decorated in neon purples and greens, with trombones and trumpets hanging off the walls.

They ordered some sandwiches, tea for Rosalie and water for Nick, and chose seats by the only window. Rosalie reached up and finger combed her curls, untangling the ones that got twisted during the parade.

Even in small moments like these, he couldn't shake his innate attraction for her. Her beauty was a given, but his attraction was beyond the outward. He enjoyed her for who she was on the inside, the person she was as Rosalie Underwood.

"Maybe I needed this more than I realized," confessed Rosalie several bites into their sandwiches. She eyed him from across the table as if seeing him in a different light. "I haven't had a chance to do anything fun in a long time."

"I never would've guessed your idea of fun is dancing in the streets."

"I don't know if I'd go *that* far. And you're one to talk—you're the one with all the moves."

Nick could feel the heat splotching pink on his bronze skin. He cleared his throat and played it off by chugging water. The last thing he wanted was for Rosalie to notice him blushing. He wasn't the kind of guy who blushed. Not normally anyway.

"Did you mean what you said to Francine?" she asked suddenly.

He choked on the next bite of his sandwich. He pounded a fist to his chest and sputtered, "Mean what I said about what?"

"You'd try your hardest to keep Ady's open."

"Rosalie, I'm already trying."

She shook her head. "You know what she meant—you know what I mean. *Really* try. Really put in the effort."

"Ady's was my mom's pride and joy. It was her dream. That means a lot to me," he answered plainly. "I'd never let it go if I could help it."

"Good," she said, smiling brightly. Satisfied with his answer, she returned her focus to her food. "Because I really think we have a shot at the restaurant competition."

"The one *you're* competing in."

"Me—or we?"

He spotted the teasing note in her voice and he marveled at her uncanny ability to rope him in even when he said he wouldn't be. The gift she had of talking him into things he thought he never could be talked into. He both loved and hated her enchanting influence.

"We'll see about that," he told her with a throaty laugh. "Better hurry up and finish our lunch. Gotta say goodbye to NOLA. We've got groceries to fridge and kiddos to pick up."

CHAPTER ELEVEN

The New Orleans trip with Nick gave Rosalie a break from the message haunting her voice mail. She hadn't listened to it, but she hadn't deleted it either. Leaving the message in a state of limbo gave her the space she needed to think about it. She didn't tell anyone, acting as if it didn't exist. There was no one to tell. Ma would go off on a tangent. Remi would cry for her daddy. The few old friends she had in Bmore were too busy to answer a crisis call. She couldn't blame them; it wasn't like she had been around for them in recent times of need.

For the briefest moment on their trip into NOLA, Rosalie considered telling Nick. He had proven himself a good listener. They had developed a rapport that felt open, even if their interactions confused her at times. At the last second she decided against it, clamping her mouth shut on the secret.

Besides, she was angry. She was furious with the man she fell so blindly in love with that she bought the lies he sold her. He had betrayed her trust and broken her heart, stomping over it after the fact. He disrespected every last vow he made on the day they eloped. He treated her like she was the problem, made her feel invisible and inadequate. She was *never* enough.

His straying was her fault. She needed to be more laidback like Erica. More of a sex goddess like Gia. More of a perfect 1950s cooking and cleaning type like the woman from his workplace affair. There was always a woman around who was "more" than Rosalie. More beautiful. More engaging. More fun. More willing to feed Clyde's ego.

At first she believed she could compete. She could fix whatever it was that had him stepping outside their marriage. After all, Ma had believed the same growing up. She had dealt with her fair share of cheaters and had done her damnedest to try to reel them in like a fisherman with bait on the hook.

But why was she competing with other women in the first place? She was his wife. She was supposed to be *it* for him. He was *it* for her. Why wouldn't he give her that same value? Why did he insist on breaking her?

The shame hung around her neck, however invisible but heavy to bear. Even with the bullshit he put her through, she had stuck around. *He* had left *her*.

No one knew the extent of how bad their marriage was. She kept it hidden from everyone out of sheer embarrassment. Ma's implied "I told you so" was bad enough. The pitiful back pats from her friends in Bmore were humiliating enough. The awkward explanations she came up with to Remi why the other woman confronted her outside the subway was hard enough.

It was time to let Clyde suffer a little bit. To ignore his existence the way he had spent years ignoring hers, making her feel small. As selfish and wrong as it was, she derived a secret satisfaction from not returning his call. From not even listening to his voicemail. Now *he* was the unimportant one. How did it feel?

On her next day off, she picked Remi up from school and took her to Main Street. With Halloween just over two weeks away, she figured it was time to shop for a costume. She had scraped together a couple of bucks from her first paycheck in order to buy one for her. Outside of Christmas and her birthday, Halloween was Remi's favorite holiday. She loved dressing up as different variations of princesses.

This year? As they strolled down the sidewalks, Remi obediently held on to her hand and told her about how she wanted to be Tiana from *The Princess and the Frog*. She described what she hoped the dress would look like, citing the bright green colors and long skirt.

"And a crown!" she finished feverishly.

Rosalie hid her worry behind a placating smile. "Remember, Remi baby, we're on a budget. Mommy can't afford the most expensive costume, but we'll get you a pretty one, okay?"

"Yes, Mommy. I remember."

The Party Haven was the place in town that sold holiday merchandise. For Halloween, the business had gone all out to celebrate the upcoming holiday. A fog machine produced rolling clouds at their feet and overhead creepy cobwebs dangled with even creepier rubber spiders. On their approach, Remi clutched her hand tighter and pressed into her side, eyes bulging as she stared at the spooky decor.

"It's okay, baby. It's all fake. Don't be scared."

"But it looks so real."

"Afternoon, folks, what can I do for you?" the clerk hooted as soon as they entered. She had rounded the checkout counter to greet them at the door. Her fire-engine red braided pigtails dangled over the front of her polka-dot Raggedy Ann costume. On her cheeks she had dotted freckles and swiped an obscene amount of blush. Pinned to her chest was her name tag, spelling out her name: Ines. "Is this your baby? She's your lil' mini-me!"

"Say hello, Remi."

Remi's grip on her hand endured. She used her left to wave hello. Ines dug into the pouch of her Raggedy Ann apron and produced a handful of chocolate candies. Both women laughed as Remi's face shone and she gladly accepted the sugary offering.

"That always wins 'em over. I keep a whole bag on me," she said.

"Thanks. It'll calm her down. The decorations freaked her out."

"Try working here. The rubber spiders still got me jumping."

They watched Remi unwrap the candies and pop them into her mouth, wandering off to a nearby kitty cat on display. The black cat was part of a witch's set, but she petted him out of interest.

"So y'all shopping for a costume?"

"I was hoping to find something affordable. I'm on a budget."

Ines leaned against a skeleton mannequin wearing a top hat. "It's rough, ain't it? Kids don't understand being broke. Especially if they weren't before."

"I've explained it to her, but sometimes she doesn't get it."

"Mine are the same. I tell 'em we're having ham sandwiches for dinner and they whine about wanting a Happy Meal. I ask 'em if they got Happy

Meal money. They know what's up after that."

A dull pang throbbed in Rosalie's chest. Her thoughts landed on the voice mail. She watched Remi walk up to a bin of costume hats and begin trying different ones on. She was going to choose an expensive costume and cry if told no. If Clyde were in the picture, he would be able to buy it for her, give her what she wanted as always. What if…?

She shook that line of thinking away. She concentrated on the searing anger. The outrage and bitterness that fueled her to stand her ground.

"If you're strapped for money, we have a loaner program," Ines explained. "Our selection isn't the greatest, but it's something. We've got the basic costumes for both children and adults. You never know, you might find what you're looking for."

"Thanks, but I doubt it. My daughter's stuck on a specific costume."

"Little girls and their love for a Disney Princess," predicted Ines with a low cackle. "We don't have any loaner princess costumes in girls' sizes, but we do have a queen costume in women's if you're looking for yourself too."

Rosalie humored the clerk with a small smile, but she was saved from providing a response. Remi screeched for her from two aisles over. She rushed over a stride ahead of Ines.

The aisle teemed with children's costumes on peg hooks. On the left were the boys' costumes, arranged by size and age. The right featured the girls' costumes, many glittering and embellished with tulle. Remi had wrangled the *Princess and the Frog* costume off the hanger and held it in her arms like fine gold. Her ponytails, one by each ear and two in the back, swung as she bounced on her feet.

"This is it! My princess costume."

Rosalie's stomach sank to the floor. Even at a glance, she knew it was expensive, priced well beyond her twenty-dollar budget. The detailing on the gown was ornate even for a child's costume. Delicately sewn leaflets orbited the skirt like a lily pad, the pastel yellow petticoat peeking from underneath. The top half was equally decorated by a sparkly waterlily-cut neckline. She eased the ornate gown out of Remi's grasp. The price tag jumped out at her. As predicted, the costume was triple her budget.

"Isn't it pretty, Mommy? Look at the sparkly beads!"

"Remi…" Rosalie rattled out a breath. "It's beautiful, but we can't afford it. Why don't we look at another costume?"

The tears were immediate. They brimmed in Remi's eyes, glazing over like glass. Her chin trembled and her nostrils flared, on the verge of eruption. Rosalie hung the costume on the peg and knelt to envelop Remi with a hug. The tantrum came anyway, exploding free in a shrill cry that was heard up and down Main Street.

"How about this cool bumblebee costume? It's from our loaner program and only five bucks to rent it out for two weeks." Ines swooped in with the assist, holding out the striped fuzzy costume complete with stinger tail.

But Remi was a runaway train of emotion. She wailed loud enough to give anyone a headache, mouth hanging open wide for maximum volume. Her dark brown skin flushed over, tears pouring down her cheeks. She wasn't ready to stop anytime soon.

What started out as guilt and sympathy transformed into frustration. Short spasms of tension shot through Rosalie, muscles clenching all over. Her lips pinched shut much like Ma's. She grabbed Remi's hand and bolted for the door. Behind them, Ines called out and said something about being around if they needed help.

Rosalie was on autopilot, too fed up for basic niceties. She strapped Remi into her car seat, ignoring the girl's cries and the stares from townsfolk on the sidewalk. For the moment, she'd had enough.

The next morning over breakfast, Ma volunteered to chip in for the costume. It wasn't that the gesture wasn't appreciated. More so that she didn't talk to her about it first. Remi had been upset with her for the rest of the night, pouting and sulking even during playtime. In Remi's five-year-old eyes, Grandmommy Lacie rescued her from her mean, stingy Mommy. She became the bad guy.

This flew over Ma's head—or if it didn't, she acted obtusely. She sipped her tea seated at the breakfast table, Remi dancing excitedly in the background, and asked what Rosalie's long face was about.

"Nothing."

"Have some tea. It'll calm you."

Rosalie rubbed her eye, expression empty. She wanted to say more than curt one-word answers, but thought better of it. With Ma, arguing was futile. She had learned that lesson as a teenager. Ma's stubbornness made any level of mutual understanding impossible. It was best to evade and avoid whenever given the chance.

She stood from the table. "I should get to work."

"But it's only eight? Why've you been headed over to that place so early?"

"I already told you. We're doing renovations."

Ma blew on her mug of tea with pursed lips. "I forgot about your little project. Well, you go ahead. I'll whip up breakfast for my precious grandbaby. You weren't gonna fix her anything but a bowl of cereal. See you after work."

Rosalie bit her tongue and headed for the door. She needed time to cool off. Between Clyde's voice mail, Remi's tantrum, and Ma's condescension, her heart felt heavy. Her mind murkier than the morning fog at the bayou. Her feet carried her to her Honda Civic parked outside. She zoned out for the entire drive to Ady's.

When she arrived, Nick was waiting for her. His smile greeting her as she walked through the door was the first uplifting feeling she had for the day. By the looks of it, he had already done much of the work required for opening, prepping the dining area and kitchen.

"You're early," she said, shrugging off her men's denim jacket. She couldn't explain the sudden flutter in her stomach, but when Nick grinned wide, the nerve-racking feeling intensified. His dimples were prominent and his wavy golden-brown hair begged for fingers to run through its strands. She looked at him and tried to ignore how the muscles in his arms flexed under his shirt.

Nick Fontaine was no longer objectively handsome. He was flat-out, undeniably fine as fuck.

Rosalie wanted to cringe at the thought. She couldn't pinpoint when she had stopped thinking of him as a boss—a boss who she thought was unqualified and out of his depth—and began thinking of him as a man she was irrefutably attracted to. When had that change happened? What was going on with her today?

She tried to shake it off, but Nick interrupted her by tossing an apron at her. She caught it and stared at him with brows raised high. He laughed.

"Apron up, chef," he teased in his throaty timbre, deep and smoky like a fine whiskey. "We've got some cooking to do."

CHAPTER TWELVE

It was *just* a cooking lesson.

Nick reminded himself this as he walked into the kitchen. Rosalie was a step behind. He could already smell the cotton vanilla on her skin. His stomach was flipping and flopping. He inhaled a calming breath and settled into his lackadaisical Fontaine stride. If he could fool St. Aster into thinking he was over his grief, he could fool Rosalie for an hour or two. He could pull off his usual cool demeanor, hiding his deeper feelings underneath.

Their trip to New Orleans hadn't helped curb his crush. The one-on-one time did anything but. Instead he got a chance to experience what it was like spending a large amount of time in the company of Rosalie—almost like a day date. The more he reminisced on the trip, the more he realized that was what it was.

The two of them had gone on a date and called it a business trip. They had traveled to NOLA under the guise of shopping at Coffy's, but had wound up doing much more. Certain moments from their day together replayed on a loop in his mind. Their dance during the street parade had felt like a dream. The secrets they shared were like strange comfort. *Finally*, someone he felt like he didn't have to pretend with…

But he had to remain professional. He was her boss. That was the bottom line.

Nick glanced at Rosalie and the small smile on her face melted any resolve in his bones. He swallowed hard, body like jelly and composure off-kilter. He didn't know how he was going to get through their lessons if a mere smile from her turned him into mush. It was embarrassing. Worse than that, it was *pathetic*.

Around Rosalie, he devolved into a schoolboy. He grew giddy thinking about her. His palms sweated. He couldn't trust his voice not to waver. His senses spun into overdrive at the slightest response from her. He was a man falling deeper and deeper for a woman he could never have.

"The kitchen is spotless," said Rosalie, clueless to his inner turmoil. She tied her apron about her petite waist and then marveled at the stainless steel appliances backdropped by the white cabinets. "Was this closing shift or did you do an extra scrub down?"

He rubbed the back of his neck and half grinned. "I figured it'd be easier for us if everything was in order."

"You mean you cleaned the kitchen for our lesson?" she asked with a rising pitch. Her teeth caught her bottom lip for a thoughtful nibble as she set out inspecting the room. She ran a finger across the countertop for the slightest sign of grease or grime. When none turned up, she rounded on him and laughed. "If I didn't know any better, I'd say you're more invested in these lessons than I am."

"It's nothing," he dismissed, passing off her observation with a cavalier lie. He grabbed his own apron and fastened it around his frame. "You forget I've got a decade of kitchen experience. I like a clean kitchen. That's all."

Her right brow arced, but she let his fib fly. She didn't object, choosing her battles wisely. That terrified him. If Rosalie was playing chess, that meant he was playing checkers. Was he that obvious? Could she tell he had feelings for her?

He swallowed again and rued the sound it produced. It was an audible gulp for their ears, and he snuck a look at her and played it off with a good-natured grin. Before she could tease him for it, he launched into the day's lesson.

"I figured we'd start off easy. Something basic that's a favorite on the menu."

"Gumbo?" Rosalie guessed.

He scoffed, yanking open the industrial-sized refrigerator. "Gumbo is beyond your skill set. You told me you burn grilled cheese, remember?"

It was Rosalie's turn to squirm. She rolled her eyes and dug her hands into the front pockets of her apron. He could practically see the embarrassed flush warming up her dark brown skin. He wanted to laugh, the sight so damn cute, but he resisted.

"I've cooked grilled cheese without burning it," she mumbled feebly.

He grabbed a tub of ghee from the rack on the refrigerator shelf and passed it off to her. "We're starting off easy. Figured I can show you how to make some good ol' fashioned cheesy shrimp and grits."

"That's what Mr. Yancy always orders when he comes in."

"We're famous for our grits."

"Didn't you used to be famous for the whole menu?"

"Once a upon time," said Nick, hitting a confident stride. He forgot his nerves and snapped into chef mode. "I need you to go to the spice rack and grab paprika, salt, ground black pepper, and our special creole seasoning— you'll know it when you see it."

Rosalie did as asked, collecting the four items. He prepped the workstation, explaining each step of the process. For as unorganized as he was in the office, in the kitchen was a different story. In the kitchen he took his workstation seriously, ensuring his ingredients, cookware, and utensils were arranged as needed. Rosalie was an attentive student, hanging on his every word and watching his every move.

He fried up the cast-iron pan and dumped in three tablespoons of ghee. Minced garlic soon joined the melted ghee, sizzling hot in mere seconds. He gestured to the shrimp they had coated in a spice mix and asked if she knew how to sauté.

"I know how to spell *sauté*. That's about it."

"There's a trick to it. It's all in the movement. Watch how the contents tips upward against the rim and then flips," he instructed with effortless ease. He dropped the half pound of shrimp into the pan. Under his expert touch, the melted ghee, minced garlic, and spiced shrimp flipped midair and landed back in place. He repeated the motion several times over, showcasing his technique. "You've gotta push the pan down, then forward. You pull back and voilà! You're sautéing. Wanna try?"

The wrinkle he loved appeared on the bridge of her nose. He encouraged her with a smile.

"It's easy. Give it a try. I promise you I've done worse than anything you can do."

"You mean cooking?"

"When I was first learning? I told you about the eyebrow incident. Lost count how many fires I've started. C'mon." Nick guided her to the forefront, sidestepping out of the way. He observed over her shoulder. "Hold on to the handle firmly. You got it. Now do the motion I showed you—tip down then forward then bring it back."

"Like this?" Rosalie attempted to mimic his smooth sauté, but came up short. The shrimp and garlic spun into the air and landed everywhere but the pan. She immediately let go of its handle with a mortified cringe and step back.

He was behind her, a brick wall to hold her in place. He balanced out her alarm with cool understanding, reaching for her arm and guiding it back toward the pan's handle.

"It's okay," he said. "Don't back off now. You were doing good."

"Are you kidding? The shrimp went flying across the kitchen."

"That's okay. You landed a couple. Concentrate on those."

"And ignore the shrimps on the floor? Got it."

"It's only half. Not so bad. Especially for a first try."

"You're trying to make me feel better."

Nick ignored how sensitive his sense of smell was, picking up her vanilla cotton scent over any other. That was the risk he took standing behind her. He shut that part of his brain off and pressed on, buckling down into instructor mode.

"Try it again," he urged softly. "Remember, tip it downward then forward and then back."

Rosalie concentrated on the measly five shrimp frying on the pan. Her grip on the handle tightened and her brow pinched in concentration as she followed the motions he directed. She dipped the pan and pushed it forward, finishing with a pull backward. The shrimp flipped midair and landed center in the pan.

"I did it!" she shrieked in both delight and surprise.

"Good job, really fluid," said Nick from behind. "You're a natural."

Rosalie snuck him a smirk from over her shoulder. "You don't need to hype me up to be better than I am."

"I promise I'd tell you if you sucked."

"Somehow, I don't doubt that either."

She twisted around, her hand pushing against his shoulder in the lightest of shoves. She caught herself a second too late, looking away.

He pretended it never happened. He stepped forward, dialed down the heat, and finished sautéing the last few shrimp. His mindset was that if he stuck to the cooking lesson, the awkward accidental touches and brushes and slipups would be forgotten. They could preserve their boss and employee relationship.

"Next is the roux," he said huskily. "You're gonna pour four tablespoons of flour into the pan of delicious sautéed drippings. That too hard or you think you got it?"

"Spooning flour I can do."

The roux had to cook for ten minutes. They stood idly by and watched it thicken.

"Have you ever thought about hiring a manager?" Rosalie asked, back against the counter opposite him. "Then you can do what you really like doing—you can cook."

"I've thought about it. Not too many options in St. Aster."

"That's true. It seems like everybody follows in their parents' footsteps."

"Is that a bad thing?"

Rosalie chewed on her bottom lip. "It is when you hate what that is. Some people are okay with taking over for their parents, but some aren't."

"You're talking about yourself. Your mom and her real estate job."

"She thinks it's best. Maybe she's right. Things didn't turn out too good when I went down my own path." Rosalie's sigh was heavy enough to slump her shoulders. "I'm back worse off than when I was a teenager. The last seven years have been a failure—except for Remi. She's the one good thing I've done."

"You should probably stop thinking about it like that. Everybody fails sometime, right? Why should you be any different?"

Rosalie considered his question. "But I have a daughter to think about. I can't *keep* failing."

"Didn't say that either. All I'm saying is you should stop beating yourself up about what happened. So you married a jackass. Millions of people do. Many of 'em stick around for longer than seven years. Maybe you should consider yourself lucky," Nick theorized. "I've known people who waste their whole lives on things like that. You've learned your lesson in seven. That counts for something."

"That's insightful of you."

Nick hazarded a look at her. She was glowing, aiming one of those pretty smiles of hers in his direction. The heat from more than just the roux warmed his flesh, leaving him flushed. Rather than continue their exchange, he diverted his attention onto the bubbling roux.

"Roux is ready. Next up is the chicken stock and whipping cream."

Thank God for distraction.

❧

Thirty minutes later, they feasted on the fruits of their labor. Their earlier uncertainty was on the back burner. Nick stopped fixating on how being around Rosalie made him feel. He was able to press pause on how his attraction to her invaded his brain and dominated his thoughts.

Rosalie seemed to do the same, choosing to ignore everything outside the shrimp and cheese grits and their conversation at hand. They had started talking about the old days, both raised in St. Aster, albeit on opposite sides of town. She dug her spoon into her bowl and fought off a laugh as he reminisced on the time he got pantsed during recess.

"Not sure if you remember him, but Freddie Avant was a little shit."

"I remember him. His older sister was a big shit."

Nick split into a loud laugh. "I'm guessing you had an encounter or two?"

"She had this bike she would ride down the block. If she saw you playing outside, you better hand over whatever you had or else she was going to knock you down and take it," Rosalie answered. She wiped her mouth with a napkin and tossed it in her bowl. "But can't say I ever wanted to be her friend, so no loss there."

"You think we would've been friends if we'd known each other?"

"I don't know if you know this, but my mom couldn't stand yours."

"She brought you by the restaurant a couple times, didn't she?"

Her eyes flickered with nostalgia. "You remember when we came by?"

"I used to help out as a kid. Not cooking or waiting tables or anything like that. But my mom used to have me help the busboy."

"And you noticed me sitting with my mom embarrassed by how much she complained?"

"She's definitely not the easiest to please."

Their laughter synced together like its own musical note. The sound reverberated off the walls of the empty restaurant, pleasant enough to lift their spirits for the rest of the day. Nick checked his watch and realized it was time to finish prep for opening.

"We've really been on this cooking lesson thing for two hours."

"And we're about to open for nobody to show up," Rosalie teased.

"You love reminding me of that, don't you?"

She rose with him from the table. "You didn't let me finish. We don't have too many customers now, but I know we will soon. The lesson was fun."

"Good. I'm glad. Now you can sauté anything you want."

"I'll get right on that. Sautéed PB&J's."

"Or sautéed spaghetti noodles."

"So I cook spaghetti from the jar! Sue me."

They were laughing again, walking toward the kitchen sink to drop off their bowls. Banter hitting its strongest stride yet, Nick couldn't resist his next retort.

"That's what we're gonna learn for lesson number two—the proper way to cook spaghetti."

"Spaghetti in a creole restaurant? That makes perfect sense."

"Rosalie, if you were really out there fixing PB&J's for dinner, you need any lesson you can get."

His latest dig caused her to gasp and she repeated her mistake from earlier. She foisted a hand against his shoulder in what was a playful shove. His reaction was innate. He caught her hand, their fixed gaze suddenly unbreakable. He couldn't look away if he wanted to, and she couldn't either. The space between them ceased to exist.

She stepped into him and he reeled her close. His eyes dropped to her lips and she took in a small, sharp breath. Another hesitant second passed them by as they left room for either to pull away.

Instead they gave in to temptation. His mouth slanted over hers. She rose on tiptoes to meet him. Her arms wound around his neck as she parted her lips and invited him deeper. His tongue obeyed, slipping into her mouth for a taste.

Nick couldn't get enough. He wanted more as their kisses blossomed. Her breathing became short little gasps that drove him wild. They stumbled backward, forgetting time and place, and bumped into the kitchen counter. The empty bowls, once filled with grits, crashed to the floor and shattered into dozens of pieces. They didn't care, too wrapped up in each other. Too enveloped to think about what they were doing and what would come after.

For the time being at least, it didn't matter.

CHAPTER THIRTEEN

"I'm surprised to see you're back."

Rosalie smiled at Ines as she walked into The Party Haven. Today the clerk wore a cowgirl outfit complete with a cowhide vest and denim skirt that stretched across her fleshy thighs. She perked up at the sight of Rosalie. The rest of the store was empty on a Wednesday morning.

"I'm surprised to be back myself," said Rosalie. She unzipped her crossbody bag and pulled out her wallet. "I'm hoping you still have that *Princess and the Frog* costume in stock."

Ines folded her arms, leaning against the store counter. "You mean the one that costs an arm and a leg? The one your baby girl threw a tantrum about?"

"That's the one."

"We've got several. What made Mama Bear change her mind?"

"I figure it's a special occasion. If it makes my cub happy, it makes me happy."

Ines cracked a smile of her own and then shrugged. "Fair enough. Gimme a second. I'll grab you one from the back. That way you're buying one that hasn't been touched by anybody else's grubby little hands."

"While you're at it," said Rosalie in another spur of the moment decision, "can I take a look at that queen costume you mentioned last time?"

Fifteen minutes later, she emerged from The Party Haven with two large shopping bags dangling off her arm. In one bag was the glittery, tulle *Princess and the Frog* costume Remi coveted. In the other, the rental queen costume that happened to fit Rosalie better than anticipated. The decision to splurge on a Halloween costume for Remi went against her better judgment.

She had created a meticulous budget and sixty bucks on a children's Halloween costume wasn't on the expense sheet. Yet, in the wake of other spontaneous decisions she'd been making, she talked herself into it. If she could ignore Clyde's call—if she could give in to an irresistible attraction for her boss and kiss him—why *not* be irresponsible and splurge on Remi?

After years of being careful and considerate of others, she was tired of playing by the rules. She was sick of giving Clyde the benefit of the doubt. She was done denying herself basic desires like any other woman. Most of all, she was tired of going through the motions.

It was time for a change. She was going to stop caring about what everybody else wanted. From Clyde to Ma to the little voice that was her conscience in the back of her head. She was going to go with intuition and whatever felt right in the moment. If that meant splurging on Remi's Halloween costume, so be it.

On her walk to her car, she passed a poster for the Autumn Festival. She lost her breath thinking about her cooking lessons with Nick. If doing whatever felt right meant another passionate kiss with him, how could she resist? She was *done* resisting, ready to take risks for the first time in years.

Rosalie tossed her bags in the back of her Honda Civic and hopped in. She was nervous about seeing Nick again, but the curiosity of what came next drowned out any hesitancy. She wanted to find out, turning the key in the ignition and pulling into traffic. Soon she would.

"What's that smirk for?" Zoe asked as Rosalie turned up at the restaurant. She finger combed her home-dyed red hair and eyed Rosalie with gossipy interest. "I know that sorta smirk. It's one of those 'I've got a secret' smirks."

Rosalie dismissed Zoe's claim with a shake of her head. She refused to lend credence to her fellow waitress's claims. Even if they were a little true. She did have a secret, and so did Nick. From across the dining room floor, their eyes met. It was the first time seeing him since what happened in the kitchen.

Her insides twisted into a pretzel. She couldn't control the reactions he drew out of her. A mere glance from him and her senses spun into overdrive. The room felt hotter and her mind foggier. She couldn't help remembering how demanding his mouth felt on hers. How sturdy his arm felt braced around her waist.

Rosalie forcefully tore her eyes away and focused on the dining area. Regulars like Mrs. Kettles and Mr. Yancy had shown up for lunch. She snatched her notepad and pen from her apron pockets and dived headfirst into waitressing.

The diners distracted her. She provided top-notch service to each table, delivering their appetizers, entrees, and drinks with a gusto that earned generous tips. Her zeal was unmatched, energy high as she failed to notice Zoe was gone on a lunch break. She didn't need anyone's help. So long as she had the tables to wait on she was satisfied. The busier she was, the less she noticed Nick's presence in the shadows.

"I love the renovations," said Mrs. Kettles, laying a ten dollar bill on the table. The tip was more than her usual. "The restaurant's coming alive. I can tell it's a woman's touch. I'm guessing that's you?"

Rosalie simply smiled and thanked the ex-schoolteacher for her patronage. She pocketed the tip and began clearing the table. Que was slow-moving and probably on a smoke break; besides, she had suspicions he kept their tips from time to time. After she finished wiping down the table, she turned on her heel to head to the kitchen, but nearly bumped right into Nick.

Her surprise widened her features. Her eyes doubled in size and her nostrils flared. She hadn't expected him to be standing right behind her. He was a tempting force, tall and broad and towering a foot over her with his intent green-eyed gaze. She clutched a hand to her heart and calmed her sudden erratic breathing.

"I didn't know you were behind me," she mumbled.

"Sorry," he apologized. His fingers threaded through his golden-brown strands. "Do you have a moment? Was wondering if I could speak to you alone…"

Oh, god.

Her already knotted insides tightened. The clench was unbearable, a deep contraction on her stomach muscles. She played it off with a curt, sharp nod, and fell in line, following him out of the dining area. She could feel others' eyes on her. Zoe as she returned from her latest break, and a couple of the diners, who stared nosily. She ignored them, trailing behind Nick with marked indifference.

Fuck them.

They didn't pay her bills. They didn't know who she was. They *didn't* matter.

Let them think what they wanted. They were going to gossip anyway. She was all too familiar with how fast word traveled around a small, close-minded, traditional town like St. Aster. As a teenager running around with a bad guy like Clyde, she had experienced her share of town gossip. She knew that once the rumor mill started churning, there was little she could do to stop it.

In the back office, the door swung shut behind them. Nick walked to his desk and plopped into his chair. She chose to stand. He seemed confused by this choice, tilting his head to the side as if tempted to ask.

"We should probably talk, don't you think?"

Rosalie folded her hands in front of her and tried to keep her head. She needed logic now more than ever. "Sure, about what?"

"Is that what we're doing?" The uppermost corner of his lips curled. "We're gonna pretend?"

"Nick, pretend what? I was on table five. Today's been a good day for business—"

"You know, as blunt as you can be sometimes, I didn't think you'd go the ignore angle," he mused aloud, relaxing into his office chair. "I figured you for a confrontational, what-the-hell-happened kinda reaction."

"If you're talking about yesterday—"

"I think you know that's what I'm talking about," he interrupted.

"It...it was a mistake. A one-time thing."

His jaw squared. "I was wrong. I crossed a line."

"We both did. It happened," she said with a shrug. "It's in the past. Time to move on."

"Just like that?"

"Just like that," she said.

"If that's what you want. If it doesn't make you uncomfortable to—"

"I'm fine. Are you?"

Nick seemed taken aback by the reversal. He nodded. "I'm good."

"Good," said Rosalie firmly. She quirked a brow, hands on her hips. "Anything else you wanted to talk about?"

"Uh, no. That was it. Sorry to pull you away from your tables."

Rosalie mock-curtseyed and then spun around to stride out of the office. Her assured footsteps made her feel powerful and confident, but the second she was out of his sight? She crumbled into herself. She paused midway down the hall and leaned against the wall to think on the exchange that just happened.

Nick had pulled her into the office to check how she was feeling. She had stamped down on every emotional response she had had since the kiss in order to appear unaffected and indifferent. Now that emotion came crashing down on her. She felt its brunt force with a sinking dread that made her groan. Confronted about the kitchen kiss, she might have lied and said it was nothing, but in reality, it was the opposite. In reality, she couldn't stop thinking about it.

Even replaying the moment in the office in her mind, she considered alternate endings; moments where she abandoned charade and rushed across his desk and into his arms. He caught her with ease and pulled her deeper into his lap. They melted together, joined at the mouth, surrendering to their magnetic connection.

That fantasy felt all too real. It was more than tempting as Rosalie closed her eyes and bit down on her lip.

"Hey, you good?"

Zoe had stopped in the hall on her way to the kitchen. Her fellow waitress raised her drawn-on brows at her, staring as if an explanation was in order. Rosalie denied her, smiling in hopes of pacifying her suspicion.

"I'm good," she said, standing straight. "Table five still mine?"

Zoe nodded and said nothing.

"Got it," said Rosalie. "I'll go check on them."

She walked off, knowing that Zoe watched her every step of the way.

That evening coming home, Rosalie's heart sank. She expected to come home and find Ma's car gone. She had claimed to have a viewing that would last hours into the evening. Yet, as Rosalie pulled up into the front drive, she spotted her Corolla parked outside the garage. Remi noticed nothing, seated in the back fussing with her favorite stuffed animal.

They entered the home to the domestic vibe of Ma in the kitchen and Henry glued to the tube. Remi slid into a chair at the breakfast table and began work on her homework. Ma asked for Rosalie's help in the kitchen. If it were anyone else, Rosalie would've gladly obliged. Since it was Ma, she held her breath, deep down aware of what she was getting herself into.

"That's not how you chop the onions." Ma clicked her tongue and shook her head, nudging Rosalie aside to show her how it was done. "*This* is how you do it. It's just chopping. It's simple as can be."

Rosalie gritted her teeth. "I was doing that."

"You're not blind, are you? Stevie Wonder could see you were doing it wrong."

"Fine. I'll try again."

"I don't know how you cooked for that man all those years," Ma mused aloud. She freed her hands of onion residue, rubbing them off on her apron. She returned to her post at the stove, wooden spoon in hand. "You were never interested in learning when I tried to show you. It makes sense now that you can't even chop anything."

Rosalie closed her eyes, the blade stuck halfway through the onion. She concentrated on breathing. If she controlled her breathing, she controlled her temper. In the background, Remi scribbled in her workbook, clueless to the simmering tension.

"Cooking is one of the biggest duties as a wife," Ma prattled on.

More tongue clicking.

Tut. Tut. Tut.

Rosalie's skin heated up hotter than the flame on the stove. Her teeth grinded at a rate that was painful. She didn't care.

"Damn shame. Never was a fan of him, but no wonder he left you."

The knife fell from Rosalie's now limp hand and landed on the kitchen tile with a loud thud. Remi stopped scribbling. Ma looked up from the boiling pot. The silence was abrupt and it was invasive, permeating every corner of the room. Except for Rosalie's ears. Her heartbeat echoed in them, pounding against her eardrums as her temper broke free. She spun around, eyes wide and nostrils flared.

"And what's your excuse? I've watched men walk in and out of your life like an assembly line my entire life!" she shrieked. "I can't keep a man, but you sure as hell can't either!"

Rosalie stormed out of the kitchen. Remi's soft murmur called after her. Ma might've said her name too. But she stopped for no one, hands trembling out of sheer anger. She sped down the hall and wrenched open the door. It swung shut behind her. Thankfully nobody bothered to follow. On the edge of the porch, she tipped her head back, nose in the air, and sucked in clean breaths.

The aftermath rained on her. The lament for her out-of-control behavior. She knew better than to let Ma provoke her. It was why she was so hell-bent on avoidance. Those strategies worked best when dealing with Ma. Even with her new decision to follow her gut instinct, how had she forgotten her ultimate goal?

Provide for Remi.

If she wanted to save up enough money for a place of her own, she needed to be on her best behavior. She needed to appease Ma as much as possible. She needed to stack every penny earned. She probably didn't need a secret fling with her boss.

And she definitely didn't need *Clyde* hanging over her head. His voice mail was a constant reminder of the past and its utter devastation. It had to go.

Rosalie slid her phone out of her jean pocket and scrolled to the voice message notification. She inhaled a sharp breath and did what she needed to do. She pressed delete.

CHAPTER FOURTEEN

Maxie's birthday was less than a week away. The finer details for her birthday party were mapped out. It would be a spook-tastic Halloween affair, complete with fun activities like a toilet paper mummy foot race. Nick had even hired a face painter. The owner at The Party Haven lent him Halloween decorations. He planned to bake Maxie's favorite cake, a recipe near and dear to Mom's heart.

Called King Cake, the fluffy dessert referenced biblical kings. Over a century ago, his great-great-great-grandmother baked the cake when they first settled into the community of St. Aster. The recipe had been passed down generation to generation, taught to Nick by Mom when he was a teenager. They were baked to perfection with cinnamon roll–style dough, and he crowned the cake with iced frosting. The more the better if it were up to Maxie. He even promised to use purple and orange frosting for her birthday.

Now if they could know with certainty if there'd be anyone attending. Maxie had refused to hand out invitations to her classmates. She claimed she didn't like them much, but Nick knew the truth; she was afraid the other kids would laugh at her. After all, she was the weird tomboy girl. Kids her age didn't usually take to her.

That was why he coveted her friendship with Remi. Maxie finally had a friend to giggle with, building sandcastles or play hide-and-seek. Remi's attendance was a given. But the other kids? Nick sought confirmation with their parents, calling them up or catching them around town.

"They're no fun, Papa!" Maxie stubbornly said, overhearing a phone call.

She had finished finger painting. The problem was, the paints got on her clothes and in her hair much more than it got on the canvas. "Me and Remi can have our own party!"

"Kiddo, you need more kids there. It'll be a fun time. Everybody will dress up."

Maxie gave him the side-eye. "Even you?"

"Even me."

"And Remi?"

"You bet."

"What about her mama?"

Nick's stomach fluttered. "Not sure. I can ask her."

"She's so pretty! Maybe she can be a princess like Remi—or a *queen*!"

"Queen sounds about right." Nick was grinning like a fool. His imagination ran away with that idea. Before he could control it, a creative vision materialized in his mind's eye. Rosalie as the sexiest queen he'd ever seen, in a lacy, corseted red little thing, jeweled crown perched atop her head. He had to chase the naughty imagery away, shaking his head.

It was shameful, completely inappropriate for him to entertain such fantasies. He had to fight his attraction for Rosalie. Find a way to squash the feelings he had developed. Stop thinking about her as anything more than his employee.

Turning off his feelings wasn't easy, though. Rosalie made him nervous. She intrigued him and inspired him. He hadn't felt this way about a woman since...

Nick couldn't remember. What that meant, he didn't know. Anytime he considered the deeper connotation, he diverted his thoughts elsewhere. In true Nicholas Fontaine fashion, he'd worry about it later, if ever.

"If Grandmama was here, would she still dress up?" Maxie asked the question that stirred him from his thoughts.

He was grateful for the disruption, as it was dangerous for him to think about Rosalie for too long.

"She would. Remember how much she loved Halloween?"

Maxie nodded, spooling tangled strands around her finger. "Now she can be an angel."

The sweet theory inspired his next smile. He tousled her already messy hair and said, "Time to wash up. How'd you get so much paint on you, kiddo? You get in a fight with the paint jars again?"

In a rare show of responsibility, Nick pulled into Ady's parking lot early. Way early. As in three hours early. The clock on his truck's dash read 8:03 a.m. On most days, he wouldn't show up 'til half past eleven, and that was *with* the intention to take a lunch. Those lazy days were behind him. Since Project Fixer-Upper began, he had dedicated himself to Ady's survival.

No more running. No more excuses. No more catnaps at his desk.

Project Fixer-Upper was about increasing profit and improving their reputation. Under his supervision, Ady's Creole Café had deteriorated into a run-down shell of its former self. What would Mom think if she walked in to find her beloved café empty?

His heart tightened into a painful clench. He had avoided wondering what Mom would think for that very reason. She had entrusted him with her life's dream and he had spent months sullying it like it never mattered.

Nick strode across the cratered parking lot, jaw set and eyes focused. Thanks to Rosalie, Project Fixer-Upper gave him a newfound sense of purpose. His heart thumped with the rhythm of determination. His strides widened, feet planting firmly on his path to unlock the front door. He wasn't going to fail Mom this time.

Coming up on the door, he wasn't expecting anyone to be standing outside. His pace slowed considerably as he took in the unknown man waiting on someone to come by. Dressed in a forgettable business suit and tie, brown hair neatly parted down the left side, the man stretched thin lips into an unnatural smile.

"Morning, Mr. Fontaine! I was hoping you would show up."

"It's Nick. Restaurant doesn't open 'til eleven."

"I'm well aware."

"Then what d'you want?" His tone hardened, and he made zero effort to return the man's smiley greeting.

"I'm Perry Langley from Yum Corp. Nice meeting you."

He left him hanging on a handshake. Instead, he produced his keys and unlocked the door. The man tailed him inside, uninvited but eager to continue being a bother. He abruptly stopped so that the man almost stepped right into him, and then he turned around with brows raised.

"I'm lost. Is there a reason you're following me inside?"

"We've sent you letters for quite some time, but we haven't heard back. I was hoping to sit down with you and discuss a profitable business offer."

"I'm not interested."

"It would be in your best interest to—"

"Not. Interested." Nick moved past Langley and flicked on the lights. Maybe if he ignored him, he would go away. He tested the theory by unstacking chairs off the tables.

But the guy remained. He stood in the same spot and patiently surveyed the dining room. Nick could see the curiosity glinting in his eyes, making mental notes about the interior of Ady's.

"Hey pal, we're closed. And I'm not interested. Are you gonna get going?" he asked rudely, unable to hold back another second.

Langley carried his briefcase to the closest table and unsnapped its locks. He pulled out a thick sheaf of papers, flipping through them like one would a book. Apparently, he seemed to think this meant something to Nick.

However, Nick wasn't amused. "Look, this is the last time—"

"Five minutes, and then I'll be out of your hair, Mr. Fontaine. I really think you'll be interested once you hear me out."

Nick zeroed in on the papers. From what he could tell, each page was stamped by a giant red Yum Corp logo in the header. The more he looked at the pages upon pages, even from afar, the more it registered with him what they were.

A contract of some sort.

"For someone in the restaurant biz, Mr. Fontaine, I'm surprised you've never heard of us," Perry said, smile smug. "Yum Corp is one of the biggest restaurant franchise holding corporations in the country. We own many of your favorite chains."

"What's that have to do with me?"

"Isn't it obvious? We're interested in your spot! We would like to partner up—*well*, not partner up exactly. But we would like to make you an offer for the restaurant."

Nick folded his arms across his broad chest. "It's not for sale."

"*Everything's* for sale—"

"I'm not interested," he interrupted, breaking into another stride. He shot toward the door, yanking it open. "Mr. Yum Yum—or whatever your name is—I heard you out. Time to go."

Perry Langley packed up the novel-length stack of papers, the locks on his briefcase clicking to a close. He obeyed Nick's demand and moseyed toward the door. On the threshold, he paused and his thin-lipped, unnatural smile returned.

"Offer's still on the table. Here's my business card. If you change your mind, call me up."

Nick snatched the business card out of his hand and let the door literally hit him on the way out.

⌒∞⌒

"Who was that guy in a suit?"

Rosalie arrived to Ady's minutes later, windswept by the October gloom. The morning was another gray dud outside, signs of rain in the weighty clouds. She shrugged off her denim jacket three sizes too big and hung it up on the coatrack. Her curls she freed from under a beanie, the fluffy mane framing her face once again.

He wanted to kiss her. Instead he focused on unstacking chairs from the tables. If he didn't look directly at her his mind wouldn't wander. He wouldn't think back to what happened during their last cooking lesson.

"Nobody important," he answered hoarsely. "Are you sure you're up for another lesson?"

Rosalie smiled wide on her walk to the kitchen. "If we're still pretending like I'm the one who's competing in the Autumn Festival, then yes."

He followed her. Her remark was bemusing. "We're not pretending anything—you are the one spearheading the Autumn Festival competition. Did you forget that?"

"It's the whole restaurant that's competing."

"Rosalie, I already told you," he said as they pushed open the flapping kitchen doors. "I don't cook for Ady's anymore. Project Fixer-Upper—the Autumn Festival—doesn't change that."

Halfway into the room, she spun around to face him. "You're teaching me Ady's menu now. What's the difference?"

"It's not the same thing."

Nick stepped around her. He couldn't face her, couldn't look into her cattish brown eyes, tempted by her pouty lips, and pretend like he wasn't entranced. He wanted to confess the feelings he had stamped down for weeks now, but knew better than to go there.

After all, Rosalie had said it was nothing.

She sighed, tying her apron about her waist. "What's the lesson today?"

Nick was at the pantry, retrieving a bag of rice. "We're doing a classic today. It's a staple on the menu. Red beans and rice."

"That doesn't sound too difficult."

"It isn't. Almost as easy as spaghetti out of the jar."

She rolled her eyes. "Are you ever going to let that go?"

"Honestly? Not any time soon," he answered with an air of honest mocking. He set down the bag of rice and cans of kidney beans. "First things first, we're gonna chop the veggies. Onions, green peppers, and celery."

Rosalie flinched as if he'd said an offensive word. "You go ahead and chop. I'll watch."

"What, do you have a knife phobia or something? Chopping is cooking 101."

"It's not my thing."

"If you're going to cook up an entire menu for the Autumn Festival, it's gonna need to be," Nick said bluntly. He guided her toward the counter with the chopping board and veggies laid out nearby. "I'll walk you through it. It's all about technique."

Rosalie gave up any protests and picked up the knife he had set out. Her resigned mood was palpable, causing him to frown. He wanted to ask why the idea of chopping vegetables seemed to upset her, but he refrained. Whatever it was, if she didn't bring it up, it wasn't any of his business.

"First thing you wanna keep in mind is to protect your fingers. You wanna hold the vegetables like this," he said calmly, slipping into an instructive role with natural ease. He reached around her and placed her hand on the green pepper so that her fingertips were safely tucked in. Her hand was so soft he hated letting it go. "To make things easier, especially if it's a round vegetable, slice it in half."

"Like this?' she asked, cutting through the green pepper with the dull blade.

"You've got the right idea. You want to make sure the flat side stays facedown. Then you start cutting."

Nick was aware of how close they were. She was directly in front of him, close enough that he smelled her scent over any fragrant vegetable. That the thick curls of her hair brushed against his chest whenever she shifted in place, or when she peeked at him over her shoulder. He swallowed his attraction and stepped away.

For a long stretch of silence, Rosalie chopped the veggies and Nick hovered in the background observing. She finished the last stalk of celery and then turned to him with a shine in her eyes that was damn adorable.

"Now what?" she asked, clearly on a rush of adrenaline.

Nick grinned. "We heat up some olive oil so we can cook the veggies."

Rosalie wiped her hands on her apron and crossed the kitchen for the stove. She moved with a sudden confidence that further turned him on. He liked seeing her this way, in the take-charge mode she assumed while at Ady's.

As if reading his thoughts, she said, "You know, part of the reason I've hated cooking was because there was always so much pressure put into it. My mother tried to teach me a few times, and it never worked out. Then with Clyde—it was always thrown in my face as a failure of mine."

"I like to think cooking should be fun. It's creating something from nothing."

She smiled. "Creating something from nothing. That's an interesting way to put it."

"It's the truth, isn't it?" Nick asked with a shrug. He had come up beside her by the stove. "All cooking is, is putting together the right ingredients at the right time to make something great."

Like them. It wasn't lost on Nick that what he described was what he had discovered with Rosalie. They were the ingredients; an experimental recipe that cooked up a delicious attraction too damn good to pass up.

It wasn't lost on Rosalie either. She had forgotten about the bottle of olive oil and the pan waiting for her by the stove. Her gaze fixed onto his face, eyes shining as the same cooking epiphany must have occurred to her too. The already-small gap between them began to close.

"I like the way you think," she said softly.

"That's a first. No one's ever told me that before."

She let out a lone giggle. "First time for everything."

Their faces were inches apart as they both gave up fighting the force that pulled them together. Nick's palms cupped the undersides of her cheeks and his pulse sped as he stared into her dark eyes. They leaned closer and their lips brushed in a teasing prelude to a kiss.

The kitchen door flapped open at the same time their names were called. Zoe breezed inside. They jumped apart. She stopped midstep, immediately thrown by what she saw—or thought she saw. Even she didn't seem sure, drawn-on brows knitted and a frown on her mouth.

The question hung unmistakably in the air. What was going on?

CHAPTER FIFTEEN

"**I**'m not interrupting anything, am I?" Zoe asked.

"No!" Rosalie and Nick answered in unison. They glanced at each other. Rosalie wanted to kick herself.

Nick elaborated, clearing his throat first. "No, you're not. I didn't even know you were here."

"Came in early to talk to you. I was looking to switch my days off."

"Right, sure. We can go talk about that. Gimme a sec," said Nick, untying his apron.

Rosalie hung back as the two left the kitchen. Though Zoe said nothing about what she had walked in on, the line in her brow said enough. She seemed to sense it was *something*.

Rosalie's face fell into her hands. She hadn't considered the possibility that someone would walk in on their cooking lesson. She hadn't thought about potential consequences as she looked into Nick's eyes and inched closer. As she allowed the magnetism between them to take control.

It was the risk of following her intuition. In abandoning rationale, she had left herself vulnerable to spur-of-the-moment mistakes. Mistakes like crossing a line and kissing Nick a second time.

Word around town traveled fast. If Zoe wanted to, she could spread what she had seen across St. Aster by the end of the day. Rosalie had decided to stop caring what others thought, but what about how town rumors would affect her reputation? How could she overlook how that would trickle down onto Remi?

She had endured St. Aster's rampant gossip before. She still remembered what it was like; the arched brows and whispers. The scandalized stares as she ignored warnings and involved herself with Clyde.

The scandal was hot gossip for months. The Underwood girl, daughter of the haughty real estate agent Ms. Lacie, had fallen for one of the most troublesome guys on the block. Shame on her. Shame on her mother. Would she follow in Ms. Lacie's footsteps? The bad relationship with Rosalie's father was a black stain even years later. Would she wind up sixteen and pregnant?

Hardly any better. Just seventeen and married. Seventeen and run off several states over, shacked up with the bad boy who stole her heart. The pregnancy didn't come until later, but when it did, it sealed the deal. Rosalie was on track to fuck up like the rest of the family.

Rosalie gathered her curls into a low, puffy ponytail. The more she analyzed the situation, keeping her past in mind this time, the more she knew she could no longer stick her head in the sand. While she refused to return to the overly cautious woman she had been, she couldn't keep acting on impulse.

She needed to find a balance.

With her mind made up, Rosalie glanced at the kitchen clock on the opposite wall. In another hour, Ady's was opening for the day. She would work her shift as usual, but by its end, she resolved to do what she needed to do. She was going to pull Nick aside to talk.

Business at Ady's that day was the best Rosalie had seen since she started working there. The lunch crowd was steady and stragglers wandered in throughout the afternoon. Project Fixer-Upper was working. The renovations they had made thus far had improved the aesthetics of the restaurant. Now they needed to focus on the food and the business side of things.

At the end of her shift, Rosalie approached Zoe. They hadn't exchanged words about what happened earlier, but she knew her coworker. Zoe was dying to know the scoop.

"You don't need to pretend like you're not wondering," said Rosalie. She joined Zoe at table six as she wiped down the tabletop. "I know you want to ask about earlier."

Zoe tossed her own rag over her shoulder and smirked. "Could you tell?"

"It's nothing."

"It sure didn't look like nothing."

Rosalie inhaled a shaky breath. "Zoe, I don't need everybody around town talking."

"Talking about what? As far as I'm concerned, ain't none of it is my business," said Zoe. She spotted the surprise on Rosalie's face and her smirk grew. "Don't look so shocked. I might like gossip, but I'm not about to air you out to anybody. What you and Nick do on your own time is your business."

"Thanks, Zoe. I don't even know what's going on. I'm hoping to figure it out today."

"Just don't forget I don't mind a juicy detail or two."

The two waitresses traded laughs before Rosalie said her goodbye. She was crossing the dining room when Nick emerged from the back office. They both stumbled to a stop to avoid colliding. An immediate air of uncertainty hung between them.

Rosalie glanced at the truck keys clutched between his fingers. "Are you out for the rest of the day?"

"I was headed to pick up Maxie."

"I was about to pick up Remi. Do you have a second to talk?"

Nick scanned the rest of the dining area. Rosalie followed him, noticing Zoe eavesdropping from table six. They turned back to face each other.

"How about we talk on our way to the school?"

Outside on the sidewalk, they almost split into opposite directions. He moved left toward his pickup truck and she moved to go right. They doubled back at the last second once they realized their error.

"How about we walk?" Rosalie proposed. She double checked the time on her phone. "We've got about thirty minutes 'til their class is out. It should take us twenty."

"Good point. It'll be easier to talk that way."

They set off on the path that led from the restaurant to the elementary school. It cut through the center of town, a long sidewalk winding past shrouded cypress trees and its feathered branches.

Rosalie had spent the day rehearsing what she wanted to say. She only hoped her mind wouldn't go blank. It was important for them to hash out whatever it was that had started to unravel between them. At his side as they strolled down the sidewalk, she chanced a glance at him, and then fired off with no preamble.

"Nick, what was this morning about?"

"You tell me."

"I was hoping you would know. It feels like things have blurred."

"Things have definitely blurred. That's what I've been concerned about—I'm your boss. I don't want to make you uncomfortable. Sorry if I have. It's on me."

"It's not just you. It's me too," said Rosalie firmly. "It's like once I'm around you, I throw all sense out of the window."

Nick released a throaty laugh. "Thanks. Exactly what I wanted to hear."

"You know what I mean. It's like I can feel myself getting carried away, but for some reason…I don't care."

"I know exactly what you mean. Probably because I feel the same way. Not sure if you realize it, but you're kinda amazing. It's been hard not to notice," he said, sticking his hands in his pockets. He had shortened his strides to accommodate her smaller steps. "*But* I'm still your boss and I don't wanna put you in that situation. It's not fair to you."

Rosalie stopped altogether. She had no idea what gave her the courageous nudge needed to voice the thought that ran through her head. She turned to him and said, "What if I want to be in that situation?"

Nick choked on his next breath as if doubting his own ears. "Your idea of a joke is cruel. You know that, right?"

"And if I'm not joking?"

"Rosalie," said Nick, staring at her with wide-eyed disbelief. "Then I'd be tempted to try a back handspring and bust my ass in the process. But I'd probably settle for a kiss."

"A kiss sounds nice."

"And you're *sure* you're not joking?"

Rosalie's head tipped backward as she laughed. "No, Nick, I'm not joking. I like you. I don't know what to do with that, or where to go from here, but…I like spending time with you."

"I'm not sure where to go from here either, but I'd sure as hell like to find out. I've been trying to impress you for weeks," he confessed with a faint tinge to his cheeks. "I know you didn't have the best opinion of me when you started at Ady's…"

"You've been trying to impress me?"

He rubbed the back of his neck. "From day one. I saw the looks you were giving me. Like this-guy-is-a-slouch sorta looks. It's how everybody in town looks at me, but coming from you? It bothered me."

"Nick Fontaine, did you agree to Project Fixer-Upper to spend time with me?"

"No! That…that happened to be a perk."

Rosalie slowly smiled watching him squirm under her accusation. She had learned over the course of the past few weeks that Nick emoted far more than Clyde ever did. He might've kept up his cool-guy act around others in St. Aster, but when he was alone with her, he couldn't help himself. Just like her.

"Are you going to kiss me or not?" she asked, challenging him with a quirked brow.

"If you're absolutely sure this isn't a joke," he teased one last time. They shared a quick laugh as they edged closer.

Nick brushed a curl behind her ear and kissed her. It started off slow, unhurried as their mouths worked against each other's at a lazy pace. She rose onto the balls of her feet and clutched his face in her hands. His wet tongue stroked across her bottom lip, sparking a shock of electricity through her veins.

Any doubts, any second guesses melted away. Rosalie stopped thinking as she lost herself in Nick's kiss.

When they broke away, they stood there for a while, still wrapped up in each other. His lips grazed her brow as she leaned into him and rested against his shoulder. The decision they'd made trickled in bit by bit.

"We're dating," Nick said aloud, stunned. His face broke into a smile. "You know that's the last thing I expected getting outta bed this morning."

Rosalie's smile matched his. "This is the last thing I expected leaving for our walk. Just promise me nothing's going to change at Ady's.

"Are you kidding? Project Fixer-Upper's still happening."

"Good. I was worried for a second."

"We're two people who happen to work at the same place," Nick answered, his hand seeking hers. "Who also happen to be dating, and who don't give a damn about what anybody in St. Aster thinks."

"That's pretty specific."

"I don't like gray area."

Their fingers threaded together as they set off down the pathway again, walking hand in hand.

"Maxie's birthday party is Saturday."

"I know. I bought Remi an expensive costume she'll be wearing."

"And what about you?"

"I'm not saying."

"I already told you about how Maxie's making me wear one."

Rosalie cut him a high-brow and curled lip kind of look. "And I already told you plopping on a plastic mask and calling yourself a werewolf doesn't count."

"Sure it does. It's the effort that matters."

"It sounds like you're making your own rules."

"Kind of like what we're doing now," Nick teased. "You're really not going to tell me what it is?"

Rosalie relished in the chance to tease him as they turned onto the elementary school's block. "You're just going to have to wait and see."

CHAPTER SIXTEEN

On the morning of Maxie's birthday, she woke with a scream. Nick's heart slammed against his chest and he barreled up the stairs. In his haste he stumbled into her room already searching for the culprit. None was to be found. Maxie sat up against the pillows, long hair tangled and eyes crusty, blinking at him in shock. At her side at once, he thought up the worst scenarios.

"Papa, I'm six years old!"

His elevated heart rate plummeted. "Maxie kiddo, is that what you were screaming about?"

"I can't believe it!" She slapped little hands to either cheek.

"I can. You've had a birthday every year, haven't you? Why so shocked this year?" He sat down on the edge of her twin-sized bed and brushed stray, uncombed strands from her face. For weeks now they had talked about her birthday; she had given him a list of wants for the party. He couldn't pinpoint what would bring a sudden bout of amnesia.

"But I've *never* been six before!"

"Good point. You're only six once."

"Can we have chocolate chip pancakes?"

"What kinda house d'you think this is?" Nick asked to her widening eyes. He rose to his feet and plucked her from underneath the covers. "We're having *double* chocolate chip pancakes—and extra maple syrup!"

Maxie's cheers rang through the house.

A half hour later, the father and daughter sat down for their stacks of double chocolate chip pancakes, complete with extra maple syrup and tall glasses of milk. He was chuckling at the sight of Maxie smudging syrup on her chin when the doorbell trilled. He made her promise to sit still as he answered the door. He expected door-to-door salespeople or his pesky old neighbor, Ms. Swanson; she routinely forgot the password to her Wi-Fi.

Opening the door, he received a jolt of delight. Rosalie stood on his stoop alongside an impatient Remi. Again, he was reminded how much they looked alike. Even their hair was styled the same, combed into puffy buns at the tops of their heads. Perched in front were crowns—a queen and her princess daughter.

Nick grinned wide. "Morning, your majesties."

"Morning, peasant!" Remi giggled.

"Peasant? Ouch!"

"Remi," Rosalie sighed, bringing a slow hand to her forehead. "How many times do I have to tell you not to call people peasant? A *good* princess doesn't make people feel bad, remember?"

"I forgot." Remi fought a smirk, lips retaining a tell-tale curl that revealed the real truth.

Nick couldn't help his laugh. No wonder Maxie and Remi got along so well; Remi had a mischievous little spark of her own. He stepped aside and ushered the two inside. He tried not to stare for long, but Rosalie looked gorgeous.

The gown she wore was a soft primrose yellow. The bust was fitted and heart-shaped in cut, but modest enough for a children's Halloween party. The silk organza skirt flowed to the floor in subtle layers. If Remi was Tiana from *The Princess and the Frog*, Rosalie was Belle from *Beauty and the Beast*. Did that make him…?

He was going to be dressed as a werewolf, after all.

Remi ran ahead to meet Maxie in the kitchen. The girls squealed their hellos, breathlessly talking over each other. Nick used the free moment, however brief, to chat up Rosalie.

"You look"—he paused for a shake of his head and another once-over—"*amazing*."

"You think? This isn't even my costume. I borrowed it from The Party Haven."

"Borrowed, huh? You sure you wanna return it? It looks so good on you." Nick stopped her outside the kitchen. The girls were nowhere in sight. He took the opening and chanced a quick but soft kiss.

"That's just what I need for my rep. Everybody to know I steal Halloween costumes."

"Let 'em think what they'll think."

"Is that so, Mr. Werewolf man? What happened to just a mask?"

He glanced down at his costume. The tufted fur was thick, heavy and cheaply made. He hadn't planned on anything more than a mask, but Maxie had talked him into it. Being the good sport he was, he agreed to make her happy.

"It's cute that you're wearing it for her," Rosalie giggled as if reading his thoughts. "And you don't look half bad either. Finest werewolf I've ever seen."

"Oh, yeah?"

"Mhmm. For sure." Rosalie confirmed as much with several small, barely-there kisses to his lips.

He was left grinning wide afterward. "You know, now that we're on the same page about what we're doing, we should probably let the kiddos know. It'll probably make Maxie's day."

"I heard my name!" Maxie squeaked from the next room over.

Two pairs of small feet rumbled against the hardwood floor. They scooted to a clumsy halt, wide-eyed and wheezing. Nick had already let go of Rosalie and began corralling them back in the other direction.

"Nothing to see here, nosy ones. Back to those pancakes."

"I can't have any pancakes or I'll ruin my dress!" Remi said haughtily.

On instinct alone, Maxie rolled her eyes and muttered, "Oh, brother."

Nick and Rosalie shared an amused smile lost on both girls.

✦

Rosalie helped Nick set up for Maxie's party. It was slated to start at noon, and they were expecting a modest group of twenty. Out in the backyard he set up foldable tables and chairs. Rosalie blew up purple, orange, and black balloons and scattered them throughout the grass. Together they decorated each table with plastic jack-o'-lanterns lit up from within by tiny bulbs. There was nothing left to handle except the food.

Last night he had stayed up late cooking some of Mom's classics. Even the breakfast's sugar-laced syrup couldn't overpower the zesty spices and herbs wafting from room to room. The chicken and sausage jambalaya, seasoned generously with garlic and chili among other spices, was a taste on his tongue. The smell was so fragrant he tasted it without a single bite. He reheated the dishes on the stove and in the oven so they'd be piping hot for the party.

Rosalie wandered into the kitchen and she froze, inhaling the aromas. "Why am I suddenly starving? That smells delicious—all of it."

"I cooked Maxie's favorites. Chicken and sausage jambalaya. Cheesy Creole Pasta. Red beans and rice. And some goodies for us adults. That's the fried catfish and boiled crawfish you smell."

"I don't know what I'm smelling. I just know I could eat every last bite."

Nick's skin warmed as Rosalie walked up from behind and hugged him. She rested her chin on his shoulder and spoke closely to his ear. Her breath tickled him in the most tantalizing way possible. The hair on his nape stood tall.

"You're probably the best cook in the state. Maybe the country."

He concentrated on the bubbling jambalaya—or tried to anyway. Her breath was still tickling his ear. He was still warm and if she didn't quit soon, other parts of him would spring to life. He swallowed hard and stirred the reddish-brown concoction in the pot. His voice a strained rasp, he managed, "I can't tell if that's sarcasm."

"Has the restaurant ever smelled this good? It smells like dried pepper and day-old shrimp when Jefferson cooks," Rosalie teased. Her hands traveled lower, leaving his chest and trailing down his abdomen. "I think it's impressive."

"You…you do?" He was hot now. Hotter than the jambalaya simmering.

"Mm-hmm. I love a man who can cook."

Nick groaned in answer. Her hands had trekked across safe territory into the danger zone. Blood surged through his body and pumped into his dick. The crotch area of his jeans became too tight and constricting. His hand uncurled from the wooden spoon and his eyes closed. Her lips skimmed his ear at the same time her fingers grazed his now large bulge.

"Maxie. Remi." He was choking.

"You hear those giggles? They're upstairs."

"Rosalie."

"Nick." Her voice was a whisper as she kissed his neck. She rubbed his package. She made him tense up and struggle for his next breath with queenly expertise.

Shit, how fast he was unraveling...

How fast he *wanted* to unravel, wanted to spin around, scoop her up, and carry her to the first private space. He was easy prey. It had been months for him and they had only been dating a week; they had yet to take things to *that* level. He hung on by a thread, sucking in a sharp breath. Eyes opening, he turned around to face her.

Her lips looked like a rose, as soft as petals, painted red, blooming into a curve. He planted a kiss on them and felt her smile spread further. His arm hooked around her slim waist and they waltzed into the center of the kitchen. Jambalaya be damned.

"What're you doing to me? You wanna drive me crazy?"

"And if I do?" Rosalie teased, mimicking a stereotypically posh British accent.

"That costume's got you feeling yourself. Can't blame you. You're fine as hell in it," he said candidly. His gaze dropped for another full view. "But you better be careful—karma just might tease you back."

"A queen answers to no one. Not even karma."

With that, nose snootily in the air, Rosalie gathered her skirt and started for the doorway. He chuckled in her wake. More and more he discovered how playful Rosalie could be. If asked to imagine her behaving like a ballsy minx when he first met her, he would've barked out a laugh. It was that ridiculous.

He was coming to find out there were many layers to her. For each one unpeeled, he fell for her a little bit harder.

∞

The turnout for the birthday party was what he hoped. Better, actually. Instead of the twenty reserved, an extra six showed up. He had planned for that possibility, setting out additional chairs and plenty of food beforehand. The party thrived thanks to the hyperactive children scurrying across the backyard in dizzying patterns.

Maxie's classmates kept up with her, running, jumping, and spinning in whatever games they played. His stomach churned even as a spectator, but he applauded their effort. After a spirited game of tag, he corralled the children for toilet paper mummy races. Rosalie stuck by his side assisting. The children wrapped themselves up in rolls of toilet paper and hopped to the finish line.

To no one's surprise it came down to Maxie and Remi. The girls scudded for first place as best as they could, given their bound condition. Mere inches away from the finish line, Remi tripped and fell chin-first. Maxie bypassed her and crossed the line to victory. The win wasn't as gallant as envisioned, though. Remi sat up and wailed at the top of her lungs.

"Shh, you're okay. It's only a scrape. We'll go inside and put a Band-Aid on it." Rosalie's circular skirt prevented her from kneeling and forced her to help Remi up by hand.

"You okay, kiddo?" Nick walked by their side, lifting his furry wolf mask. His eyes fell on Remi's chin, rubbed raw and red. He didn't realize Maxie was huffing to catch up until she bumped into him. The four of them entered the kitchen to patch up a tearful Remi. "I've got a first aid kit in the drawer by the fridge."

"Remi, don't cry," Maxie mumbled. "I fall all the time. It'll stop hurting."

That did little to soothe Remi, who sat on the chair at the dinner table and dissolved into another cry. Rosalie seemed equipped for the little one's meltdown. Calm and quiet, she kept her arms around her in a motherly embrace. It took another minute or two, but Remi's cry hiccupped to a stop.

"Cool Band-Aid. I almost want one." Nick grinned at her after fixing the bandage to her chin. She blinked back at him from under her thick, wet lashes. Slowly, she smiled at him.

"Look, Remi, now we're twins!" Maxie excitedly lifted the leg of her pants to show Remi the neon green Band-Aid on her kneecap. "Wanna go play now? We'll be real careful!"

Just like that, the girls skipped off. Nick and Rosalie shook their heads.

"Crazy, huh?" he asked, hands on his waist. "One sec, the world's ending. Run for your lives. The next sec, everything's okay. Let's go play!"

"I've learned it's best to let them cry it out. You know, get it out of their system."

"Makes sense. Wish my troubles were solved with a cry."

Rosalie smirked and elbowed him in the ribs. "You just have to make a joke out of everything, don't you?"

"Isn't that what you love about me?"

"Love. Hate. Who really knows?"

They had inched closer, coming together for another stolen moment of affection. His mouth hovered over hers, intent on giving her a taste of her own medicine. He hadn't forgotten about earlier. In fact, he had been thinking up ways for payback. She had it coming.

It was a kiss that never was. Their eyes closed and their heads angled, but the phone on the table buzzed. Rosalie threw a glance over her shoulder and then froze. Her features flattened at once, like she saw something too confusing to compute.

"What is it? One of those scam numbers? They call me every day."

She sighed and gave a small, wry smile. "I wish it were them. It's him."

"As in…?"

"Clyde," she finished for him. She picked up the phone and held it in her palm, staring at the screen. "If you'll excuse me. I guess it's time we talk."

CHAPTER SEVENTEEN

"**W**hat do you want, Clyde?"

"I knew you'd be heated."

"I wonder why. It's almost as if my husband walked out on me and our daughter."

Clyde answered her with what sounded like the long drag of a cigarette. She imagined him blowing smoke, reclining on the couch. His drink on the lamp table beside him. Hennessy with a splash of Coke. The game playing on the TV. The scene unfolded in her mind's eye down to the last detail. For seven years, when he bothered to come home, this had been the case. She knew better than to believe anything about him had changed...

"I'm hanging up," she said when his smoke-blowing grew impudent. "Goodbye, Clyde—"

"Ros. Don't be like that. Hear me out."

"Hear you out? I've been hearing you out! I've heard you out for *years*. When are you gonna do the same for me? When are you gonna care about what I have to say?" she snapped, one word after another barreling past her lips. She started pacing the length of Nick's living room. Her pitch brittle, she couldn't hide the emotion in her voice. "You left me. You left Remi. You threw us away. Like trash."

"Shit was rough. I can't make excuses."

"There are no excuses—"

"So it don't matter that I needed time? I mighta left, but you did too. Packed up and left Bmore like nothing. Came back and you were gone. How's that supposed to make me feel?"

Rosalie hung up. She couldn't handle another manipulative word. She tossed the phone as if it were hot to the touch, letting it tumble onto the sofa cushion. Her pacing continued. Her skirt flounced against the floor, so long that sometimes she stepped on its hem. A frustrated growl revved up in her throat as she bunched the gown about her knees and dropped onto the couch.

The good day had soured. Her mood darkened and she pursed her lips into a tight line. It took her a second to notice Nick standing in the doorway. Any other time, she would've smiled at him, but her agitation ran too deep.

"You having an argument all by yourself?"

"I don't feel like joking around right now. I should go. The party's almost over. Remi has that scrape on her chin…"

"How about we sit down and just relax?"

Her right brow reached a peak. "Relax? Are you serious?"

"Sure, I am. Why not? The party's winding down. Some of the other parents are watching the kiddos. I need a break. You look like you need one too. Let's sit here and chill." Nick strolled over, shrugging with hands in the pockets of his furry wolf costume. He collapsed onto the empty sofa cushion beside her. His decompressing sigh was immediate. "Feels good to actually sit down."

He was right about that. It *did* feel good to relax against the sofa's pillowy cushions. The queen gown might've looked regal, but it was also uncomfortable as hell. Plus her heels, while kitten in height, pinched her toes. Her next breath mimicked Nick's sigh and she kicked off the sparkly shoes.

"That's more like it," Nick laughed. "Here, let me help you."

Her eyes closed as his large, warm palms smoothed the curves of her cheeks. His touch, however slight, soothed. In an unhurried manner that only Nick could pull off, his fingertips padded over her skin and into her hair. He unclasped the barrette holding her crown and high bun in place, and let her thick, coarse curls fall free.

Curl by tight curl, they tumbled down to frame her face. Big and bouncy, completely untamed and softer than a cloud. His dimples pierced his cheeks as he smiled at the end result, looping his finger in one.

"I've been waiting to touch your curls since I met you. So damn sexy."

Somewhere along the lines, he'd leaned forward and she'd licked her lips. The prelude to their kiss was another half second of their eyes stuck on each other, lids lowering. Her heart fluttered at a cadence faster than the speed of sound, but it was a good kind of fast. A blissful, delighted, even pleasantly nervous kind of fast.

Nick's kisses tended to do that to her. Almost like she was a teenage girl again, rediscovering love…

Rosalie ended their kiss with a soft smile. Nick's fingers were back to caressing her hair, his strokes relaxing. His curiosity tilted his head into a slant.

"What is it?" he asked.

"Nothing. Just you make me feel better. Thanks."

"I don't mind. It's a job I'll take any day. Feel free to talk about whatever it was." He studied her face as if each feature was worth a reverent gaze. "I've never been married, but I've got ears. I can listen."

She gave a light shake of her head. "It doesn't matter. He doesn't matter. Not anymore. If he thinks he can call and I'm going to drop everything for him—he's wrong. Fuck him."

"It's sexy when you cuss. Do it again."

They wound up seated on that sofa in a fit of laughter by the time they realized they should return to the party. On their feet with reluctance, they headed for the squeaky sound of children's voices. Rosalie stopped him at the glass sliding door.

"By the way, I've been thinking. We need to start planning our official menu for the Autumn Festival. Figure out what we're going to cook."

"What *we're* going to cook?"

"Nick, stop fronting. We both know you're going to compete with me," said Rosalie with a roll of her eyes. She laughed at his resigned sigh. "It's two weeks away."

"Yes, boss. We'll start ASAP."

"Tomorrow ASAP?"

He caved. "Yes, *tomorrow* ASAP. We'll be ready."

That evening, Remi was beat. Rosalie carried her up the porch steps and through the door. Though it was only five o'clock, it seemed like she was ready for bed. After hours of play and mouthfuls of cake, she wasn't surprised. The five-year-old had expended every ounce of energy in her little body.

"Say hi to Grandmommy Lacie and then we'll go run your bath."

Remi nodded sleepily and trudged down the hall like a zombie. Rosalie trailed at a distance, headed for the kitchen with automatic wariness. For days now she had been avoiding Ma whenever able. Their last argument left them at a stalemate. Ma wasn't bending and Rosalie wasn't breaking. Neither would give anytime soon.

"Grandmommy Lacie," Remi murmured in a sleepy sigh. She teetered straight into Ma's arms and hugged her tight about the thighs. "I missed you, but I had so much fun!"

"Aww, sweetie, I missed you too. The house felt so empty without my grandbaby."

"I had peanut butter cups and fudge cake and I tried a crawfish!"

Ma simpered. "Yummy. Sounds delicious. Your lil' tummy's prolly too full for my cooking, isn't it?"

"Yep! I'm very full, Grandmommy." Remi confirmed with a sharp nod. She giggled, sticking out her belly and rubbing the tiny pooch. "I can't eat anymore today."

"Well, your mommy better get you changed into your jammies then. But what's that on your chin—a sticker?"

The breath in Rosalie's lungs emptied. She shot forward to collect Remi and steer her toward the door, but Ma wasn't about to let it go. Her eyes narrowed and the pinch of her lips told Rosalie everything she needed to know. In that single flash of a look, Ma said a thousand scolding words.

"You hurt yourself, sweetie?"

"I fell when I was running," Remi answered in clueless innocence.

"Remi baby," Rosalie cut in softly, "let's get you upstairs in that bath."

"Shoulda known that would happen. Shoulda known you'd get hurt and then it'd be brushed aside like nothing."

The slick comment dug under Rosalie's skin. It tensed her muscles and stiffened her bones. Her breathing went ragged, her next inhale coming up short. She squeezed her eyes shut and counted backward from ten. Remi glanced at both of them, frowning.

"Let's go upstairs." Rosalie's voice was tight, each word clipped.

"I wonder about you sometimes, Rosalie. I really do. I wonder how could things have gone so wrong? I tried my best—I really did," Ma mused aloud for their open ears. She returned to the mashed potatoes on the stove. Adding salt and stirring, she sighed. "But you wind up proving again how irresponsible you are."

"Don't start."

"I wouldn't start if you didn't give me good reason."

"I'm tired. Remi's tired. I don't have the energy for this today."

"But you have all the energy in the world for that man you're seeing," Ma retorted with a squawking cackle. "Do you have any idea what everybody around town is saying? Or do you care at all? And those books—the real estate books—have you even opened 'em? Have you taken one look?"

Rosalie's temper, seconds ago quivering on the edge, about to let loose, died out. She shoved it down far enough that it couldn't be reached. No matter what antagonistic shit Ma said to try to spark an argument. She wasn't going to fight in front of Remi. She wasn't going to give Ma that satisfaction. Cooling off, body unwinding to a lax indifference, she shrugged off the hurtful insults.

"If we're not welcomed here anymore, I'll find somewhere else to go."

"I never said that, now did I? I love having my grandbaby here."

"Just not your daughter," Rosalie said darkly. "It's okay. I'll start looking for another place. I'll be out of your hair. Remi too. We're a packaged deal."

"Don't be dramatic. You're fine staying here. All I'm saying is think about how you're making yourself look. All after you married Clyde. You ditched that fiasco for a whole 'nother messy one. Might as well've stuck it out with him."

Rosalie grabbed Remi by the hand and marched out of the kitchen. They stomped their way up the staircase as best as Rosalie could, given the long gown. Inside the bedroom, Rosalie tugged open the chest of drawers and collected Remi's pajamas. Remi hovered uncertainly at her side, still confused by the confrontation downstairs.

"Mommy, why were you and Grandmommy Lacie yelling?"

"Because…because…" Rosalie shuddered out a sigh. "Your mommy and Grandmommy Lacie don't get along sometimes. Mommy's going to start looking into other places to stay."

"But where else will we go? We don't got any money."

That was the reality of the situation. Rosalie was broke. Her wages from Ady's had managed to keep her afloat thus far, but only barely. She bought bargain brand everything and scrimped with coupons for most purchases. The little stack she put back into her savings wasn't enough to sustain them for long.

But what other option did she have? She couldn't stand living under Ma's roof much longer. She couldn't give her any more satisfaction at her failure. The sore topic reached deep into her core, her greatest insecurity. Ma knew that. She understood that and proceeded to use it against her for cruel amusement.

"We'll figure something out," said Rosalie, stroking Remi's coarse mane. "I promise, baby."

Remi's bottom lip poked out. "I don't like when Grandmommy Lacie is mean to you."

"I don't like it either."

"Is it true, Mommy? What Grandmommy Lacie said. You and Maxie's daddy?"

The question was the last thing Rosalie expected from Remi. She anticipated questions about bath time or what story she would read her before bed. She didn't expect Remi to pick up on that detail from her argument with Ma. Especially since Nick hadn't been mentioned by name.

Remi wasn't upset about it. Far from it, as judging off the curvy twist of her little mouth, she was smiling.

Rosalie smiled too, caressing Remi's chin. "It is, baby. It's true."

CHAPTER EIGHTEEN

"Nicholas, funny seeing you around here."

"Mrs. Kettles, no kidding. I'm so used to seeing you at Ady's."

"I like what you've done to the place. The looks of it anyhow. The food's still…" she trailed off as if thinking up a polite remark.

"It's okay. You can be honest. The food's not so good." Nick lightened the atmosphere with an easy laugh. It worked like a charm, disarming Mrs. Kettles's tightly wound features. She straightened her second set of eyes, the glasses looped around her neck by stringed beads. As with most women in St. Aster, his dimpled grin and intent green eyes cast a trance over her. "But what if I told you Ady's is making an official comeback? Delicious food included."

"What kind of official comeback? That's a little hard to believe."

"Believe it. Next week at the Autumn Festival. We're setting up a booth of all of Ady's classics."

Behind her thick glasses, Mrs. Kettles's eyes widened. "Like the old days?"

"Better see you there, Mrs. Kettles." Nick sealed his flirtatious advertisement by winking. His lips blew a whistled tune and he pushed his shopping cart forward.

Not even a minute later, reading the labels on aspirin bottles in the medicine aisle, he overheard Mrs. Kettles's chatty exchange with what sounded like Macy Greene, wife of store owner Gary. Greene's General Store hired family and local teens only. Macy often stocked the shelves. She was unloading a box of detergent when Mrs. Kettles gossiped in a loud whisper.

"See Nicholas Fontaine over there—he's saying Ady's is making a comeback."

"Comeback how?"

"He's gonna have a booth at the town festival."

"Is he now? Who's cooking? His lazy self?"

"Shh. He's right over there. Don't want him to overhear you."

Nick whistled and pretended he was none the wiser as he eavesdropped on the older women's gossip. He selected the generic brand of aspirin and tossed it into his cart.

Mrs. Kettles and Mrs. Greene had moved on to talk about him and Rosalie.

"Lacie's gal and him are a thing."

"Already? She been in town for, what, a month now?"

He didn't care to hear the rest. The wheels on his cart squealed as he rolled it into the next aisle. Along with his whistle, the squeaking wheels drowned out the gossip. He couldn't deny the ladies had a point about him. So he was lazy. Or had been. The whole town knew it, recognized as much when months after Mom's passing, he slouched about town without a care in the world. No fucks given about the restaurant. He never liked to focus on the reality of how others perceived him, but it was impossible now.

He was a failure. He had let Mom down. He had fucked up.

But he wasn't about to hang around and listen to Mrs. Kettles and Mrs. Greene trash-talk Rosalie. He could tell where the conversation was headed. He understood their thought process. The basis of their traditional values that drew them to quick judgment. From there he could work out what they thought about Rosalie. How they felt about his relationship with her.

Town gossip never bothered him. He hoped Rosalie was the same.

Nick spent a couple cents under a hundred bucks shopping that afternoon. He thanked the cashier and walked out of Greene's General Store thinking about Rosalie. It'd been a day since he'd seen her given her day off and the way their shifts worked out. She was scheduled for the whole afternoon. He considered stopping by Ady's *just* to see her.

Stuffing the shopping bags into his truck bed, Nick laughed off how preposterous it was. Never had the compulsion to be around a woman stayed on his mind like it had with Rosalie. His only comparable relationship was with Desiree. It could've been time's cooling effect, but he couldn't think up an instance where he'd felt half the urge. Desiree was his great measure for love and relationships, a constant comparison whenever dealing with the women in St. Aster.

But when it came to Rosalie, there was no comparison. Rosalie was in a realm of her own.

Nick finished unloading his shopping bags into his truck bed. His mind wasn't made up on whether he'd stop by the restaurant. The option turned over in his head as he checked the time on his watch. School wasn't letting out for another two hours. He had no other pressing obligations.

He was walking around to the driver's side of his truck when watchful eyes weighed on him. Across the street, loitering in front of Ms. Maple's Coffee Shop and Bakery, Perry Langley from Yum Corp waved at him. He waited until the coast was clear and then strolled to Nick's side.

"Good afternoon, Mr. Fontaine."

"Look, we've been over this—"

"Yum Corp is ready to make you an official offer. You don't have to decide now," interrupted Mr. Langley. He fetched an envelope out of the breast pocket inside his suit jacket. "I think you'll be pleased with the amount we're offering."

"Your offer is a scam. What makes you think Ady's is gonna be any better with your company?"

"We've been over this, Mr. Fontaine. Yum Corp specializes in rebranding restaurants just like yours. Do you know how many we've turned into successful franchises?"

"I don't have time to entertain your sales pitch. I have to go."

"That's alright. I'll follow up with you in a few days. It's a lot to think about, but I have a feeling you'll make the right decision."

Perry flashed him an artificial smile, his teeth visible even from underneath his bushy mustache.

Nick ignored him, hopping into his truck. He had no clue Langley was still in town, let alone that he was out and about in the same area. The coincidence was more than odd, but he couldn't help his curiosity. He waited until the man sunk out of sight in his rearview and then tore open the envelope.

His eyes widened staring at the number on the offer letter. Never in a thousand years had he imagined he would sell Ady's. Even if he had spent the last year since Mom's passing slacking off. He still never thought he would sell the restaurant.

But he had to admit the numbers were tempting. The dollar sign held his attention. He mused on the offer for the briefest minute and then shook the thought from his head and started up his truck engine. His answer was still the same. He wasn't interested.

꒰ ✿ ꒱

Popping in at Ady's was perfectly harmless. That was the lie Nick told himself, pulling into a parking spot outside his restaurant. The truth was he wanted to see Rosalie. He had called her last night, but she hadn't answered. He figured she and Remi were still recovering from Maxie's birthday party. He was too. Both he and Maxie went to bed early for a second night in a row.

Ady's saw slow business that afternoon. He sauntered through the door whistling a light tune on his lips.

"Nick," Zoe said, penciled brows on the rise. "You're here on a day off?"

"Is that surprising?"

"Well, it's you. So yeah."

He shrugged off the waitress's dig. "What can I say? People change, Zoe! Ady's is about to too. You'll see."

She snorted. "And I'm gonna go back to my natural hair color."

"I see your roots coming in," he ribbed. He glanced around the dining area. "Where's Rosalie?"

"Last I saw her she was camped out in your office on that laptop. Lotsa numbers."

Nick found her doing just that. Rosalie sat hunched over the restaurant laptop, fingers punching the keys. Her teeth gnawed away at her plump bottom lip and she muttered different figures under her breath. There was a crease between her brows and her curls frizzed presumably from the day's earlier drizzle. He grinned, using the next couple of seconds to savor the sight of this beautiful, brilliant woman. She inspired him to be better than he was. He could prove the naysayers like Mrs. Kettles and Zoe wrong.

"I see you watching me," Rosalie said suddenly.

He barked out a laugh. "I couldn't help myself. It's sexy seeing you like that."

"Like what? Driving myself crazy over a budget?"

"Only you can pull it off. What budget are you working on? I thought we already crunched the numbers for Ady's—" Nick must've caught Rosalie off guard, because as he walked around the desk, she snapped shut the laptop. He cut off his next step, tilting his head. "What'd you close the laptop for? I was just gonna see your brilliance at work. I bet you've found some other way to save Ady's money."

Rosalie wrinkled her nose. "Okay, maybe I was working on a different budget."

"What kinda different budget?"

"A personal budget. I'm going to have some unforeseen expenses," she confessed. Her attempt at an even tone failed, a slight waver in her voice. "Sorry for using the office computer for that. The library's computer lab is being remodeled."

"No apology needed. Use the computer anytime you want. You're the boss, remember?" he teased. When that did little to cheer her up, he leaned against the desk and frowned. Now that he had a closer look, he noticed some things different about her.

Her usual crisp blouse was in need of ironing, rumpled as if the fabric lived without a hanger. Her curls were less defined, lacking their standard luster. Though she still looked gorgeous, skin a smooth and deep sienna brown, he saw the traces of bags under her eyes. She hadn't had a good night's sleep last night. His concern mounted as a constriction in his chest.

"Rosalie, something's wrong. Want to talk about it?"

She rubbed her brow and sighed. "Just another fight with my mom. More crap about how I fail at everything. Even as a mother. I let Remi get hurt."

"It was an accident. Kids fall. They get cuts and scrapes. It's what they do."

"She sees it as me being inattentive. It doesn't matter anyway. I told her I'm finding somewhere else to stay."

"Like where?"

She shrugged. "I can't keep staying there, Nick. I'm walking on eggshells every day. I'm tired of dealing with it. I've been crunching some numbers, and I can afford the Cypress Inn. If I cut gas on the car, I can afford it."

"Then how would you get to work? How would Remi get to school?"

"I'd walk to work and then walk her to and from school. If you let me work it into my schedule. I'll work an extra day to make up for the extra time I'm gone," Rosalie answered. She smiled as an afterthought and attempt to quell his concern. "It'll be okay. I'm used to being on foot. I was for a while in Baltimore when I couldn't afford to fix a dead engine."

"The Cypress Inn is on the outskirts of town."

Not to mention it was a flea trap. The motel was known as a regular stop for truckers, but also for unsavory guests up to no good. Several times throughout the year it made the ten o'clock news for a prostitution or drug arrest. The thought of Rosalie and Remi staying in that place for even an hour caused him sharp chest pains. While her choice was hers to make, he hoped he could talk her out of it.

"It would only be temporary. I'm saving every other penny I can. I calculated my new budget. If I save two hundred bucks a month, I'll be able to afford one of those one bedroom apartments on Lawson Street. It'll only take me four months."

"Rosalie, you can't live there for four months. You should stay with me and Maxie. We have an extra bedroom—you and Remi can have it. Stay there as long as you like 'til you're back on your feet. It was Mom's, but I've renovated the room."

"I don't think that's a good idea. You're already my boss."

"We're co-bosses," Nick said quickly. "And I have the space. And you and Remi don't belong at the Cypress. And…and…" He inhaled and plucked up the courage for candor. "I care about you both too much to not offer it. Stay with us, please. I won't sleep at night knowing you're there."

"Nick, I care about you too. But it's better for me to find my own place to stay. I'm still planning things. I'll figure it out."

"Okay, I understand. Just know the room's there if you need it."

"I appreciate that. I really do. It means a lot that you care."

"Tell you what? How about we give the girls what they've been asking for," said Nick, collecting her smaller, softer hands in his. "They've been wanting to do a movie night for how long?"

"A movie night, huh?"

"Doesn't that sound like a good distraction from your mom? Picture it. Nice home-cooked dinner. Two giddy little girls. A flick to sit back and watch. Some wine."

"Now that you mention it, that does sound like what I need right now."

"I want you relaxed and stress free."

Rosalie's slimmer fingers slipped between his thicker ones, and she rose to her feet. Standing on tiptoe, she tilted her chin and placed a sweet kiss on his mouth. He was already grinning like a fool when she said, "I can't wait."

Later that night, it took some considerable time to cool Maxie's and Remi's engines. The kindergarteners did exactly as Rosalie predicted. They launched into a cheering, clapping, dancing bout of celebration. At one point, Maxie tripped on her own two feet and fell on her bottom. Nick enjoyed their enthusiasm, but he had to call for an end to the craze on the basis of their clumsy little feet alone.

Rosalie insisted on helping with dinner. Nick didn't fight her on it. Mostly because he wanted the kitchen time. The girls played outside, their overzealous shrieks a constant sound. Right now, they ran in circles amid their giggles, all in an attempt to catch a flittering butterfly. That was going to keep them busy for a while. He and Rosalie had a moment to themselves.

"Since you insist on helping, we're gonna treat tonight like another cooking lesson. Guess what's for dinner?"

Rosalie eyed him suspiciously. "You know you look up to no good without even trying, right?"

"That's because I'm always only up to no good."

Against the kitchen counter, they backed up, arms linked around each other. Between their busy day at Ady's and picking the girls up from school, and dealing with their immediate spastic energy, the two hadn't had any alone time.

"It's an easy one. Even you can cook it."

She poked him in the chest, nose scrunched. "I'm a better cook than you give me credit for. I didn't burn those sautéed shrimp, did I?"

"True. You did really good."

"You're supposed to be teaching me. So teach me."

"Alright, let's get to work then. Those girls are gonna be in here starving in no time." Nick's arm around her waist guided her toward his pantry. He explained that Monday night's dinner was Cheesy Creole Pasta. Maxie was a picky eater and the pasta was one of her favorites. He held up the box of fettuccine and rattled it. "Guess why I said it's right up your alley?"

Rosalie rolled her eyes, a smirk stealing across her lips. "The spaghetti out of the jar thing. It's only the five-hundredth time you've brought it up."

"The sauce might be a problem. I make mine from scratch."

Another poke. This one to the side. Ever ticklish, Nick swallowed a laugh. "Okay, chill! I'm about to show you. It'll change your life. You'll be cooking this for Remi—and anyone else—for years to come."

Side by side as partners, they chopped the vegetables and grated cheese. Nick noticed her technique with the grater was botchy. He offered gentle suggestions, demonstrating the proper slide and glide technique second nature to him. Rosalie said nothing. She mimicked him silently and proved a quick learner on attempt one. His grin followed, bright and proud.

"We've got the fettuccine boiling. We've got the shrimp and sausage sautéing. The cheese we've finished grating. Guess what we need to do next?" Nick watched as Rosalie flipped the shrimp and sausage with near expert-like ease on the pan, the garlicky scents rampant in the kitchen. She really was fast to pick up on things. It wasn't that she couldn't cook; it was that she'd never been taught properly how to.

"The sauce," she predicted in answer.

"That's right. It's a concoction Mom said has been in the family for a century."

"I'm sure it's better than jarred spaghetti sauce."

"Much better. We're going to take the white wine and whipping cream and add it to this other skillet. Mix in the seasonings. Then the cheese."

"How much of each?" She looked over her shoulder at him.

He shrugged. "Here's what I say; it's how Mom and everybody else in my family cooks too. Go by instinct. A pinch of each and taste test. Another pinch or two. You'll figure it out as you go."

"You just have to make it more difficult," she huffed. But she followed through with his suggestion. She took a pinch of black pepper and sprinkled that in. Next, she added paprika and cayenne pepper. She stirred the tiny grains into the creamed white wine and then brought the spoon up to his lips. "You're my taste tester. How's it taste?"

"You're on the right track, chef. Maybe a little more cayenne pepper. But not too much—the girls won't be able to eat it."

"Just a pinch. Off instinct." Rosalie was smirking as she speckled extra cayenne pepper and whisked it into the sauce. In no time they had the sauce heating up over the stove's flames. The shrimp and sausage were sizzled and sautéed, neatly set aside for the time being. The fettuccine softened in the pot of water, butter, and salt.

They were on a slight kissing detour. Her arms looped around his neck and he tasted the rich butter on her tongue from their samples. Somehow she made anything taste better. Even butter, an ingredient he didn't think could get any tastier.

"Mmm, I can't believe it's *not* butter," he mumbled against her lips.

She giggled, breaking away. "You're so silly. Back to cooking or we'll burn the house down."

"Good point. And those girls are gonna be in any second. Maxie's always starving after she plays."

"Then we better wrap this up," Rosalie said, overseeing the cream. Her skills on display, she stirred the sauce without his direction, and turned off the burner for the pasta. She was no longer checking with him. She knew she had it in the bag. He stood back, arms folded, and his chest swelled out of pride. As if reading his thoughts, she thanked him. "You're a good teacher.

I've never been able to get much done beside burnt grilled cheese. Now I'm sautéing and whisking. I might as well be the new cook at Ady's."

From behind, he brought his face next to hers and kissed her cheek. "You're taking over all of our jobs. Zoe's. Jefferson's. Mine. Who's next?"

Rosalie answered him with a shine in her eyes that made her even sexier. She dialed down the heat on the skillet with the sauce and dramatically kissed her fingers to her lips.

"Voilà! Dinner is served."

CHAPTER NINETEEN

"Mommy, this is yummy. Are you sure you made it?" Remi asked, spooling noodles around her fork.

Nick and Rosalie burst into laughs. Minutes into dinnertime, both girls had slurped half their bowls of fettuccine. As it turned out, they were both loud eaters, noshing on the pasta dish with the smack of lips and clang of silverware. Maxie in particular happened to get involved in her meals, licking any runaway sauce off her fingers.

For their part, Nick and Rosalie were two glasses of wine in. They laughed easier, smiled wider and moved slower. The dinner itself was a welcomed break from outside stressors, the foursome able to sit down and unwind over good food. And it *was* as yummy as Remi said it was—the most delicious meal Rosalie ever cooked.

A self-satisfied grin reached either corner of her lips and she sipped more wine. Even if it was a silly thing to be proud about, it didn't make it any less gratifying. She thought back to Ma's reprimands, calling her lack of skill unwifely. Clyde's complaints about her subpar abilities as a housewife during their marriage. The criticism had been used against her time and again, provided as evidence why she was somehow less than other women.

The truth was, she wasn't less than anyone. She was worth as much, flaws and all. Whether or not she knew how to cook. Regardless if Ma thought she made a proper wife. The acceptance she sought in Clyde now meant nothing. At least that was the level of bravery the wine's warm cloak brought her.

"Kiddo, are we playing a game where we pretend napkins don't exist?"

Nick grabbed the dinner cloth and handed it over to Maxie. "Use your napkin."

"Papa, can we have a sleepover?" Maxie asked between another finger lick.

Remi gasped. "Oooh, can we, Mommy? And we can tell spooky stories!"

"And go trick-or-treating together!"

The girls spitballed off of each other. Rosalie picked up her wineglass and gave a small toast to Nick, whose thoughts reflected hers. Let them chat it up and tire themselves out. No use trying to stop their imaginative chats once they got started.

Dishes in the dishwasher, they headed into the living room to start the movie. The girls parked themselves on the rug in front of the TV. Nick dropped onto the sofa and patted the cushion next to him, wiggling his brows. Rosalie giggled, still feeling silly from her two glasses of wine, and curled up at his side.

Minutes into the movie, they caught the girls throwing them furtive glances. Even in the dim room, where the only light was blue and emanated off the TV screen, both could be seen with little hands cupped over their mouths. As soon as they realized Rosalie and Nick noticed their sneak peeks, they rushed to face the TV screen again. They pressed their hands harder against their mouths to stifle what sounded like girlish giggles.

Nick paused the movie and said, "Something funny, girls?"

"No," they answered in singsong unison.

Nick and Rosalie smirked at each other.

"Girls…" Nick trailed off in a mock stern voice.

"You guys are gonna catch cooties," Maxie confessed. She fell backward onto the rug as she erupted into a fit of giggles.

Remi joined her, rolling onto the rug at her friend's side. "Ew, gross! My mommy's not gonna catch cooties."

"Yes, she is! Look how they're sitting all smushed."

The movie was forgotten about as Nick and Rosalie enjoyed the ridiculous scene playing out in front of them. The girls proceeded to bicker about who was giving who cooties and ended up accusing each other of the fabled germ. Within seconds they were coughing from laughing themselves delirious, sprawled out on the rug on their bellies.

"Okay, okay, girls, time to calm down," Rosalie called out above them. "Nobody's giving anybody cooties."

"Right," agreed Nick.

Remi and Maxie sat up with lingering hints of amusement shining on their faces.

"Are you and my mommy getting married?" Remi asked Nick in unabashed curiosity. Maxie squeaked and clapped a hand to her mouth again.

"Well," said Nick slowly, "I like your mommy very much. But it's a little soon to throw the *M* word around."

"Remi, remember what we've said about asking people questions?"

"But I was just wondering!"

"Would that make Missus Rosalie my mama?" chimed in Maxie. "Then you could braid my hair! Papa has me looking crazy."

"Hey, kiddo, I'm still learning. Gimme some credit." Nick rose from the couch to pick her up off the ground for a retaliatory tickle. "How about we get back to the movie? And later we'll sit down and talk about what's going on over cookies?"

Rosalie's heart warmed, watching as the girls cheered and then bolted upright to continue the movie. She hadn't told him, but something about seeing Nick in Dad mode tugged at her heartstrings. He was effortless with Maxie, jokey and playful but adoring. That translated to Remi as it was obvious how much she liked him. He had won her over.

"Mr. Nick, can we have the cookies now?" Remi asked, eyes bulging with hope. Maxie perked up too.

"What do you say, boss?" Nick deferred to Rosalie with a humorous wink.

Her smile was small. "I don't think I'll ever turn down a movie snack."

"Good point. We can't be watching a movie without snacks to munch on. I'll grab us some," said Nick to the three. He headed for the door leading into the kitchen, but hung back for one more tease. "By the way, everybody knows it's *girls* who have cooties."

In the week that followed, Nick and Rosalie held more cooking lessons before and after their workdays. Before their shifts, it was in the kitchen at Ady's. After their shifts, it was in Nick's kitchen at his home. Though he had already admitted he would cook the menu for the Autumn Festival, Rosalie insisted their lessons continued. She wanted to know how to prepare the dishes served at Ady's.

It was about more than the contest now. She had never known cooking could be relaxing. Any past attempts were laden with stress and tension. Clyde insisting she cook holiday dinners or have dinner on the table by the time he got home. Never mind that she had classes and her part-time job, or that she cared for a colicky Remi while he kicked back and watched his games. Holding Remi in one arm, frying pork chops with the other, and glancing at the open textbook on the kitchen counter was a memory she preferred to forget.

Cooking now was different. Instead of an economics textbook splayed on the counter, she had a wine bottle corked open for casual sipping. Rather than Remi's fussy cries bouncing off the walls, she listened to her spells of convulsive laughter from the yard. In place of Clyde reclined in the next room like a king, by her side stood Nick, cooking with her as a duo.

It was nice to think of it as a hobby. Something she did to decompress. Creating a delicious meal by combining different ingredients, blending these flavors together. A *choice* she made on her own, pleased by the end creation. Never had she considered it possible, but she preferred the surprise of it.

"You add a little extra something to this?" Nick asked, scooping a spoonful of gumbo to his mouth. He smacked his lips together, savoring the spices, mulling over the combination. His eyes brightened by his last swallow. "Did you just improve one of my mom's recipes? Tastes like you added extra thyme."

"Nope," she said, tight curls shaking with her head. "Your palate is slipping, *chef*."

"Oregano?"

Rosalie boasted a broad grin. She had no intention of revealing the secret ingredient. Glancing at Nick, she saw the amusement creeping onto his features. His dimples were beginning to appear, but he fought them off. He loved it when she teased him as much as he loved to tease her. She loved it too.

"Listen, if your gumbo recipe becomes more popular than mine," he said, stalling for the rest. He scratched his head, fingers dug into his cropped golden-brown waves. "I don't know how I'm gonna feel about that."

She gave off a quick laugh. "There's a new chef in town. Everybody's going to see it at the festival."

"I can tell you're serious." Nick poured a couple more droplets into her glass and then his. He was relegated to the salad and biscuits that night, choosing the hands-off instructor approach. If she needed help or had a question about the recipe, he was there to step in. Unfortunately for Nick, he wasn't used to being in the background in the kitchen. It seemed to occur to him last second he forgot to check the oven. "Shit, the biscuits! You're distracting me."

"Amateur mistake. How long have you been a guru in the kitchen again?"

"Looks like somebody's coming for my title," said Nick, stepping up beside her. He touched the small of her back and kissed the apple of her cheek. "You've come a long way in a month, you know that, right?"

"That's because it's easy to cook when I'm not being told how hopeless I am."

His brows lowered in concern. "Ms. Lacie?"

"Who else? She's never let me forget how *unwifely* it was that I couldn't cook. According to her, she can't blame Clyde for leaving," said Rosalie in a show of candor. "It's my fault."

"No offense to your mom, but it sounds to me like she's projecting."

"Don't tell her that. She knows everything."

"If she knew everything, she'd know how amazing her daughter is." Nick eased her away from the stove for a second, his hands stealing her by the waist. "It's her loss. Your gain."

"Oh, and what am I gaining?"

"Look at everything you're doing," he said. "You're overcoming every roadblock that's been put in your way—you're refusing to give up. You've made Ady's a better place. You've helped me want to make Ady's a better place. Everything you're doing—it's working, Rosalie. It doesn't matter if Ms. Lacie gets that. *You're* gonna come out on top."

Gooseflesh tingled on Rosalie's skin as she gazed into Nick's eyes. She trailed the angular outline of his jaw with her finger and said, "Thanks for believing in me."

"No. Thank *you* for believing in *me*. It started with you."

"Well, if you insist I take credit." Rosalie interrupted her own giggle by placing a sweet kiss on Nick's lips. He seized the opportunity to pull her in closer for more, raining warm kisses first on her mouth and then her cheek and neck. She squirmed in his arms, loving the sudden burst of affection but also pushing him away.

They were lost in their battle of teases and laughs, failing to notice the two nosy four-foot-tall girls watching. Remi and Maxie had come in from their evening play surprisingly earlier than usual. Most nights they cooked together, they had to drag them inside for dinner.

"What's up, girls?" Rosalie asked. She had escaped Nick's clutches and turned to the stove to dial down the heat on the big pot of gumbo. "Everything okay out there?"

"We wanna help," Maxie announced. She had sticks of grass tangled in her wavy strands and a splotch of dirt on her chin, but she didn't seem to care. In contrast, Remi looked as clean and put together as when their play began. Her curly puff on top of her head was as neat and bound as earlier, and she had nary a grass stain on her overalls.

Rosalie smiled at the opposites. "How about you both be my helpers? Your papa's fired, Maxie."

"Hey, I've been doing a great job on these biscuits. They're a little crispy, but...they're still edible."

"We'll scrape the charcoal off," Rosalie joked to the girls' laughter. She shooed him toward the door. "Go set up the table. Me and the girls got this."

Remi and Maxie snickered as Nick literally threw in the towel. He tossed his kitchen rag onto the counter and admitted defeat, outnumbered three to one.

"Fine, I can handle that. I see I've been voted off the island."

"Buh-bye, Papa!" Maxie giggled and waved.

Once it was only the three of them, Rosalie turned to the girls and offered a twinkling smile. They waited intently for what she had to say, fascinated by what they perceived as her prowess in the kitchen.

"First thing we do in the kitchen is wash up."

The girls lined up at the kitchen sink as she helped them scrub their hands with soap and water. After they toweled off, she explained what they were cooking for dinner.

"Can I have a cooking blanket like that, Mommy?" Remi studied the apron she wore with interest.

Rosalie smirked. "It's called an apron, Remi baby. We'll get you and Maxie one, okay?"

The girls bounced on their feet with fervent nods.

The rest of dinner prep was a team effort. Rosalie walked Remi and Maxie through simple kitchen tasks. They kept the mood fun, a stark contrast to what Rosalie remembered as the scolding kitchen work when she was a child. Toward the end, Nick joined them, back from setting the table.

After dinner, they decided to go for a walk around the bayou. Now well into autumn, the days were shorter and the nights were longer. The wind harsher, carrying an incessant chill, they bundled up in their jackets and marveled at the distant sun sinking below the vast wetlands.

Remi and Maxie skipped a couple steps ahead. Rosalie and Nick strolled behind them at a lazier pace. From the bits and pieces Rosalie picked up of their conversation, they were chatting about their favorite cartoon. The adorable quality of their instant and natural friendship put a smile on her face. Glancing at Nick, it was the same. He was listening in on their chat, hands deep in his pockets, his expression light.

"We should do these evening walks more often," Rosalie said, the brittle leaves snagging underfoot. They crunched as her boots pushed through their piles. "Plus, we need to walk off all that food and wine."

"Smart plan. Bonus is that it uses up their last bit of energy."

Rosalie chuckled. "Also true. So I take it we're going with my gumbo recipe for the festival's competition?"

"Your gumbo recipe wins," Nick conceded, but he snapped his fingers and pointed at her. "But we're going with my King Cake."

"Fair. It *is* delicious."

"We should probably add something like our crab cakes too."

"With tangy mustard dipping sauce."

"How could we forget the dipping sauce? It's half the magic," Nick said. "I think we're ready. Our menu's gonna show 'em we're not messing around."

The girls were kicking piles of leaves. Rosalie stopped to face him, the smile on her lips reflecting in her bright-eyed gaze. "I never would've guessed how good we vibe off each other. We make a pretty amazing team, don't we?"

Nick gripped her chin and answered her with a tender kiss.

Yes, they did.

CHAPTER TWENTY

Halloween night, they took the girls trick-or-treating. Maxie and Remi scuttled ahead of them in their werewolf and princess costumes, their pails full of candy. Nick hung back on the sidewalk and watched them cross the yard, Rosalie pressed against his side. They listened as Remi shrieked "trick-or-treat" and Maxie howled like a werewolf.

"Maxie makes a great werewolf," Rosalie said.

"She gets it from her papa."

"I'm sure that's it. Because you were a great werewolf."

Nick grinned wide. "Best there ever was."

They moved on to the next house when Maxie and Remi returned with pails overflowing with their latest treats. Nick stuck his hand into Maxie's plastic pail and fished out a Kit Kat bar.

"Hope you don't mind, kiddo," he said, biting into the chocolate wafer. "I have to check your candy to make sure it's safe for you to eat."

"Papa, get your own!" Maxie stuck her tongue out and skipped ahead of him.

Rosalie waited until the girls were out of earshot and then clicked her tongue. "Every parent knows you wait until they're asleep *then* you raid their candy."

"Guess it wasn't included in the parental handbook."

For the next two hours they walked the neighborhood of St. Aster, giving the girls a chance to collect a generous bounty of sweets. Being an evening in late October, there was a shiver-inducing chill in the air that had them huddled close. Whenever they crossed a home decked out in Halloween decorations, they stopped to admire the spooky creativity. The girls loved the home with a wicked witch on broomstick hovering off the porch. Rosalie thought the one with the mock cemetery was the most impressive. Nick's personal favorite was Mr. Hebert's home. His use of eerily carved jack-o'-lanterns speckled across his front path was unparalleled.

It was past nine o'clock by the time they circled back to Nick's house. The girls dragged their feet over the threshold and Rosalie helped them out of their jackets. Nick tossed his keys on the console table and double checked the locks on the front door.

Since it was Halloween, they had decided to give the girls the sleepover they had spent weeks begging them for. They had set up a tent in the middle of Maxie's room for the girls to sleep in, creating the illusion of camping.

"Are we gonna get to tell spooky stories now, Papa?" Maxie asked.

Remi shuddered on the spot. "I'm kinda scared…but I wanna hear them!"

"Everybody change into your jammies. It's been a long night," said Nick. "Then we'll get you some of your candy and you can tell some spook-tastic stories under your night-lights."

Together in parental unity, Nick and Rosalie ushered the girls up the stairs so they could change out of their Halloween costumes. The girls were already up past their bedtimes, which meant their scary stories in the tent lasted about fifteen minutes. Then they were out, spilled over onto their sides fast asleep.

Nick eased the door shut and whispered, "Thanks for agreeing to this sleepover. I left the guest room with everything you'll need. Even set out an extra wool blanket in case you get cold. Or you can wake me up and tell me to turn up the thermostat. I keep it on seventy-two."

He realized the longer he talked that he was rambling. He noticed the humor unfolding on Rosalie's face. Her expression livened up as her lips curved and she wrinkled her nose. He fell silent, insides wrought with nervous energy, and his hand shot to the back of his neck.

"I mean, you tell me what you need. You're the guest."

Rosalie rested her hands on his chest, her alluring brown cat eyes turned up on him. "I was thinking we could enjoy some time to ourselves."

Nick grinned. "I bought a new bottle of pinot noir."

Alone in the kitchen downstairs, they did their best to keep the noise to a minimum, but it was difficult. They gathered at the kitchen counter and uncorked the bottle of wine, letting the berry liquid flow into their glasses.

The mood between them was a content sense of ease. Things were working in their favor now more than ever, as they devoted each day to improving Ady's and exploring their connection.

Though they hadn't officially labelled their relationship, he had never been happier. He wanted Rosalie by his side. He wanted her as his girlfriend. He wanted to keep spending his days with her at Ady's and his nights with her in his home.

The grief that had kept him weighted down for the past year was still there, lurking in the shadows. Ady's months-long money troubles were still around, in dire need of the business to start raking in a real profit. He wasn't foolish enough to believe in magical solutions. But the new outlook on life was helping. The one that Rosalie helped inspire in him.

Nick cornered her somewhere between the fridge and dishwasher, his hands quick on her hips. Almost as quick as the pace of his own heartbeat. All Rosalie had to do was aim a teasing smile his way and she got his blood pumping. He savored the split second before their kiss. The millisecond where the gloss in Rosalie's eyes intensified the spastic energy in his stomach, and he inched closer to capture her lips.

She readily accepted his kiss. Hands knotting in his shirt, she pulled him into her. The curves of her body fit his broader frame so well. He could feel his skin go flush. He could feel her go breathless, only kissing him harder, on her usual tiptoe as if about to float above ground at any given second.

He helped her. He wreathed his arms around her small waist and plucked her off her feet. He was carrying her, lifting her up into his arms. Her legs sought his waist and they walked like that across the kitchen. The rest of the house was silent, which meant even the soft smack of their lips and puffs of their breaths sounded loud. Even the pad of Nick's footsteps thudded louder as he hauled her off to the nearest private space.

The pantry awaited them in its dark seclusion. Nick set her down long enough to listen for the girls one last time and ease the door closed. She had surrendered to a wave of unexpected giddiness, cupping a hand over her mouth. He understood her laughter. Only they would hide in a kitchen pantry to mess around. And it was so fitting given their time together in the kitchen.

Nick gently pried her hand away and replaced it with his lips. His tongue followed in light flicks against her own. She let a moan slip out, but he promptly swallowed the sound. They had to be quiet. They had to make as little noise as possible so as not to wake the girls. Besides, the forced silence made it that much more challenging. That much naughtier as his hands slid under her shirt and palmed her breasts.

Any semblance of coherency faded as unfettered arousal sprang to life. He could feel himself go hard, his erection like rebar. It strained against his jeans, a thick imprint now begging for freedom.

Rosalie pulled away from their heavy kisses and dropped her gaze to take note of the bulge in his jeans. Hers landed on his belt buckle and he sucked in a breath. He stood still and watched her hands work him free, in a clear grapple to not lose himself too soon. He clenched his eyes shut and bit back a primitive growl when she took him into her grasp. She kissed him, stroking him nice and slow—torturously slow.

"Rosalie," Nick breathed hoarsely. He failed to hold off his next groan. "Are you sure? We could go back into the living room and—"

"Do you have a condom?" she whispered in interruption. Her mouth stretched into a minxy smile as she watched his own hang open in surprise.

It vanished the next second for a lopsided grin. He nodded and dug for his wallet. The condom wrapper crinkled obscenely in the pantry silence, but the anticipation thrilled them. She grabbed hold of his shirt and tugged him to her mouth. Over the course of the next thirty seconds they faced off in a match of who could undress the other faster.

She dropped his jeans to his ankles and he kicked them away. He lifted her blouse over her head and she reached backward to undo her bra. Together they helped her shimmy out of her jeans. Then her panties. Their eyes wandered. Even in the dim light of the pantry, they drank up what they could of each other's bodies.

Her teeth raked her bottom lip, scanning the length of his sturdy build. His strong arms and flat abdomen speckled by a trail of his golden-brown hair. Her eyes landed on his member last. It was hard and thick with a slight curve, crowned by the glisten of pre-cum. She couldn't resist another moment. She gripped him a second time, working into a steady rhythm.

Nick's eyes fluttered shut and his jaw tightened. He was holding back another moan. She smirked as he began to unravel. If she kept stroking him just a little bit longer, he would blow then and there. Right in her hands. Refusing to give in that easily, he tore open the package and rolled the condom on. Their kisses heated up again as he backed her up against the only wall without shelves. Her naked flesh felt so good on his.

But when her legs notched his waist and his length pushed into her?

There were no words. His mind went completely blank as her wet heat surrounded him. He could think to do nothing but hold Rosalie in his arms and crush his lips to hers. Their kisses hungry and sloppy, they began to move.

The sensations enveloped them. Her clench around him as he slipped deeper. His warm tongue explored her mouth and he savored the taste of her. Pleasure spread through every inch of his body like a current of unbound electricity.

In mindless rhythm, they worked for their climax. Nick's thrusts became harder. He earned breathless gasps out of her. His fingers snaked low, rubbing her swollen nub that was sensitive to the slightest touch. He nudged her closer and closer to the finish line. He could feel it in the quake of her body. How hot and slippery her skin became.

Rosalie's grip on his nape tightened and she buried her head into the crook of his neck.

She erupted in a silent, shuddering orgasm that had her stiffening up underneath him. If not for him she would've collapsed to the ground in a puddle. He wasn't far behind her, as her kneading warmth drove him over the edge. He planted a palm against the wall, his other arm barely holding her up, and he thrust a final, hard time.

An immediate gratification sprinkled over them. Eyes stuck on each other, they rode out the seconds-long wave of pleasure together. It felt much longer, as they stood nestled against the wall panting hot against each other's dewy skin. As they caught their breath, cadences back to normal, they shared small, satisfied smiles.

"How about that pinot noir?" she whispered in jest.

He barked out an unexpected laugh that bordered on loud. It no longer mattered as they bent and gathered their clothes. From outside the pantry, the house was still silent. The girls slept soundly. The time on their phones told them it had only been eleven minutes since they snuck off into the dark pantry.

Clothes righted again, they opened the pantry door. The bright lights of the kitchen felt more blinding than earlier.

"We should probably get cleaned up," said Rosalie, hand slipping into Nick's.

He had fixed a near-permanent smile onto his face. "Clean up now, wine later?"

"It's like you read my mind."

Rosalie spent the night in Nick's bed. After the wine, they tittered and tottered upstairs with fleeting affection expressed in between. On the second-floor landing, Nick rubbed his neck and his accompanying chuckle revealed his nerves. He was thinking what she was thinking. But staring at each other in the middle of the hallway, neither wanted to say it. She caved first with a tipsy, teasing smirk and suggestive glint in her eye.

Fast forward another two hours, they lay in the naked afterglow of another session. Real exhaustion set in. On their sides, cheeks cushioned into their pillows, they engaged in easy conversation and the occasional yawn. Nick played with her curls. His touch was gentle and considerate, much like it had been during their slower, second lovemaking.

With a tight curl circling his finger, he asked her about her plans. "No real estate license. No Mrs. Lacie's. What's next?"

"What do you mean what comes next? I'm still a waitress at Ady's, aren't I?" she chided him with a slow raise of her brows. "Unless I've been fired and you haven't told me."

"I can't think of anything you'd ever do to be fired."

"Are you sure about that? I slept with my boss. Twice."

Nick erupted in a throaty laugh. His pale green eyes brightened. As his laugh faded but his stare persisted, he couldn't help studying her every feature, mesmerized that this amazing woman was in his bed.

His physical attraction to her went without saying, but he had discovered a deeper connection with Rosalie. She inspired him in more ways than he had told her. From her brilliance to her determination and tenacity, he wanted to be the man at her side, working to turn the tides in their lives. Prove the naysayers wrong.

Nick's palm slid from her curls to her cheek. His timbre deepened from drowsiness but he hung on, enjoying their pillow talk. "I love working with you. We're partners."

She scoffed, assuming he was joking. "Partners?"

"Yeah, partners. Sounds good, right?"

"You mean…business partners?"

"Rosalie, look how far Ady's has come in a few weeks. It's all you."

"It was both of us."

"Exactly. That's why we're partners," said Nick boldly. "You've gotta stop questioning me."

He was lost in laughter as she sought revenge and swatted him.

"Are you nervous for the festival?"

"Nope. I think we're gonna be great. We're gonna show everybody up."

"Kind of cocky, but I like when you are."

He wiggled his eyebrows at her. "Yeah?"

"Sometimes. Don't let it go to your head."

"Never would," he said, pulling her closer and dropping a kiss on her cheek. "Besides, if we win, accepting the trophy is all you."

"If? Or *when?*"

They were smiling as sleep rippled over them and they began to drift off. Within seconds they were goners.

It was the best night's sleep he had in months.

"Double chocolate chip pancakes on the griddle," Nick announced to the household.

The girls were up and groggy at the breakfast table. Their hair was a disheveled mess that Rosalie volunteered to sort later. In their jammies, Maxie's green and Remi's pink, they talked about how much fun they had trick-or-treating last night. Rosalie sat with them and listened, clutching a mug of coffee.

Nick's smile was in secret. He stole glances in their direction every so often, switching between the griddle on the stove and the three at the table. The Sunday morning felt perfect, too good to be true as they got ready for a delicious breakfast.

He sensed Rosalie approaching and winked at her from over his shoulder. She drew that kind of constant playful, jokey reaction out of him. He wanted to spend his time making her smile—making her laugh. He wanted to make her happy.

"Need any help?" Rosalie came up from behind and wrapped her arms around his chest.

"Sunday breakfast is all me. I need you to sit back down with the girls and prepare for the best pancakes of your life."

"I thought we talked about your cockiness last night."

"And you still doubt me every time," Nick said, sliding the four pancakes off the griddle and onto the waiting plate below. "Remember the grits? Or the King Cake? Or the—"

"Point taken," Rosalie cut off, using his own phrase against him. "I'll go have a seat. But I've never been a big fan of chocolate chip."

"You will be. Right, kiddo?"

From the breakfast table, Maxie jerked straight in her chair at the sound of her name. "Yes, Papa—bestest chocolate chip pancakes ever!"

"See?" Nick boasted.

Rosalie shut him up with a quick peck. She was headed for the breakfast table when a heavy knock beat against the front door.

"I got it. I got it—" Nick started, but Rosalie was faster. Already by the kitchen doorway, she insisted she answer. He relented, knowing that once she set her mind to doing something, she was going to do it. He turned his attention back onto the pancakes.

"Next year I wanna be a vampire!" Maxie bared her teeth as if it made her look scary and not adorable, given the missing ones in the front.

Remi scrunched up her nose. "That's not a fun costume."

"Remi, you only like princess costumes!"

"Nuh-uh, next year I wanna be a fairy!"

"Boring!"

"Girls, get along," Nick warned from the stove. He turned off the burner and dumped the last few pancakes onto the plate. "If you can't, guess what?"

"Chicken butt!" Maxie giggled. Remi tried to resist but she gave in too, joining her bestie.

Nick laughed along with the girls and then he heard it. Beyond their silly giggles, there were voices in the hallway. A *man's* voice he didn't recognize. His stomach contracted as his carefree good mood was paused. He told the girls to stay put and left the kitchen to check on Rosalie at the front door.

He was a few footsteps down the hall when the sight of Rosalie alarmed him. She was standing frozen in place staring at two people on his stoop. He didn't recognize who they were at first, but as he moved forward he put two and two together.

Suddenly, Rosalie's shocked stare, like a fish out of water, made sense.

The visitor was Ms. Lacie, along with a man who he had never seen before. He knew who it was anyway.

Rosalie's ex-husband, Clyde.

CHAPTER TWENTY-ONE

Rosalie couldn't think of a single thing to say. She stared, gobsmacked and speechless, at the last two people she expected to find knocking on Nick's door. She wished for it to be a dream—some horrible nightmare that she would wake up from any second, but in her gut, she knew it was real.

Clyde was back in St. Aster. Why she didn't know. What could have possibly motivated him to breeze back into her life after months of radio silence?

Ma was the first one to speak. "Morning, Rosalie. I thought we would find you here."

The insinuation was clear. The lift in Ma's thin brow spoke for itself. The judgment in her low tone. It was Sunday morning. Rosalie and Remi hadn't come home last night. Now she answered Nick's door in her pajamas with the buttery scents of pancakes wafting in the air.

An inexplicable element of shame anchored in Rosalie's stomach. She searched for a bold retort or the courage to slam the door in their faces, but she came up empty. She could think to do nothing but stare at them like she had been frozen in time.

"Ros, mind if we talk?" Clyde asked.

"That's probably best for everyone," Ma agreed.

Still, Rosalie said nothing. She tried to swallow, failing due to the block in her throat.

"Is everything alright?" Nick joined the fray with a clueless concern. He stopped at Rosalie's side in what she recognized as solidarity, but ultimately made the situation that much more complex. He glanced from Rosalie and then to Ma and Clyde. "I thought I heard more than one voice."

"What's up, man? I'm Clyde." Clyde held his hand out to shake Nick's.

Rosalie watched as the two men's hands clasped on to each other's for a brief if not tense handshake. She inhaled a weak breath and cobbled together her best attempt at speech.

"Nick, do you mind giving us a second?"

"Daddy? Daddy!"

Remi's high-pitched squeak drowned out any of the adults. She had heard Clyde's deep baritone trickling halfway across the house and had wandered into the hallway. As soon as she saw him, her eyes bulged and she gasped louder than she had on any Christmas morning. She dashed toward him, knocking anyone in her path out of the way.

Clyde opened his arms for her and called, "My baby girl! Gimme some kisses."

Rosalie stood back aghast as Remi threw herself into his arms without missing a beat. It was as if the year of hell hadn't happened, and he hadn't walked out on them on a whim. Like she hadn't cried for hours wondering where her daddy went. For Remi, he was back, and that was all that mattered in her five-year-old worldview.

"Are you sure you're okay?" Nick muttered, easing her to the sidelines by the elbow. He dropped his voice so no one else could hear. "You look like you've seen a ghost."

"I...I didn't expect..." Rosalie swallowed against the stubborn block in her throat. It had started to ache. "I guess I should go."

"You don't have to—" Nick started, but Ma cut in.

"Sundays are days for families," she said matter-of-factly. "Rosalie, you should do what's right, and spend it with yours."

Rosalie hated that Ma was right. Not because Clyde was *her* family, but because he was—and always would be—Remi's. She couldn't deny her daughter time with her father. She also couldn't waste time waffling on what to do with co-parenting their daughter.

When Clyde disappeared and Rosalie filed for a default divorce, she had done so knowing even with the judge's ruling, she might never receive real support for Remi again. That Remi might not even see her father again. Many months of missed child support payments and visitations later, here he was like nothing happened.

"Remi and I need to get dressed," Rosalie said suddenly to the group. She steeled her voice, ridding it of any wavering. "We'll be down in a second. Then we can talk."

She couldn't bear to look at Nick. His penetrative pale green eyes were on her, following her every step, but she ignored him. Consumed by the shock and stress of Clyde's reappearance, she couldn't handle seeing any confusion from Nick. She pried Remi out of Clyde's arms and carried her up the stairs. She hadn't a clue what she would say when she came back down.

⌘

The four of them went for a walk at the park. Remi refused to let go of Clyde's hand. She swung off his arm in a fluttering excitement that rivaled a spastic hummingbird. For his part, Clyde humored his daughter with chuckles and half-hearted replies to her rambling.

But it was nothing like Nick. It was nothing *genuine*.

After a few minutes, Remi bored him. He wanted her to run off and play and give him space. Rosalie could tell; she had always been able to tell. In their Baltimore days, he spared her ten or fifteen minutes of daddy-daughter time before he gave up and told her to play with her stuffed animals.

Remi didn't know better; she couldn't spot his disinterest. Rosalie saw right through him.

"Baby girl, why don't you go play on the jungle gym and leave the grown folks talk?" Clyde asked.

"But, Daddy, I wanna play with you!" Remi begged, tugging on his hand. "Can you push me on the swing?"

Even Clyde didn't have the heart to deny her plea. He sighed, scrubbing a hand over his bearded face, and then he let her drag him across the playground. Rosalie and Ma stayed put, standing in a tense silence thickened between them.

"He's back for his family," said Ma. "You should give him a chance."

"He's back after he abandoned us?"

"People make mistakes—*men* make mistakes, Rosalie. Nobody's perfect. Least of all, you."

"What goes on between Clyde and me is none of your business," said Rosalie, ignoring the insult. She couldn't deal with Ma's critical opinion of her right now. She already knew what Ma thought of her. "You don't have to be here. I'll handle Clyde."

"Clyde asked me here for your reconciliation."

Agitation bubbled in Rosalie's chest ready to burst. She bit down on her tongue and tried to keep a lid on the emotion that had her overheating on the spot. It was no use, as she gave in and let it pop to life. She sprang forward without a word to Ma and stormed across the playground.

If Clyde thought he was going to pressure her to take him back, to curry favor with Ma and win her over, he was epically mistaken. He saw her coming, but chose to ignore her. He pushed a giggly Remi on the swing, now in a sudden show of dad of the year.

"We need to talk. Now," said Rosalie coldly.

"I'm with my baby girl. It can wait—"

"No, it can't. Right now, Clyde."

In their seven years of marriage, rarely had she taken a firm, authoritative tone with him. The change threw him for a loop. He dropped his hands to his sides and stared long and unblinkingly at her. Remi's swing started to lose momentum and she twisted to ask him to push her higher.

"I'll be back, baby girl," he said at last. "Ask your grandma to push you."

Rosalie spun on her heel and Clyde fell into step beside her. Ma watched them go, staying behind with Remi. In seconds thanks to Rosalie's fast stride and Clyde keeping pace with her, they were far out of earshot from the playground.

"Wanna grab a drink?" Clyde asked.

"I don't have time for a drink with you. This is strictly business."

"So let's sit down over it. Or is that against your new independent woman front?"

"Ms. Maple's. Across the street."

Rosalie agreed to the coffee shop for one reason only. Clyde might've seen it as an opportunity to humanize their talk, but she saw it as a reason to keep others around them. Considering Clyde's history of explosive behavior when she tried to call him on his shit, she needed people around to prevent that unsavory turn.

Once seated at the coffee shop, Clyde took off his ball cap and rubbed his scalp. "Look, mistakes were made. I'm not perfect. Never said I was. Neither of us are perfect. We had our problems. We had some good times too. Remember those?"

"The divorce is final. The good times don't matter anymore."

"I never signed anything."

"I didn't need you to," she told him. She kept her expression stern, not to be swayed by his manipulative tactics. "You were gone long enough—I filed for a default divorce. A judge finalized it. Did you think you were going to walk out on us and I'd stay and wait for you? I'd keep your name?"

"Nah, never said that—"

"Because you also think you can come back like nothing happened. Like you were gone for an hour at the store. You expect me to drop everything for you? I have a *life* here."

Clyde's bushy brows rose and the threat of laughter played across his face. "You got a life here? You sure about that? 'Cuz let your ma tell it, you've got some job waiting tables and some dude—*your boss*—you're getting dicked down by. That's what you want Remi to be caught up in?"

"It's none of your business. *That's* what you don't get. I'm free to do whatever the fuck I want," she spat in a tone angrier than she wanted. She hated when she showed him emotion; it usually led to her spiraling out of control, and him gaining the upper hand. Her firm, detached approach worked best with Clyde. Before her breathing could outpace itself, she inhaled a steadying breath. She gripped her coffee and fixed him with her coldest stare. "Clyde, it's over between us. You're not going to guilt trip me or use Remi to convince me to take you back."

"You're gonna have her grow up like that, huh?" he asked.

"Like what?"

"Like you. No father around. Just her ma raising her. She's gonna be looking for that love elsewhere."

The low blow dig was meant to hurt her, and it accomplished its job. Rosalie fell silent, brain short-circuiting. She hadn't viewed the situation from that perspective, but with Clyde unloading it at her feet, she was forced to think about what that was like. She plunged into the past, years of trauma as a young girl wondering why her father left home. More years as she grew older resenting Ma for it. Those years in high school, deep in a boy-crazy phase, where she first noticed the cool older guy named Clyde from around the block. The rest was history…

"I work today. I've got to go or I'll be late. Remi's staying with my mom," she said in a mechanical tone. Her body language matched. She rose with limbs like boards and her walk was a rigid gait for the door.

Clyde didn't call her back, but instead let her go. He knew his words would be on her mind nonstop.

And he was right.

❧

Rosalie showed up late to work. It was unlike her, but Clyde's arrival had knocked her world off-kilter. The first thing she wanted to do was seek out Nick. They needed to talk about what was going on with Clyde. As soon as she moved in the direction of his office, Zoe swooped in for the interception.

"I've been here since opening. Break time. You cover the lunch regulars."

She could hardly protest, given her tardiness. She tied her apron dutifully around her waist and spent the next hour waiting on the usual lunchtime diners. Busy delivering food to tables, she was on the opposite side of the dining room when a man in a business suit walked in. Before she could ask him if he was dining in, he disappeared down the back. He was going to Nick's office. Did Nick have a business meeting he hadn't mentioned?

The mystery was forgotten about the moment Mrs. Kettles raised her arm and flagged her over for a refill on her soda. Rosalie rushed over, working as if on autopilot. She was too stuck in her head to truly put forth her best effort.

Her brain felt overstimulated, crowded by thoughts of Clyde and the bombshell he had dropped on her lap earlier. She hadn't been able to stop thinking about it. What if Clyde had a point? What if she was dooming Remi to follow in her footsteps?

If there was one thing she wanted even more than providing for Remi, it was ensuring her future was a good one. Better than hers. That she didn't make the same mistakes she had...

"You taking your break?" Zoe asked when she finally returned. She joined Rosalie at the soda machine and poured herself a cup of root beer.

"That sounds good. I need to talk to Nick."

"You didn't see the guy in a suit? Your boo thing boss has a visitor."

Rosalie frowned as curiosity rippled through her. She untied her apron and ventured toward the back half of the restaurant. Nick's office door was closed. The closer she stepped, the clearer it became that he and the man in the suit were talking.

She couldn't help herself. She hovered outside the door and listened for a few seconds.

"Mr. Fontaine," said the mystery man, "it's days before the Autumn Festival. I understand you think you'll be able to pull off some landmark victory, but it's not going to change the state your restaurant's in."

"My restaurant's just fine. We've been making renovations."

There was a condescending tick in the man's tone. "Yes, your little improvements have been a step in the right direction, but let's be honest: you're not much of a business man, Mr. Fontaine. The damage is done. Ady's will never recover to what it used to be. Not without professional help."

"Not interested."

"I have a new proposal for you. Have you read the last offer letter?"

"Why would I when I told you I wasn't interested?" Nick asked back.

Rosalie had promised to only eavesdrop for a couple of seconds, but now she was too puzzled to walk away. She held her breath listening outside the door, trying to make sense of what was going on. Who was this man and what offers had he made to Nick for Ady's?

"I suggest you open the letter, Mr. Fontaine. Here's a copy," said the man.

The tear of an envelope and rustle of a letter unfolding sounded. "The offer has gone up. Add another zero."

Nick's sharp intake of breath was audible even through the door. Several seconds went by where neither man said a word.

"You said add *another* zero?"

"That's right. We're confident we'll be able to profit off of the little buzz you've started to create. The entire town is excited about Ady's. We are too— we just want to commodify it."

"Commodify it? What does that mean?"

"Ady's has franchise potential in the right hands. I'm giving you an out now before it's too late. Don't squander away this opportunity. I'll be back tomorrow. Last chance before the offer's off the table."

Rosalie jumped back as the office door shot open. The man strode out in his crisp business suit carrying a briefcase. He barely noticed her, nearly walking right into her with a thoughtless apology.

She couldn't be annoyed; she was too busy digesting the conversation she had overheard. Nick appeared in the office doorway with his hands burrowed in his trouser pockets. He was seeing the man off, only to notice Rosalie in the hall.

"I didn't know you were around," he said slowly. "Were you...were you listening?"

"You're selling Ady's?"

"No."

"That's not what it sounded like."

"Can we talk in my office?" Nick stared beyond her, where at the end of the hall two women pushed open the door to the ladies' restroom.

Rosalie was still processing her shock as she obliged Nick and joined him in his office. He dropped into his chair and pressed the pads of his fingers into his eyes. She chose to stand, in a pacing mood.

"Who was he, Nick?"

"Perry Langley. He's with Yum Corp. It's some franchise holding company. They own a bunch of restaurant chains."

"And," she said, swallowing shock, "and they want to *buy* Ady's?"

"Yes. He's made a few offers."

"A few offers? For how long?"

Nick leaned back into the chair and shrugged. "Maybe a couple weeks?"

"You haven't told me. You're thinking about selling, and you haven't told me."

"I'm not thinking about selling. I never said that. Don't put words in my mouth," he said in a gruff tone she had never heard out of him before. "Langley's shown up a couple times trying to convince me to sell. It's not me looking to do business. He shows up unannounced."

Rosalie turned her back on him, folding her arms across her chest. She couldn't deny it felt like a betrayal of some sort. Even if he claimed he wasn't considering going through with it. Just last night he said they were *partners*. She had spent weeks at his side, devoting hours to Project Fixer-Upper. Why had he never mentioned this Yum Corp offer? Not at least once?

"You know how much this job means to me," she said. "And you kept this from me."

"Do you want me to be honest?"

"Please."

"It crossed my mind maybe once. Twice at most. But it was never anything I seriously considered. You haven't been here the past year, Rosalie," he explained from his desk chair. "You don't know how much of a struggle it's been trying to keep Ady's afloat—"

"You're joking, right? Obviously, it's work running a restaurant! Nick, *really?*"

He rose out of his chair. "I already told you I'm not gonna do it! Why are you ignoring that part of the conversation?"

"Because I can't believe you've kept this from me. For weeks. How many hours have we spent talking about Ady's? I sat down with you and figured out a comprehensive budget for the next few months! I worked overtime trying to clean this place up! I enrolled us in a damn competition hoping it'd boost sales!" Rosalie snapped, gaping at him in knitted brow disbelief. "And you couldn't pause for one sec and tell me about this?"

"I'm not the only one keeping secrets around here."

Rosalie recognized the bitter undercurrent immediately. She saw the sudden tightness in his mouth. He was upset with her. Just as upset with her as she was with him. She fell a step back, at a loss for words.

It was hard to believe twelve hours ago they were over the moon, tangled up in the sheets in each other's arms.

"What secret do you think I've kept from you?"

"Clyde didn't show up from nowhere," said Nick. "I want to be understanding about the situation, but the guy's turned up on my doorstep. You're going off with him. What am I supposed to think?"

"I didn't know he was going to show up."

Nick sighed and said, "I don't wanna believe you did, but whatever's going on, it's how you wanna handle it. I'm not gonna stand in your way. Don't feel guilty on my part. Do what you gotta do."

"Where's this coming from? What does that even mean?"

"I want you to be happy. I don't want what's going on with us to complicate everything else you've got going on. It's a lot on your plate. I saw that this morning," Nick said, taking a step closer. "You tell me what you want."

Rosalie's heart pounded against her chest so loud she couldn't hear herself think. The thumps distracted her, muddling her brain further. She couldn't make sense of anything that was being said. Anything that she had overheard earlier.

She just wanted to go off somewhere quiet and bury herself under blankets and think.

Looking up, she saw Nick's normally dimpled, handsome face was taut and square. She knew then what her answer was, knew their attempts at communicating had broken down. She swallowed the lump of hurt and ignored the sting of tears in her eyes.

"I guess I need time to figure things out."

"How long?"

"I…I don't know. I didn't plan on any of this. I need to figure out what's best for Remi."

"I get that. But I was serious about what I said earlier. I wasn't gonna sell."

"Nick, you know how much I need this job," she said wearily. "You chose to keep me in the dark. Now you're backing off because Clyde's here. I don't know what to think."

"I'm not backing off—I just don't want you to feel stuck with me—"

"I can't finish this shift. I'm leaving early."

Rosalie denied him eye contact as she turned to go. She was no angel, but she was sick and tired of the tug-of-war in her life. She was over Clyde's manipulation and Ma's insults. She was done toiling hard to make Ady's a better place. Finished fighting for a restaurant she believed in more than Nick himself.

CHAPTER TWENTY-TWO

"**H**ow'd I screw shit up?"

Nick groaned, lying awake late Sunday night in bed. He had screwed up meeting with Langley from Yum Corp. He had screwed up his role in Rosalie's life. He had made a giant fucking mess of things. The worst part was that he didn't know how to patch any of it up—or if it even could be fixed. He recounted for the dozenth time how he had messed up that badly...

When Clyde and Ms. Lacie showed up on Sunday morning, he wanted to support Rosalie. He was trying to help get her through the awkward spot. He knew what it meant for her. Though she hadn't confided much about her marriage, he understood that it wasn't an easy situation. Her contentious relationship with both Clyde and Ms. Lacie was rife with tension.

At the same time, he didn't want to stand in her way. She had decisions to make. A young daughter to think about. As he stood back and watched Rosalie walk out the door by Clyde's side, he couldn't help noticing how they looked as Ms. Lacie described—*a family.*

His jealousy pooled thicker than expected in his stomach. He couldn't unsee the three of them, and he couldn't forget how it made him feel. He didn't like the thought of Rosalie back with Clyde. What could he say? He was human. Just a man.

He spent the morning at Ady's stewing. Perry Langley's greedy visit hardly helped. Rosalie showed up and tempers ran high. Frustrations formed. He carelessly blurted out things he didn't mean. In a way he instantly regretted as he stood there and witnessed her walk out of his office, and also what felt like his life.

She hadn't returned his calls. She hadn't even answered his text messages. Zoe mentioned she mumbled something about calling in sick tomorrow. He wanted to see her. He needed to explain what he meant when he said he wanted her to do what she thought was right.

He wasn't trying to push her away. The thought they had reached an end to what was a still a very green relationship disappointed him. The situation only served as a reminder of how bad he was with expressing himself.

It always called back to Mom and her passing. He had spent an entire year bungling how he handled his grief. Running away from expressing that part of himself in favor for hiding behind a mask. It was what he did whenever confronted with tense situations. He disassociated from his true feelings and played it off. He said and did the wrong things.

He fucked up.

But how to fix things? Could they even be fixed?

Nick dug the base of his palms into his eyes, teeth bared and clenched. His relationship with Rosalie meant a lot to him. More than he had allowed himself to muse on for too long. He had been unbelievably happy with her, working side by side. True partners.

Now the Autumn Festival was two days away and he was alone.

He wished things were like the movies; he could uncover a time machine and travel backward to undo the damage he'd caused. It didn't matter if that was never his intention. He hurt Rosalie and lost her trust.

That night Nick fell asleep with his phone in the palm of his hand, in the middle of sending another text to her. Deep down hoping that she would soon answer.

⌘

Maxie broke into a cry when she found out about his fight with Rosalie. She asked him if Rosalie and Remi would be coming over for their usual Monday night dinners—Cheesy Creole Pasta now a staple. He tried to skirt around the issue, but Maxie was a smart cookie. She figured it out based on the strange Sunday encounter with Clyde.

Nick tried everything to soothe her. He cooked her favorite breakfast. He let her wear her favorite clothes to school, patchwork overalls and her Godzilla T-shirt. He promised her an hour of cartoons when she got home. Nothing worked. The distress flushed her tan skin in a pink tint and her eyes were puffy and rubbed raw.

When he dropped her off at school, he hoped to run into Rosalie. No such luck. He exchanged brief words with Maxie's teacher, Ms. Gumbel, and checked the parental crowd. He couldn't find her. Had she decided to keep Remi home a day? Did Clyde have anything to do with this?

The muscles in Nick's stomach contracted. The same tension locked up his jaw. He squeezed his eyes shut and blocked out the jealous imagery that had been plaguing him since Clyde showed up. The imaginings of the three of them cozying up as a family, deciding to give things another shot. It made him sick to think their relationship was over. Just like that.

In his truck, he withdrew his phone and debated for the dozenth time what to say to her. He wanted to call her again, to hear her voice. That might've been too much. He had already tried that three times. She was clearly upset with him. Another sincere text was a better bet. His fingers hovered over the screen's keyboard as he crafted a careful message.

Hey, hope you and Remi are OK. just wanted to check up on you.

He waited for what felt like forever on a reply. It took a couple nerve-racking minutes, but one came, short and succinct.

We're okay. Thanks for checking

Nick's brows pushed together. He was hoping for more. Some sort of in on a conversation. He typed out another text anyway.

Are you free? Was hoping we can talk…

He inhaled a Hail Mary prayer breath and waited for her answer.

Busy the next couple days. Sorry to use sick days. Hope Zoe's okay covering.

The response was oddly impersonal and cold. Even for text. He stared at the screen for a long moment and couldn't feel anything. His earlier nerves dissipated for a hollow numbness. Was Rosalie already over their relationship? Had she already moved on from him?

He had no clue. Before he could torment himself over the possibility, he received another text message. This one wasn't from Rosalie. Instead, Langley's message dashed his hopes once again.

Mr. Fontaine, I will see you soon at the cafe. I'm looking forward to doing business!

Nick groaned audibly to no one but himself. He had forgotten about the follow-up meeting with Yum Corp. For a quick second, he considered standing Langley up. He thought about sending a text demanding he leave him and Ady's alone. But the more he sat there and thought about it, the more he realized that he should show his face. He had something to say.

⤫

"Thanks for meeting with us, Mr. Fontaine."

Nick hesitated to shake Langley's hand. He wasn't alone like Nick thought he would be. Four other men in suits, all identical by way of neat, coifed hair and plain features, stood behind him. Their biggest difference? Their ties. Each one was a different color or pattern. That was it. That was the defining difference between them.

He motioned to the biggest table Ady's had to offer. It was their family table, boasting eight encircling seats. He took a seat as far from them as possible, leaving an empty chair on either side. The suits didn't seem to notice. They leered at him with creepily blank eyes. He focused on Langley.

"We understand that you're interested in the offer we've made," said Langley coolly. He opened a manila folder and revealed what looked like a twenty-page document. On the front it had the Yum Corp logo, the happy, hungry face with a spoon in its mouth. He slid it across the table to Nick. "This is the contractual agreement. Feel free to take your time looking through it. If you have any questions, I brought Rob Garish here. He's one of our finest attorneys."

Nick's brows scrunched into a line. Glancing at the man Langley referred to, he discovered Garish was the one with the emerald green striped tie. He would've guessed the guy with the golden yellow polka-dot tie…

He looked down at the contract in front of him. The print was small and the paragraphs long. It went on and on for pages and pages. He flipped through it quickly and the laugh forming in his throat wheezed its way out louder than called for. The suits glanced at one another and back at him. He picked up the contract and held it close to his face, admiring its density.

"You guys really went for it. Look at this thing—it's like a dictionary."

"It's a standard business contract," Langley said. His mustache hid half his mouth, but judging off the curve of his bottom lip, he was frowning. "I assure you, Mr. Fontaine, that there's nothing too off the wall in there. If you read page seven, paragraph 4B, you'll notice your lump sum payout. I'm assuming that's what matters most to you, right?"

Nick flicked to page seven, paragraph 4B. Just as many zeros as last time. He laughed again.

Langley produced a ballpoint black ink pen. "If it's too much for you to look through, we can always explain it to you aloud as you sign."

"Who said I was signing?"

The clueless stares around the dining table were enough to make Nick snort in stifled laughter. His brows rose high onto his forehead and he let a wide, dimpled grin speak for him. Did these fools really think he was going to sign the contract as they explained what it said?

"Mr. Fontaine, you're under no pressure at all to sign. I was offering an alternative. If you're overwhelmed by the length of the contract, we can break it down for you."

"Because you're trustworthy." Sarcasm oozed from his low register.

"Well, we're not here to swindle you if that's what you're—"

"I've told you how many times now?" Nick interrupted, kicking back his chair and standing. "I'm not interested. Not today. Not yesterday. Damn sure not tomorrow or any other day. So you guys can go. Maybe try the burger joint down the block. They might wanna sell their souls. But Ady's? It's not for sale—it's never gonna be for sale. Got it?"

Nick felt their bemused gazes follow him toward the door. He propped it open and swept his arm for them to take their exit. They got the hint loud and clear. One by one the suits passed him by, straightening their ties and smoothing their already slicked hair back. Only Langley stopped at the edge of the threshold to address him.

"You're missing out on a great opportunity."

"No, I'm not," said Nick, composed. If possible, his grin widened. "My great opportunity is *here*."

He waved Langley and the rest of his Yum Corp suits goodbye, and with his foot, nudged the door to a swinging close. He took a look around Ady's dining room, wall-to-wall, eyeing the cavernous space that was his own. That was once Mom's. He couldn't, and wouldn't, give it up. Even if he wound up owner, manager, waiter, and cook, a one-man army trying to keep it open, he would.

But he hoped it wouldn't come to that.

Nick unstacked the chairs from the rest of the tables and headed to the kitchen to prep for opening. In the back of his mind, he was thinking about what he could do to make things right.

～∞～

Come closing time, Nick called Ellie to check on Maxie. The babysitter had picked her up from school and helped her with homework. At the time of Nick's call, she was about to feed Maxie dinner. She mentioned Maxie's uncharacteristic behavior. Unlike Maxie's usual hyperactive antics, she was lethargic and sullen. When asked if she wanted to watch cartoons, she shrugged and mumbled.

Nick's breath hitched in his chest. He hated it when Maxie was upset. It wasn't often, but when it happened, it was like a dagger straight to his heart. He had failed Maxie in some capacity. How could he not feel responsible for that?

He sulked on these thoughts and started on mopping. The day itself had been a long and hard one. Though he'd had a self-assigned victory in his meeting with Langley and Yum Corp, he still faced an uphill battle. The Autumn Festival was coming up. His relationship with Rosalie was in shambles. The rollercoaster of emotion was difficult to sort out. He was used to a flat line of mediocrity, of do-nothing days with slacker tendencies.

"You've been acting weird."

Nick dunked the mop in the bucket and looked up. It was Zoe. She was about to call it for her shift, purse on her shoulder and pack of cigarettes in hand. He shrugged and wrung the mop, squeezing out the excess water.

"Look, if it's about the Autumn Festival, it's gonna be okay," Zoe said. "So what if we don't win? Everybody knows Ady's gone."

Nick said nothing again, sloshing the wet, soapy mop around the floor. Zoe wasn't giving up.

"This about Rosalie? Heard her ex is back in town."

"I'm sure everybody in St. Aster knows."

"Did y'all break up? Judging by how down in the dumps you look and how Rosalie said she's gonna be out the next couple of days, I'm guessing that's a yeah. I never talked about you with her, but if my opinion's worth anything? I think she really likes you."

"I thought so too."

"You try talking to her?"

"She's been busy."

"With her ex?" Zoe asked aloud. She flipped hair over her shoulder. "Listen, I don't know what happened between y'all. Maybe I shouldn't say anything. I just think you shouldn't give up 'til you've had your say—'til y'all have talked it out."

Zoe left him on that note. Nick finished the rest of cleanup by himself. He flicked off the lights and locked up the building. Now November, it was already dark out. The street lamps lit the unoccupied streets and sidewalks. Most of town was home by now.

Nick was on his way to his truck, digging in his jacket pocket for his keys. The neon pizza sign from across the street was too bright to ignore. He chucked a glance in Doughboy's direction, expecting to see Joe Schmoe in the window. His stomach dropped and his feet stopped. Across the street, visible in the glowing window of Doughboy's, were Rosalie and Remi.

Not just Rosalie and Remi but *Clyde*. The threesome sat in a booth by the window and ate dinner.

Like the family that they were.

Nick didn't want to stare. It wasn't his place. None of it was his business. Not anymore if he and Rosalie were through. Still, he swallowed with difficulty against the lump in his throat. He found the resolve to keep walking, crossing the pavement to his truck. He had the answer to the question he had asked himself over and over again since his fight with Rosalie. He had screwed up for good.

CHAPTER TWENTY-THREE

Remi beamed looking between Rosalie and Clyde. Though pizza was one of her favorites, Rosalie had never seen her look so happy. She was a direct contrast to Rosalie, who barely touched her pizza and drank two Diet Cokes. The dinner wasn't her first choice of an outing, but she wanted to give Remi what she asked.

The truth was, she had no intention of being with Clyde again. She had spent the day trying to clean up the confusing mess. That started with her planning a way forward.

She sat Remi down and explained in layman's terms that Mommy and Daddy weren't getting back together. They both still loved her, though. The revelation seemed to confuse Remi, as a hundred little question marks popped up above her head. She didn't cry and she didn't protest, but she did make sure to ask if Clyde was going to be around.

Cue their family dinner. Clyde was heading back to Baltimore in two days' time. Remi begged and begged for the chance to go to Doughboy's together. It was supposed to be their last family event. Instead it wound up worrying Rosalie that she had once again fed into the idea that there was a possibility she would give Clyde a second chance.

If Remi didn't believe it, Clyde seemed to. More than once he mentioned his love for not only Remi, but for Mommy too.

"I love my girls," he said from over the rim of his Coke. The ice chinked against the glass and he munched on a few chunks. His dark eyes twinkled staring across the booth table at them. Remi ate it up. "I'm gonna miss you."

"Daddy, don't go," Remi moaned.

"I've gotta, baby girl. Baltimore is home."

"Then I wanna go! Mommy, can we go?"

Rosalie never broke eye contact with Clyde. Her voice was leveled. "Remi, we talked about this earlier, remember? Maybe for one of the holidays."

"But I wanna go now!"

"Sorry, baby. You heard your mommy." Clyde gave Remi's small hand a quick and sympathetic squeeze.

"Clyde, don't start."

"Start what?"

"I thought we agreed dinner would be chill."

"It is chill. I'm chill. Our baby girl was just asking a question—can't she ask a question?"

Rosalie glanced to her right and saw Remi eyeing her. Though they resembled each other, like mother and daughter in terms of features, she couldn't interpret what Remi thought. Her mouth was twisted in a deep frown and her nose was wrinkled. If she had to guess, she was making sense of the exchange between her parents. She was deciding Clyde was right...

"We should go. It's getting late and I can't keep Remi home from school another day," said Rosalie. She dug inside her purse for her wallet.

Clyde waved her off. "I got dinner. Am I still allowed to pay for my family?"

Turning him down would only be another point deduction in Remi's eyes. Rosalie conceded without a word. The argument that would ensue wasn't worth it. Dinner was about to be over. She had driven herself and could arrange to discuss future custody with Clyde over the phone.

The waitress, Allison Porter, checked on their table. Her face said what was on her mind. The teenager found the situation scandalous. Her mouth curled into the type of gossipy smile Rosalie had seen others in St. Aster wear. As if her existence in the small town couldn't get any more salacious. Now she was a divorcée who returned to town with her small daughter in tow, dated her boss, Nick Fontaine, and days later, went on dinner dates with her ex-husband.

Rosalie was aware how it looked to the rest of town.

"What about tomorrow?" Clyde asked, jamming his debit card into his wallet. "We can hit up another spot."

"No. We can't afford it."

Remi whined at once. Her legs thrashed against the bottom of the booth and the whimper she gave sounded like she was liable to tear up any second. Rosalie ignored the pre–temper tantrum signs. She had compromised on dinner for one night. She wasn't going to compromise a second night.

"I'll pay."

"No, thank you," she said. "Once was enough."

"Nobody said you've gotta be there. It'll be me and my baby girl—just the two of us."

"No."

"She's my daughter." Clyde's baritone remained low, but it deepened to a rumble. She knew him well enough to understand his meaning. To the untrained eye, he seemed harmless, reclined against the pleather booth cushions. In reality, his own temper was stirring. He didn't like it when she tried to control the situation. He was the man and saw it as his charge. "I can take her out whenever I want."

"We don't have a custody agreement. I don't feel comfortable—"

"It doesn't matter what you feel comfortable with."

"I'm her mother—the one who has been there every day of her life," Rosalie snarled before she could stop herself. She sucked in a breath and sat up straighter. She had to keep her cool. He wanted her upset. Besides, glancing at the other tables, people were starting to take notice. She couldn't afford a scene. "Look, we'll talk about it later. It's getting late."

"You really think you're controlling shit now? 'Cuz I walked out once?" He released a chuckle deep from his belly and snatched his ball cap off. He found the idea ludicrous. "She's my daughter and if I wanna keep her out longer, I can. You don't get to dictate it."

Rosalie nibbled on her tongue. On her left, Remi's whine continued, now with tears brimming. She hated when they argued. In front of her, Clyde was spun up and ready to keep pushing her buttons. He wanted a confrontation on the matter. He hoped to force her hand and get her to relent.

"She's also a five-year-old child who has a bedtime," said Rosalie matter-of-factly. "It's 7:00 p.m. We have to get home and get her ready for bed."

"Home? You mean that shitty little room in your ma's house?"

"*Stop* using that language in front of her."

"Or else what? What're you gonna do?"

Rosalie popped to her feet, grabbing Remi's hand. She wasn't going to put up with his disrespect another second. Even for Remi's sake. She cut off Allison returning to clean their table and beelined for the exit. Clyde was quick to follow. The nosy eyes of everybody in the restaurant followed too. A show was about to happen.

"Maybe I'm gonna take it to the courts 'cuz this is bull," Clyde ranted behind them. He cared little that they spilled onto the sidewalk and passed more strangers. His point was going to be made. "Get primary custody so I can have my baby with me all the time."

Remi started crying. Rosalie strode as fast as her short legs allowed. She didn't look back at him. Seeing his angry face would only tempt her to respond. He wanted a reaction and she was giving him her retreating form instead. Otherwise, her mind was empty. No real thoughts or a concrete strategy materialized. She just wanted to be out of his presence.

Clyde had never hit her before. He had initiated plenty of midnight screaming matches and other behavior that was calculating and aggressive. He had slammed doors and broken things. He had left both she and Remi in tears. But he had never crossed that line. In that moment, speed walking to the car with him on their tail, Rosalie wasn't sure what his intention was.

She hurriedly unlocked the Honda Civic and plopped Remi into the car seat. She rounded on him to ward him off. Her eyes narrowed and her nostrils flared as she spoke to him in the coldest, most forbidding voice she could muster.

"You go ahead and take this to court. We need a legal custody agreement," she explained. "Until then, Remi is my daughter and she's in my custody. I'm not going to let you manipulate the situation. I'm not going back to you. We're *done*."

"So you gonna tear up our family? For what? Some creole dick?"

"Think what you want. I don't care. Good night, Clyde."

Rosalie ducked her head as she dropped into the driver's seat. Clyde stood on the sidelines inching closer as if to bang on the window, but she ignored him. She hurried to start up the car and drove away.

⁓

Remi wouldn't speak to her. The moment they were home, the girl flopped onto her bed and buried her face into the pillows. Her muffled cries chipped away at Rosalie. The sound was the worst in the world. The most heartbreaking noise to Rosalie's ears.

She gently lowered herself onto the bed beside Remi. At first she offered silent comfort. Her hand rubbed circles into her back and she let Remi cry it out. The tears needed an escape and Rosalie understood what upset her. Many years ago, she had been in Remi's place, utterly confused by the interactions between her parents.

"Shh…Remi baby, it's okay. Everything's gonna be okay."

"Nuh-uh. You always say that. But now Daddy's *gone*!"

"Remi—"

"You made him mad!" Remi rolled over, puffy brown eyes teary and angry. "You made Daddy mad and now he's not gonna be my daddy anymore! He's gonna go away again!"

"He'll always be your daddy. You'll see him again as soon as we figure out an arrangement."

"He was mad! He's gonna go away. He's not gonna come back."

"Calm down, Remi. Please stop yelling at Mommy, okay? We can talk about it," she said softly. "I know you're upset. Daddy upset me too. We're going to try to make a new arrangement work, but please remember we love you. That's what matters most."

Remi rubbed her fist against her eye. "I don't like when Daddy's mad."

"Me neither."

"It's scary. I just wish you and him could not be so mad anymore."

"We'll try, baby."

"Mommy."

"Hmm?"

"Why don't you wanna love Daddy?" she asked curiously. Tears and snot shone on her cheeks and under her nostrils. Rosalie grabbed a tissue and wiped off both.

"Daddy hurt Mommy's feelings, baby."

"But if he says sorry?"

Rosalie inhaled a steadying breath, the used tissue crumpled in her enclosed hand. "Sometimes sorry doesn't fix things. Sometimes someone does something so mean and hurtful that you can't forgive them anymore."

"Like what? Did Daddy call you a bad name?"

"No, baby."

"A boy called me a poopie head and I cried, but Maxie punched him and then he said sorry. And now we're friends."

"It's not the same thing, but thank you for trying to make me feel better."

Remi rubbed her eye some more and sat in silence. The gears in her brain turned over their conversation as she tried to understand. Rosalie was thankful for the brief reprieve, exhausted by the day's back and forth. She stroked Remi's thick curls and untangled them with her fingers.

"I'm sorry, Mommy."

"For what, baby?"

"For being mad at you 'cuz Daddy was mad. I just wanna be like before."

"I forgive you. Do you forgive Mommy? I'm sorry everything's been like this. I promise I'll do better. We'll be a team, okay?"

"Okay."

Rosalie kissed her cheek. "Good. Let's get ready for bed. I'm pooped."

Remi giggled and bounced off the bed to choose her jammies.

⚜

Rosalie couldn't sleep that night. She waited until Remi fell asleep and then quietly drew the bedroom door closed. Ma and Henry were already in their bedroom for the night. She crept past their door and down the staircase.

At first she intended on curling up in the living room, but once there, she found the confines of Ma's house too restricting. She threw on her denim jacket and slipped her feet into her boots and braved the night's cold.

She knew where she was going as soon as her foot struck the porch's creaky floorboards. She needed a long walk to process what had happened earlier with Clyde. How she was going to move forward starting tomorrow.

The bayou was different at night. It was dark and difficult to see. She flicked on her phone's flashlight and shed light on a path through the thick green brush.

For a long time, she walked. Her pace fast, she put as much distance between herself and Ma's house as she could manage. The frothy waters of the bayou emerged from around the bend. At night rather than green, it looked black, reflecting the moon in its ripples.

The soundtrack hadn't changed; wetland critters were loud in their humming and buzzing. She welcomed the background noise as she plopped down on the bench by the abandoned cabin. She sat there for an indeterminate length of time, staring so unyieldingly at the water that she zoned out. She traveled deep into her head and sorted out her thoughts.

The snap of a twig brought her back. Her hand curled around her cell phone and she shone the flashlight in the direction the noise came from. She assumed it was a mirage. She was seeing things. There was no way…

"Hey," said Nick, drawing cautiously closer. "I was out for a walk and saw you pass by. What are you doing out this late?"

"I could ask you the same thing."

"Rough night. I asked Ellie if she could babysit a couple extra hours because…because…" He stopped there, sighing deeply. "I needed time to think."

"Me too." For as mad at him as she had been in the last two days, she couldn't help relating.

"Seat taken?" Nick gestured to the empty space next to her.

She shook her head and he lowered himself onto the bench. She instantly jumped back to over a month ago, where they had shared a bench at the school playground. The first real time they had achieved a personal breakthrough. The simple dinner outing that had slowly peeled back another side of Nick she hadn't been expecting.

Now, seated next to him, it was hard to believe everything that had happened. In the span of a month, they had gone from a disagreeing boss and employee to being friends and then lovers and partners. They had given up on these developments after the first big roadblock, emerging from the other end alone. She was still upset, but another part of her hated to think things would end on that note.

"Surprised to find you out here."

"Things have been tough lately," she explained. "I had dinner with Clyde tonight. We got into it. Not that I ever expected anything different from him. It's just difficult trying to do what's best for Remi."

"I owe you an apology," he said in earnest. "I'm sorry for how I acted on Sunday. It's not acceptable. I should've been there for you. I wanted to be, but I blew it. I screw up because I'm bad at handling heavy stuff. I let myself think it was okay to pull away because you might've been going back to Clyde. Even if you are, it's your right. It's not my place."

Rosalie appreciated the apology. She could hear the strain in his voice. Nick struggled with expressing himself and that only further worsened their breakdown in communication.

He continued. "And I should've told you about Yum Corp. Perry Langley—he's been contacting me for weeks. You deserved to know about it. I wasn't going to do it, but I should've told you. That job is important to you. I kept saying you were my partner, but I didn't act like it. I'm sorry, Rosalie."

"Do you know what I've realized?"

"What? That I'm a jerk?"

She understood his hopeful attempt to sprinkle in some humor. It was how he handled situations where he felt awkward, but if he was unloading his thoughts, she wanted to too. Regardless, she played along, sneaking him a sideways smirk in the dark.

"Maybe," she said quietly. "But that's not what I meant. We both *suck* at communicating."

"Good point."

"You should've told me about selling Ady's."

"Believe me, I know that now."

"But I should've tried harder to understand what you were trying to say about Clyde and me," she admitted. "You were in the dark. I can't be mad you jumped to conclusions—but I wish you hadn't."

"It's been a weird past few days."

"I didn't see any of it coming. I never thought he would show up."

"I'm sorry I implied you did. I know it was out of left field."

Rosalie shifted on the bench to look at him, even if the shadows engulfed most of his face. "Nick, I was hurt when I found out you didn't tell me about Langley. I was hurt about Clyde being here. It was all a lot for me to deal with."

"Tell me how I can help."

"By sticking with me," she answered. "None of this is easy. I just need someone to listen sometimes, if that makes sense?"

"My ears are still open. I hope I didn't lose your trust."

"You didn't," she said. Any tension in her shoulders lessened as she felt his hand seek hers in the dark. "I've been struggling a lot, Nick. Remi comes first. She's like most little girls; she loves her daddy so much. She doesn't see his faults—and I don't expect her to—but it's been hard on me. I don't want to be the bad guy. I don't want to be the one who keeps her from him."

"So you went for dinner with him tonight," he filled in for her.

"I hoped it was harmless. Then I realized Clyde wasn't here just for Remi. He was in St. Aster to guilt me into getting back together with him. You know what's worse? He almost got in my head."

At her side, she could tell Nick's posture stiffened. That it was something difficult for him to hear. He kept his tone neutral next time he spoke. "Sounds like he realized what he was giving up when he walked out on you."

"He's used to me being a fool over him. I was for seven years. I've taken him back more times than I can count." Rosalie broke into a wry smile as she reflected on her relationship with her ex. "But he doesn't get that I'm not that woman anymore. I've changed. I'm never going back to that life. I want to fight for my own, with Remi."

"I've gotta be honest. That's a relief to hear. You worried me when you walked out of Ady's. Then you wouldn't answer my calls. Your texts were short. I didn't know what to think."

"I pulled away because it felt like you were pulling away. Now that I think about it, we were both doing the same thing."

"I'm not good at relationships," Nick confessed, squeezing her hand. "The last real one I had was Maxie's mom, and that was a train wreck. Don't even know where Desiree is these days."

"I can't talk. My marriage with Clyde wasn't any better."

"But the past's the past. We've still got our futures. We've still got *now*."

Relief swept over Rosalie listening to his uplifting words. She relished in the warm feel of his hand clutching hers and leaned closer into him. She had missed resting her head against his broad shoulder.

"Where does that leave us?"

"I still have the same feelings for you, Rosalie. I'd like to pick up where we left off—put a real label on it. Boyfriend and girlfriend if the boyfriend has anything to say about it."

His humor at the most unexpected moments still managed to produce soft laughs out of her. This time was no different as she released a quick snicker and pressed her lips to his neck. She placed a trail of kisses that served as her answer.

"Seconds back together and you're already driving me crazy."

"I can't help it. I've missed you," she murmured.

"Two long days apart. It was rough."

"For the girls too. Remi's been upset."

"Maxie almost turned down a chance to wear her Godzilla T-shirt to school. Her *Godzilla* T-shirt."

"Wow, sounds serious," said Rosalie, sitting upright.

Nick's hands swept the curve of her cheeks and he bent forward to kiss her brow. "It was very serious. Now we can make up for it."

"There's something we've got to do first."

"Like what?"

"Are you serious?" she asked, raising her brows. "Like do what we've been planning on doing for weeks now?"

Nick grinned. "Win the restaurant competition at the Autumn Festival."

CHAPTER TWENTY-FOUR

"**R**eady?"

Rosalie's face warmed up with a smile. "Ready."

"Let's do this. It's gonna be an all-nighter," he warned, slipping on his apron.

"Are you kidding? I was a finance major—I'm familiar with all-nighters."

Nick and Rosalie split course in the kitchen. He went left and she went right. He pulled out the necessary ingredients to get started on boiling crawfish. Rosalie on the gumbo. They traded ingredients like mind readers, swapping paprika for pepper and whipping cream for ghee. Within an hour, every burner on the stove was going. The blue flames heated up their delicious concoctions.

They met halfway for high-fives, riding the tenacious wavelength they had developed together.

"Two hours down, who knows how many to go?" Nick laughed.

Rosalie checked on her gumbo, stirring it under meticulous supervision. "It doesn't matter. We'll sleep later."

"Like when we're dead?"

"Exactly."

"Or we can take a vacation," he proposed, coming up behind her. "Picture sandy beaches and cool ocean waters."

"Sounds amazing—*after* we win."

Nick turned her around in his arms and searched her gaze. Her relentless determination spurred him on, lighting a fire in him that burned longer than any flame in the kitchen. He kissed her, swallowing the sweet vanilla taste of her. Her nimble fingers grazed the length of his chest. Even the light touch was too much for him. His baser instincts started to kick in, sprawling beyond his control.

The fragrant spices from the gumbo saved them. Rosalie broke from him and hurried to check on the pot. He inhaled a cool breath and reoriented himself to focus on the cooking. It was crazy how easily he lost his wits around her. For tonight at least, they had to double down and prove themselves in the kitchen.

"Tastes amazing," said Rosalie. She held up a wooden spoon to his mouth for a taste test. "What do you think?"

"I think an amateur chef might've mastered my mom's recipe," he replied.

She beamed. "No one cooked better than Ady."

"Maybe not. But you're coming pretty damn close."

"You think we have a chance, Nick? Tomorrow…"

He saw the hope alight in her brown eyes. "I know we have a chance. Let's do what we do—cook this food to the best of our ability. The rest is in everybody else's hands."

Rosalie nodded, rejuvenated by his quick call to action. They returned to the burners on the stove and the chopping boards on the counter to finish their recipes. The night wore on and they toiled away as a team. Two chefs working in sync to create the scrumptious dishes on the Ady's menu.

Nick couldn't remember the last time energy surged through his body while he cooked. Beside Rosalie that night, he felt invincible. He pulled out all the stops, showing off every trick from his culinary arsenal. For the first time since Mom passed, he cooked her menu without the heavy tug of grief. He slipped back into the old Nick—the man whose passion for cooking was an untamed explosion of creative artistry.

And Rosalie was by his side every step of the way, sharing in his reawakening. Her newfound expertise was just as inspiring. Together they worked in tandem through the night.

The morning of the St. Aster Autumn Festival, they got up early and drove to the town square. Though they had reviewed the setup of their booth, they wanted no room for error. Nick yanked off the large tarp covering their booth and flipped over their sign, spelling "Ady's Creole Café" in loopy green scrawl.

He fought through a yawn as by his side Rosalie flicked on the Crock-Pots. Each one was full of Mom's precious recipes. Each one hour's worth of late-night slaving over the stove. They had trudged upstairs half-asleep before their faces even hit the pillow. But the hard work was worth it.

In the pit of Nick's stomach, instinct told him so. It didn't matter if the crowds paid their booth dust or if their dishes were met with criticism. He had picked himself up by the bootstraps, for once being a proactive business owner, and he had *tried*. He had given it his best effort. Thanks to Rosalie, he had woken from his grief-heavy stupor long enough to realize that he needed to fight to keep Ady's open. To keep Mom's dream alive.

And he was going to. He would fight 'til the bank foreclosed and forced him to nail the Out of Business sign on the front window.

Rising up to meet the responsibility had always terrified him. He had decided no effort at all was better than failure. Now he understood how wrong he had been. Mom wouldn't have left him Ady's if she hadn't believed he could do it. He was Nick Fontaine, top graduate of the Savoy Culinary Academy, head chef at Ady's Creole Café for four years, and now he was the owner.

He folded the tarp into halves and looked up over at Rosalie. She lifted the glass cover of the first Crock-Pot and checked on the chicken and shrimp gumbo. Since they had gotten back together, their relationship was stronger than ever. They were now an unbreakably united front.

"I'll finish setup. Why don't you take a break? You only got a couple hours." Nick slid an arm around her waist and kissed her brow. They had woken up so early they hadn't even said goodbye to the girls. Ellie had shown up for her daylong babysitting, looking pale and groggy herself. If he was tired, he knew Rosalie had to be.

She stood her ground, stirring the gumbo. "I'm good. Festival starts soon."

"It starts in two hours. We've got time for breaks. Go get a coffee." Nick slipped a twenty-dollar bill into the pocket of her men's denim jacket. "While you're at it, get two. Large. Extra dark roast. The whole works."

"You've yawned fifty times this morning. Are you sure *you're* okay?" She smirked, giving him one of her usual nudges in the side.

Nevertheless, she was gone in seconds, off to go find the coffee booth and cure their fatigue. Nick concentrated on setting up the rest of the six-by-eight stall. He double replenished their disposable supplies of paper plates, napkins, and plastic cutlery. He jotted down the price points on the giant chalkboard hanging off the front of their booth window. He was wiping down the counter when Rosalie reappeared in step with Zoe clutching coffees.

"Eleven o'clock Mayor Allen himself kicks things off," Zoe mumbled over her coffee cup. "Then it's a few hours of everybody wandering around like chickens with their heads cut off."

"Right, to explore the booths and taste test for the competition." Rosalie handed Nick his coffee. As requested, it was piping-hot, large and black. Her own she was almost finished with. "How are the customers voting?"

"It's by the tokens they've given at the festival entrance. Whichever booth has the most tokens wins. But votes won't be announced 'til later. Usually it's around five," Zoe explained. "You don't remember, Nick?"

He strained his memory for any recollection. "It's been years since I've, uh, showed up to one of these."

"I come every year for the shopping," Zoe said. "You're gonna be the big star today. Everybody's gonna be talking."

"C'mon, it's not like Nick went anywhere. Who cares?" Rosalie rolled her eyes.

"That don't matter to anybody. No offense to you, Nick, but I'm sure you know what everybody's been saying."

"Ignore her," Rosalie insisted.

Nick offered no reply for either remark, choosing to swallow the hot coffee instead. Zoe prattled on about the town gossip and Rosalie rolled her eyes a second time. He didn't know what else to say, but to admit that Zoe had a point. People had talked. The word around St. Aster was known. He was a slacker and Ady's was failing.

But starting today, he was going to prove them wrong.

The festival grounds filled up in waves. Come ten o'clock, for each quarter of the hour, another drove of festivalgoers wandered onto the square. The festival volunteers pressed play on the sound system and the speakers blasted the ever-cheerful chords of holiday music. The booths lined either side in their autumnal glory, bright oranges and golds the color scheme. Other autumn staples like strewn leaves, plump pumpkins, giant squash and stacks of hay littered the festival site.

Jefferson and Que showed up in solidarity to cheer them on. The cook and busboy had checked out the other booths and wanted to report what they had observed around the festival grounds.

"We were over at the Burger Shack's booth and they ain't got nothing on us," Jefferson said. "You should see 'em—scrambling to get their shit set up last minute."

Rosalie rested her hands on her petite waist. "We've been here since 8:00 a.m."

"It's in the bag," Que said, stroking his sparse goatee. "Nobody's even close. Maybe you were right, Nick. All that comeback talk."

The cook and busboy waved goodbye after another couple minutes of chatter. Not long after that the festivities officially kicked off. The mayor gave his speech. The festivalgoers began crowding around various booths, lining up with tokens ready. From their own, Nick spotted several he was curious about.

There was a booth for cold weather accessories like scarves and gloves. Another booth for beautiful glass Christmas ornaments. More than a couple themed picture booths for family photos. Even a pumpkin booth, where anyone could go to fulfill their pumpkin desires; you name it, they stocked it.

"I never knew pumpkin spice toilet paper was a thing," Rosalie said aloud, mirroring his thoughts.

He shot her a sideways grin. "I want to know who's tasting their toilet paper."

Their first real customer of the day turned up as they were laughing. Up until that point, many had strolled by with curious glances. They were surprised to see Ady's with a booth set up. More surprised to see him behind the counter. That alone wasn't enough to order off the menu, though. Ady's had earned its poor reputation for its subpar food fair and square.

It didn't offend him. It only meant that when their first customer did approach, he worked extra hard on giving his best. He ladled a generous serving of gumbo into the container and delivered it to Clementine Browning. She quietly but gratefully accepted the warm bowl, spoon already between her fingers. She returned minutes later once satisfied by the food to cast her vote, dropping her token into their inbox.

"That's one vote for us."

Rosalie glanced around the crowded festival. "More will come. You see all the looks we're getting? Or is that because we're together?"

"With St. Aster? Could be either or could be both."

They dismissed the possibility with a quick peck on the lips. Another customer on the other side of the counter cleared her throat. It was Mrs. Kettles, the older woman prodding her glasses up the bridge of her nose. She showed off a prickly smile as soon as Nick greeted her.

"You really did set up a booth. Good for you, Nicholas. Adeline would be proud. How about a medium of that gumbo? It smells just like it used to way back when."

"It's courtesy of Rosalie. You're gonna enjoy it." In his tried and true charm mode, Nick winked and grinned, eliminating whatever critical bone was left in Mrs. Kettles. By the time she left, midswallow of the gumbo, she was nodding her head. She had dropped a token into their inbox. He checked on Rosalie. "Looks like that gumbo might be our biggest hit today."

"You don't have to tell everyone I made it."

"Why not? You did. But you still haven't told me the secret ingredient."

"And I'm probably not going to."

"What if I bribe you?" Nick wiggled his brows and elicited a laugh out of her.

"Bribe me like, how?"

"You'll find out when the time's right. I've got some things up my sleeve."

"Nick," Rosalie said, pointing at the booth window. "Our next customer."

His tan skin hardly concealed the light pink flush that crept up. He had a penchant for getting carried away, particularly where Rosalie was concerned. The customer waiting on him was actually the Duval family of five. He waved hello and welcomed them to the booth. It was as he took their orders that he noticed. Behind the family stood a small, growing line of customers…

Three o'clock swung around, and Nick and Rosalie were running low on food. Ady's had gone from nonexistent patronage to a continuous line for the last few hours. Some came back for seconds. Others for thirds. He served Clementine Browning her fourth cup of gumbo that day and whistled watching her go.

It was déjà vu. He was reliving Ady's golden days in real time. Seeing the booth flourish before his eyes was like having Mom around again. He inhaled a deep, far-reaching breath and released it with a newfound sense of ease. The road ahead was an uphill one, but it was doable. The restaurant was going to be saved.

During a five-minute interlude where the line thinned some, Ellie brought by Maxie and Remi. On their heads they wore matching orange beanies stitched to resemble a pumpkin. They showed him a strip of silly pictures taken in one of the photo booths.

"Took them by the pumpkin shop and they wanted these really cool fuzzy pumpkin beanies." Ellie gestured to the trio's identical hats. The teenager looked as excited as the kids, for once out of her shy and reserved shell. Her smile showing teeth and her tone upbeat, she told them all about their day. "Then we saw the photo booth and we had to take pics."

"Papa, I stuck out my tongue like this!" Maxie exclaimed, demonstrating how she posed in the booth. The second pose included bunny ears behind Remi. She giggled mischievously afterward. "It was sooo much fun!"

"Sounds like it, kiddo. Hungry? Wanna a slice of cake?"

He and Rosalie traded off time with the little ones. For the first ten minutes of their visit, he took his break and she held down the booth and customers. They switched places afterward, with Rosalie sitting at the bench across the walkway. The girls sat on either side and they ate their cake.

"How's the booth going, Mr. Fontaine?" Ellie asked. She hovered on the sidelines as Nick served a couple crab cakes. "Every customer's been dropping in tokens."

"Hoping that's gotta be a good sign."

"When is the winner announced?"

"Sometime this evening," said Nick, counting the dollar bills in hand. He gave the couple their change and thanked them for coming by. The next customer at the window forced a shallow intake of breath from Nick. He had opened his mouth to greet her only to discover Ms. Lacie. He hesitated a second, stammering on his words, "Afternoon, Ms. Lacie. What can I do for you?"

"I have a lot to say about your relationship with my daughter," she said tersely, straight to the point. "I won't air dirty laundry right now—not when we're at the festival, but I'd appreciate you coming by. *Both* of you."

"I'll run that by Rosalie. It's her say."

Ms. Lacie's pinched smile spread across her face. She eyed Nick with what felt like blatant distaste and then turned around and disappeared into the crowd. Ellie stood by watching.

"What was that about?" The nineteen-year-old placed her earlier jubilance on hold.

"What was what about?" Rosalie asked. She walked up flanked by Maxie and Remi. Her ten-minute break over, she reclaimed her spot behind the counter with Nick. "Did I miss anything?"

Nick waited until Ellie herded the girls out of earshot before he answered.

"Your mom came by," he said, scanning the area for any sign of her. She was long gone. "She wants us to sit down and talk later."

"I refuse to let her ruin today. She can wait 'til we're ready to talk. I don't live on her timetable. She knows that," said Rosalie resolutely. She aimed a bright smile at him. "Today's about nobody else but us."

⌒∞⌒

The second Mayor Allen announced the results to the food booth competition, Nick blacked out. His body numbed and he stopped thinking.

But his legs still worked. They carried him through the crowd, gradually prodding his way to the front. In passing he overheard a mixture of loud applause and hoots, but also the muttered opinions of those keen on gossip. At the stage, the festival volunteers beckoned him up the steps. His haze ended halfway up. Where was Rosalie?

The crowds had separated them. He scanned the audience, searching for her familiar warm face. He spotted her almost instantly. She stood out among the crowd like a literal spotlight shone on her, and his heart fluttered. He wanted her up there with him—his partner through Ady's comeback.

The audience gasped when he jumped off the rickety staircase and dashed for her. They parted to make way for him, eyes peeled to watch his quest. He reached her faster than he anticipated. His arms opened and she let out a shriek as he lifted her off her feet. Their mouths met halfway in an impassioned, celebratory kiss.

His feet spun them in a small, fast circle. Rosalie held on by gripping his shoulders. Still they never broke apart for air. She tasted sweeter than the King Cake they enjoyed earlier. He swallowed the sugary taste, yearning for more— *always* more with Rosalie. He would've kept going had they not stood encircled by half of St. Aster.

They separated with breathless smiles and hands linked between them. Aware of the many watchful eyes, he ignored each one and concentrated on her. He wanted to celebrate the win with no one else. It was *theirs.*

"Ready to go collect our prize?"

Her nod was sheepish but eager. "Let's do it."

Together as a couple, as bosses and as chefs, as partners at the restaurant and in their relationship, they strode toward the stage to claim their victory.

CHAPTER TWENTY-FIVE

After the festival was over, Rosalie decided it was time to deal with the tension with Ma once and for all. She had shown up to the festival to try to sour her day with Nick. Rosalie was no longer going to bite her tongue. Enough was enough.

"Tea?" Ma asked at the kitchen counter.

Rosalie's and Nick's eyes snapped to each other. They both shook their heads side to side. Ma poured three mugs anyway. The light trace of lavender had its usual effect on Rosalie. Her anxiety doubled and left her feeling restless, but she refused to back down now.

This conversation with Ma was one that needed to happen. She could sense it. Either they would emerge with a new understanding, or it would be the opposite. They would be on worse terms than before. If she guessed based off of Ma's behavior, she chose the latter. Everything about how Ma acted told her she hadn't changed her mind. Her stubborn and uncompromising nature went nowhere.

"Are you sure I should be here?" Nick muttered under his breath. He leaned close to Rosalie for permission. "If you two want a moment alone—"

"You can stay, Nick," Ma said, overhearing him. She set the mugs down on the table in front of them and nursed her own in the palm of her hand. "I'll be quick. Here it goes: I didn't want you two together."

The blunt delivery shocked her. She spent the next two or three seconds gaping across the table at Ma. She hadn't expected that quick of a revelation. If anything, Ma usually chased around the bush as long as possible. Known to speak in riddles, she used subtext to communicate more often than not. For her to flat-out deliver her intention was different.

The shock soon fell away for hot irritation. The wispy evening breeze wafting in through the kitchen window was no longer enough. Rosalie massaged a hand to her forehead and let it sink in. Ma hated her relationship with Nick. It fit perfectly with her reasoning for turning up on his doorstep with Clyde by her side.

"It was you," she sighed. "You brought Clyde back to St. Aster."

Ma sipped her lavender tea, eyes discerning. "That's right. I got a hold of him and told him he had to come get you. You were making a mess of things."

"I was making a mess of things? It's *my* life!"

"You've been reminding me since you were fifteen. I know that, Rosalie. But that doesn't change the fact that you make piss-poor decisions at every single turn. I hoped things would be different when you came back to St. Aster. It was more of the same."

"Because I was making my own choices? Because I didn't want to be a real estate agent?"

"You don't think long-term. It's hard to watch from the sidelines. I contacted Clyde's mother, Erma, and explained the situation. She reached out to Clyde and he wanted to try again," Ma explained. Her features relaxed, the sharpness in her expression no more. "I'll go ahead and say it: I was wrong."

Rosalie opened her mouth to argue, but then stopped herself. Another surprise from Ma. She hadn't expected her to admit fault—exactly the opposite. Rosalie readied herself to counter Ma's justification, but she fell silent and blinked out of confusion. Those three words had never been in her vocabulary.

"I'm sorry," Ma went on. She focused on Nick. "Nick, I don't know you well enough to judge, but I did—I used your reputation around town for being a lazy slacker against you. I didn't want you to drag my daughter down with you. I've been down that road."

Nick found Rosalie's hand in a show of solidarity. He only acknowledged her apology with a stiff nod. Ma smiled.

"Your loyalty's to her. I get it. I just wanted to let you know. Now if you don't mind, I think Rosalie and I should chat alone now…"

"Are you okay?" Nick checked in with Rosalie, glancing at her. "You tell me what you want."

"It's fine. You can go ahead."

Nick half rose out of his chair, pausing long enough for a kiss to her brow. She and Ma sat mute at the table and listened to the disappearing pad of Nick's footsteps. The thud of the door closing followed. Only then did Ma clear her throat and speak again. Lips pinched into a smile, she eyed Rosalie with an unfamiliar wistfulness.

"I look at you, and I see so much of myself. You don't even know it."

"We look alike, but the similarities end there." Rosalie's guard wasn't down. She held strong, refusing to be fooled by one apology.

"I don't think they do. Your grandma Opal isn't here to tell you, but I ran away when I was young. I was fifteen."

Rosalie knitted her brows. "Grandma Opal never mentioned…?"

"We made peace before she passed. She didn't want to drudge up the bad times. Our relationship was complicated. I hated her for a long time. Then I *became* her," Ma mused, tea mug forgotten in her hand. "I raised you like you were a burden, but really, I was angry with myself for letting my life turn into what I didn't want. I was young and single, a teen mom with no man to show for it. Your father came and went as he wished."

"I remember. I was little, but sometimes his car starting woke me up in the middle of the night."

"I tried to fix. I figured, if I can't have him, I can have *somebody*. I've spent the last twenty years of my life trying to please a man—many different men—and I have nothing to show for it."

The crack in Ma's voice revealed her sincerity. She paused, no longer able to continue. She blinked back what seemed like tears and shuddered out a breath. Rosalie's stony exterior thawed seeing Ma like this. It was a realer display of emotion than she could remember seeing. In truth, her insides ached witnessing Ma unravel. Even slightly. She had always been so stoic…

"I broke up with Henry," Ma whispered.

Rosalie's eyes widened. "You broke up with him? Is that why I don't hear him snoring on the couch?"

"He took his things this morning and left." Ma used her shirtsleeve to wipe her tears. She avoided Rosalie's gaze. "I'm going to mess up my makeup. I've a showing in an hour."

"I hated the men you brought around," Rosalie said in quiet honesty. "I *hated* them. I hated you. I didn't know that you couldn't control Pa leaving us."

"I picked the wrong man. I've picked all the wrong men. And I've sat here and judged you for the same."

Rosalie sacrificed her pride and reached across the table. She patted Ma on the hand. "I've made mistakes too. I ran off with Clyde. I let him treat me like shit the entire time. But getting back together with him isn't going to solve my problems. It's going to make them worse."

"You're right. I realized what I had done when I heard about him acting a fool the other night."

"You heard about that?"

"Of course I did. You forget St. Aster has a pulse for gossip? The whole town knows about your argument at Doughboy's."

"I should've known. It doesn't matter. It's over between us. If Clyde wants to be in Remi's life, he's going to have to agree to a court-ordered custody arrangement."

Ma's smile was small. "That's also what I've realized. You've learned your lesson. You're twenty-four and you *know* what you're going to tolerate. I never learned that lesson."

"It's never too late."

"Maybe."

The two sat there appreciating the first real progress made in years. The big breakthrough their relationship needed. Ma understood where she went wrong. Rosalie saw her in a different light than she expected. She only hoped that the progress would continue into the future.

Ma dumped their mugs of cold tea into the sink. "Tell me about him. You two have that look in your eyes. You know what look I'm talking about. That gaga type of look. It was obvious at the festival."

"Really?" Rosalie winced and laughed all in one go.

"Yes, really. Things seem good between you."

"They are. I really like him. But I want to take it slow. One day at a time."

Ma folded her hands in front of her and shared a wish that rounded out the surprises for the day. "How about we do that? We've never been close, but maybe we can work on it. Take it one day at a time like you two."

Rosalie smiled wide. "I'd like that."

CHAPTER TWENTY-SIX

Nick and Rosalie stood back and admired the Now Hiring sign plastered in the restaurant window. With business surging, they needed as much help as they could get. According to the budget, they could afford two new hires. Until then everybody stepped their game up and helped out wherever they could.

Before opening and after closing each day, Nick and Rosalie handled the managerial side of things. Rosalie taught him what she knew about accounting. Her major in finance proved to be invaluable as she walked him through the basics and answered his questions.

Elsewhere, Project Fixer-Upper lived on. They hit up the thrift store and picked out pieces of cheap but workable furniture. Nick got a deal on paint at the hardware store and they carried the furniture out back. Alongside Zoe, Jefferson and Que, they set to work fixing the wobbly legs and painting the worn finishes.

Rosalie even got Ms. Lacie, who happened to be an excellent sewer, to patch up cushions for the armchairs they'd bought. Those they dragged into the corner of their new lounge. Decked with four armchairs, a coffee table, and a bookcase, the enclosed space was their new area for customers looking for ambient vibes.

"Browning's gonna love this," said Nick, appraising the boxed-in area. "It's a good space for people who just want to sit alone and eat some dessert."

"Like your famous King Cake and banana bread pudding?"

"Speaking of dessert, might be time for some."

She smirked at him, dusting her hands off on her jeans. Their earlier painting had them marred in different colors. Her left cheek had been accidentally smeared by a coat of mustard yellow. She even had some on the knotted head wrap she wore. She looked cute like that, paint smears and all.

He chuckled, his insides topsy-turvy. She still made him nervous, a true feat for a cool as cucumber man like himself. He had accepted that the pleasant nervous energy wasn't going away anytime soon. It was a marker for how on his toes Rosalie kept him.

Even as they called it quits on renovating for the day and moved into the kitchen for a spur of the moment snack, he couldn't stop relishing in his good fortune. Ady's was on the up and up, and now that they were back on track, they had started turning a profit. More and more each day, he adjusted to his role as a business owner, finally accepting the responsibility for what it was.

Best of all? The frisky woman under his arm. She surprised him heading into the kitchen, fisting his shirt and pushing him against the fridge. He started to laugh, but she sooner silenced him with her mouth. Right away he forgot about the dessert they were going to whip up. Her lips, sweeter than any other sugar he had ever tasted, were a dessert of their own.

He held her flush against him and their kiss reddened with passion. They tangled themselves together, Rosalie practically levitating off the floor. She wound her arms tightly around his neck and halfway hung off him, a laughably light load for him to bear. His attention was elsewhere, hands busy gliding a path down her body's petite curves. She gasped her surprise when he filled both with the supple cheeks of her backside, and squeezed.

Her fingers tightened on his shirt and she slipped her tongue into his mouth. His pulse was rushing at rapid speed. In no time, his breaths turned ragged and his baser impulses begged to come out and play. His hand was down the back of her jeans and panties much to her moans when an ounce of logic trickled in.

"We should probably take this to the office," Nick muttered. He broke away long enough to survey the stainless-steel appliances around them. The kitchen had been sanitized during closing shift. "Don't know about you, but I'm not interested in another cleanup."

"You're right. Things *do* get messy."

The tease was tantalizing. He groaned as Rosalie buried her face into his chest, muffling her girlish laughter. He couldn't waste another second. He grabbed her hand and bolted for the kitchen door. Their dash down the hall outside was a blur. In seconds they slipped into the office breathless and giddy. Though the restaurant was empty, technically closed for the day, there was still a sneaky element to their impromptu romp.

Unfettered adrenaline burst through Nick. He and Rosalie kissed their way through the office, navigating the filing cabinet and the desk blind. They fell into his desk chair with hands all over each other. Rosalie landed on top, her curled up form a welcomed weight in his lap. She kissed him until his lips numbed. It was a thrilling kind of numb, a tingly marker of their affection. He tried to keep up.

She leaned back and undid the buttons on her shirt with fast fingers. His next breath stuck in his throat. Her shirt split open and offered him a delicious sneak peek preview of her breasts. They stared at him from over the rim of her bra cups. He worked both fleshy, pert mounds free. Her eyes fluttered to a close as his palms filled with their soft weight. He rolled her nipples between his fingers, adding a light pinch that earned a jaw-dropping moan out of her.

Nick barely had time to grin before he sought her lips. Their mouths found each other again, their own private language. In those heated kisses they spoke many words no one else but themselves would understand. He seized the opportunity to speak with his body and its movements. His hungry mouth and pair of eager hands; both dedicated time to worshipping Rosalie.

Together they fumbled their way through the rest of their clothes. Rosalie yanked his shirt over his head and he helped her wiggle out of her denim. The pile on the floor beside the office chair grew until they sat naked. His eyes shot to hers as the condom wrapper fell away and he slipped the rubbery encasing onto his member. She held his gaze, foreheads pressed together. He sucked in a breath the second she sunk down onto him.

It happened faster than he thought. The slippery hot sensation consumed him as he paused to relish how wonderful she felt. Pleasure zinged through his entire body. A groan revved up in his throat. She seemed to share the same sentiment. She purred, coming undone in his lap. The friction between them was tantalizing as they discovered a rhythm.

The chair rocked with them. Back and forth again and again. The motion was as fluid as theirs, a seesaw of pre-orgasmic bliss. They rode it until the wheels fell off, rocking harder the closer they edged toward release. Nick grit his teeth. In need of distraction, he smashed his mouth to Rosalie's. His member had started to twitch inside her, and he counted down the seconds.

He met her halfway, pumping up into her silky wet goodness. He held on as long as he could before he had to surrender. His hands squeezed her ass cheeks the second he let go. He released a strangled growl torn from the base of his throat. Rosalie kept going, pulsing and tightening around him as if to drain his very life essence. She tapped out seconds behind him.

He was there to catch her, sweaty and breathless. His arms engulfed her, holding her close to his chest as they panted back to normal cadences. Her forehead touched his in the seconds it took them to come down from their highs. He grinned, staring straight into her cattish brown eyes.

"That wasn't so messy," he joked.

"Nick, shut up."

He laughed, running a hand up the petite curve of her side. "Just saying. Next time maybe—"

"No," she interrupted with a kiss and a smile. "Ady's just earned its reputation back. Last thing we need is to sully that by fucking in the kitchen."

He agreed, but he laughed anyway. "Point taken. A man can hope though."

"A man should get dressed," she said, sliding off his lap. "We have a visit to make."

"Rosalie, I was talking out of my ass—"

"Nick, you should. It's important. I'll be there with you."

Her gaze was honest and earnest. He sighed and conceded her point, running a hand through his cropped golden waves. "Alright. Just...just gimme a sec."

"Thanks for coming."

"I don't mind," said Rosalie, holding his hand. "Remember that time way back when, you came with me to see my mom? It was an awkward talk where she admitted to sabotage?"

"You mean last week?"

"*Was* that last week?"

He appreciated her attempts to lighten the mood. As it was, his nerves rattled uneasily in his stomach. His heart hung heavily in his chest. The urge to pretend to be calm and collected lurked under the surface. He resisted the old habit, choosing instead to be as vulnerable as he felt. He showed Rosalie that side of him. The nervous, uneasy smile and the wavering breath. His clammy palm that she didn't seem to mind holding on to. He was pretty sure his bronze skin paled to a dull beige entirely unlike him.

She gave no indication any of it bothered her. Actually, she offered soothing affection. Her featherlight caresses eased the antsy flutters inside of him. The soft lilt in her voice helped him inhale a centering breath again. By his side, just her energy alone encouraged him to stand strong and keep going.

The St. Aster Cemetery was vacant that deep into the evening. They crossed the grassy plains columned by dozens of gravestones and shrouded by cypress trees. The sun had already begun to set, ending its run of pale light for the day. Now a breeze kicked up and brushed cool against their cheeks.

When they came upon the gravestone belonging to Mom, they stopped. Nick gripped the bouquet of flowers he'd bought earlier at the florist. The inscription on her gravestone jumped out at him as poignant as ever. He lost his breath and failed on his next inhale. Instead he choked on air and brought his fist to his mouth, biting his knuckle.

Adeline Marie Fontaine
Beloved Mother, Doting Grandmother, Renown Chef
The flavor she brought to the world is still being tasted
Rest in Peace (1966–2017)

The rush of emotion hit him all at once. His teeth digging into his knuckles failed to stave off the cry. It burst free with a choked breath and the tears flowed. The deep sadness he felt in her absence had consumed him for so long it rose to the surface for the first real time since her funeral. He let it out. However ugly and however messy, the heavy grief that weighted him down now pelted to freedom.

And that was what it wanted. To be heard. To be seen. To be *felt*.

The flowers loose in his grasp tumbled to the ground. Rosalie's arm coiled around his shoulders as much as possible given her short reach. He didn't notice at first, seconds ticking by. His eyes closed and he swallowed against the soreness in his throat. The anchor-sized anvil tying him down was gone, lifted as if by the grace of Mom herself.

He felt lighter. He felt better. More at peace than he remembered in recent memory.

"The restaurant's gonna make it," he whispered under his breath. He crouched close to the earthy grass and laid her flower bouquet properly in front of her grave. His smile was small and sad, but also tinged with hope. "I'm gonna make sure Ady's lives on."

On the walk to his truck, he pulled Rosalie close and pressed his lips to her brow. His nose by her thick curls, he caught a whiff of her conditioner. The nutty aroma of shea butter was now another delightful scent he associated with her. He couldn't help but indulge a second inhale. Rosalie drew away slightly, confused by his greedy nose.

"What are you doing?"

"Don't move. Your hair smells really good."

"Are you serious right now? It's half covered in a head wrap."

"Still smells amazing," he said huskily. The teasing could be heard in his voice. "Just like the rest of you."

"You're obviously buttering me up," she laughed.

"That a bad thing?"

They made it to the truck trading teases. He was behind the wheel and she was giving him shit. He didn't want it any other way.

CHAPTER TWENTY-SEVEN

Rosalie never thought she would see the day. Baby steps were still being taken, but for forty minutes straight, she and Ma shared close quarters without a single argument. They collaborated, working side by side in the kitchen. The occasion was Saturday night dinner. Ma had asked Rosalie, Nick and the girls for a dinner at home.

If it had been a couple of weeks ago, Rosalie would have invented an excuse not to participate. Dread would have flooded her insides as she scrambled to think up any reasoning. Any excess time in Ma's presence always spelled trouble. It always meant an impending argument. She wouldn't have predicted things would change anytime soon.

But *baby steps*. That was still the stage they were in. Still cautious around each other in fear of stepping on the other's toes. One look at Ma and she saw the effort. She was trying, brick by brick lowering that wall that had been up her entire life. Rosalie tried too. In small ways, like joining Ma in the kitchen while Nick and the girls played outside.

Years ago, growing up under Ma's roof, she avoided the kitchen as if allergic. The kitchen was the spot in the house where their fights happened. Something about the room ignited their tempers, and they burnt faster than any food cooking on the stove. The spot near the breakfast table would be where she stood when she snapped and decided she had enough. She ran out of the house, seventeen and angry, and never looked back.

'Til now. Rosalie snuck a smile at Ma. She grated the cheese block in her hand and appreciated their silent treaty. The cease-fire, mutual peace they had decided on. That they were working toward. Regardless if it took them years, these were baby steps in the right direction, with an end result well worth it.

"Who taught you to cook like this? Couldn't've been me," said Ma, scraping the peeler across a misshapen potato. "Was it that cute boyfriend of yours?"

"Don't let him hear you say that. His head is already big enough."

"How's things at the restaurant coming along? I heard from Mr. Hebert that the gumbo is tasting better than ever."

"Thanks to Nick."

"Not thanks to just Nick."

Rosalie paused mid-grate and quirked a brow at Ma. "He's the head chef."

"But he's not the only one who's been cooking, right?"

"Well...no..."

"And a little birdie told me, Ady's improving the way it has wasn't all Nick either."

"I made a few suggestions." Rosalie shrugged it off, returning to grate the last quarter of the parmesan cheese block. She hadn't given thought to who was responsible for Ady's recent success. As far as she was concerned, it didn't matter so long as it continued earning revenue. That meant she got paid and when she got paid, she could save, save, and save some more. Providing for Remi was still the goal. "Anyway, I'm glad business has picked up. Now I can keep saving for my own apartment."

"Rosalie, what I'm trying to say is, Ady's is a success again because of you. It was your smarts and your determination, wasn't it?"

Ma's kind words were a surprise. Rosalie forgot about the cheese grater for the second time in minutes. Her face slackened and the expression must've clued Ma into her shock. She touched a hand to Rosalie's shoulder in earnest compliment.

"I'm being serious," she added. "You don't give yourself enough credit. Maybe because I never gave you enough. But if you turning Ady's around is proof of anything, it's proof you can do whatever you set your mind on."

"Thanks, Ma."

"Do you want to know how you can thank me?"

Rosalie hesitated on asking. For the briefest second, she wondered if she would bring up the real estate licensing exam. "You tell me. How can I thank you?"

"Keep doing what you're doing." Ma spotted the lingering confusion and simpered. Back to peeling the potatoes, she elaborated. "Rosalie, I'm talking about doing what you want. Your instincts are right, aren't they? They've been leading you to the decisions you've been making, right? Keep following them."

"I think I will. I've kind of realized I enjoy Ady's more than I thought I would. I've never seen myself in the restaurant biz, but…"

"Who knows?" Ma finished for her.

Rosalie's mouth widened in a smile. "Yeah, who knows?"

At dinner, they piled food onto their plates and engaged in light conversation. Ma hadn't stopped smiling since Remi and Maxie launched into a long story about their day at school. She ate up their words as well as the chicken parmesan on her plate. Rosalie relaxed and savored each bite, for once appreciating Ma and Remi's bonding.

Before it caused anxiety. She wanted Remi to love her grandmommy and wanted Ma to spend time with Remi. Yet, it had been a struggle due to their tumultuous past. She hadn't felt open enough to sit back and watch the bonding unfold. It was a beautiful sight, seeing Remi giggling and Ma's dark eyes brighten.

Under the table, Nick gripped her thigh. His touch elicited an automatic shock. Down her spine it traveled as an electric reminder of his feelings for her. Likewise, her feelings for him. The happiness they had discovered in each other. She sent him a secret smile and he understood her intent. She couldn't wait until they got home later, and were finally alone.

"I squirted milk from my nose, like this," Maxie said, chugging juice for demonstrative purposes.

Nick cut in. "Kiddo, no! No nose juice squirting—not in Ms. Lacie's home anyway."

"I'm sure it's impressive," said Ma in fairness.

"No, it's not. It's gross!" Remi wrinkled her nose, a mirror image to Rosalie.

Everyone around the table laughed, recognizing the resemblance. The rest of dinner carried on, as the fuller they became the blither their mood. They indulged one of Ma's cherry pies and felt their bellies ache in fullness. Thoughts were shifting to calling it a night, but Rosalie's ringtone chimed louder than their voices.

"It's Clyde," she said, staring down at the caller ID.

Nick straightened in his chair. "What could he want at this hour?"

"You don't have to answer it," Ma said sternly. "He can call back at a normal hour tomorrow."

Rosalie scooted her chair back. "I'll answer. Just a few minutes. See why he's calling. Excuse me."

⚬∞⚬

On the porch, Rosalie paced its length. Crickets and other night bugs chirped in the shadows, the incessant noises disruptive enough. Then there was the beat of her own heart echoing in her ears. She ignored the outside noises and held the phone securely in her hand.

"What is it now, Clyde?"

He had left St. Aster more than a week ago. He hadn't said goodbye. Certainly hadn't asked about custody arrangements or child support for Remi. As promptly as he showed up, he vanished from town like a figment of their imaginations. Once again, she was left to glue together the pieces for Remi, explaining why Daddy didn't hug and kiss her first.

"I'm back in Bmore," he mumbled.

"That's great. I assumed that when you didn't call."

"You could've call—you know what? Never mind. I'm really not tryna argue."

Rosalie quit pacing and sighed. "Me neither. I'm *tired* of fighting. It's the only thing we did."

"We had good times."

"Sometimes. But we fought way more. You know that."

Clyde's breaths deepened over the phone. At first she assumed he was dragging a cigarette again, but soon realized he had swallowed some air. He was as stubborn as she was. He hated admitting wrongdoing. Another major problem in their marriage.

"Look, I called 'cuz we've gotta figure something out with Remi."

"I want you in her life."

"I wanna be in her life."

"Then you can't keep walking out of it, Clyde," Rosalie lectured. "It's confusing her. I need her to be able to rely on you."

"We've gotta get the courts involved. Make it official."

"Agreed."

"Maybe we can do summers."

"Remi would love to see you for summer vacation."

"And child support. She's mine. I owe it to her."

"The money for her would be a huge help. I couldn't afford to take her back-to-school shopping this year, so she's wearing last year's stuff. She's growing out of it."

"I can't do my baby like that. I'll transfer you some money for now."

Rosalie nodded to him, even if he couldn't see. "I'll let Remi know."

She hung up with her ex-husband feeling like it was the best conversation they'd had in a long while. They were no sooner to resolving their old marital issues. Clyde had yet to take responsibility for his cheating. He had yet to apologize or express regret over how profoundly it hurt her. In truth, he probably never would.

But that was okay. Clyde had agreed to be an active father to Remi. That was all she cared about. She no longer needed, nor wanted, his apology. She had moved on to bigger and better things. A bigger and better life. A future that was undoubtedly brighter.

CHAPTER TWENTY-EIGHT

"**P**apa, read us a bedtime story!"

Maxie and Remi wore their pajamas, hair plaited thanks to Rosalie. They had returned from Ms. Lacie's after 10:00 p.m. for another sleepover. Way past the girls' bedtime. Stuffed from the big dinner, they didn't protest getting ready for bed. He didn't need to ask Maxie to grab her things for her bath. She did it on her own. Same for Remi.

Into Maxie's room they raced to grab a Dr. Seuss book. Nick lifted his left brow, glancing to Rosalie.

"Who's going to bite the bullet?"

"You're kidding, right? I braided their hair. You're narrator."

"Point taken. You joining us for *Green Eggs and Ham* hour?"

Rosalie smiled and gave a nod.

The four found spots in Maxie's eclectic bedroom. Her twin-sized bed was covered in an emerald green comforter representing her fascination with Godzilla and her toy chest was a plastic rocket ship. On the wall were posters of her favorite Disney Princess, the red, curly haired girl who shot arrows. Her name escaped him. But he smirked sitting at the foot of her bed and cracking open the Dr. Seuss book.

His girl marched to the beat of her own drum. She had grown to like her hair neat when Rosalie styled it, but she also still appreciated dinosaurs and frogs. Her favorite color was green and she wanted to be a vampire next Halloween. Mom would laugh at the boldness of it all, and he took pride in that too.

Curled up on her beanbag by the window, Remi was a welcomed surprise for Maxie. The fellow kindergartener was a mini-Rosalie in looks, as heart-faced and curly-haired with a nose that scrunched up at any given moment. She balanced Maxie out. Her first real friend in her life. For that he was grateful.

Rosalie cuddled Remi until her lids couldn't stay up another second. Maxie was out not long after that. He read the last couple of pages in case they half listened and then kissed his kiddo on the forehead. Rosalie had lifted Remi into her arms to carry her to the guest room. The last thing Nick did on their way out was flick off the lights.

He smiled at Rosalie when his bedroom door opened and she slipped inside. He was waiting on her. His arms enveloped her smaller frame and she buried her face against his chest. They treasured their private moments at night. The days were spent focusing on the girls and the restaurant, but once alone, it was their time.

"We might need to think about getting your mom in as head chef."

Rosalie rolled her eyes. "I'm sure that'll work out. Sounds like a great idea."

"Better yet, let's make you head chef." He treated her to a sweet kiss, cradling her face in his hands. He couldn't wait until they slipped beneath the covers and spent the rest of the night together. Tomorrow they would sleep in. Another lazy Sunday morning. "You've mastered how many dishes now?"

"Oh? And what would that make you?"

Nick nuzzled her, letting his lips glide over her skin. "Busboy or something. I don't know."

Rosalie giggled as they inched to the bed, still tangled up in each other. Finally, he grew impatient and plucked her off her feet. She dug her head backward into the mattress unable to hold in another laugh. He was swooping in on top of her, planting kisses all over. Their play was just getting started.

"Busboy, huh? Wouldn't that put me in charge?"

He brushed a curl from her brow and his dimples emerged on his cheeks. "It's whatever you want, boss."

"I like the sound of that. Roll over."

Nick loved the sultry element to her voice and he obliged as asked. He rolled onto his back and Rosalie pinned him with her thighs. One on either side of him, he was in heaven. He lay back and looked up into her beautiful face, the blood in his veins circulating on a fast track to arousal. She planted her hands on his chest and teased him a smile.

"I think I like us being partners better."

"Anything sounds good as long as you keep sitting on me like this."

She convulsed with laughter and leaned forward for a warm kiss. "You've got your wish."

The next day they woke closer to noon than the morning. The girls yawned and dragged their fuzzy socked feet into the kitchen. Nick and Rosalie fared little better. They had spent the night in a lover's haze exploring each other's body. By the time they fell asleep, it was 3:00 a.m.

Now they were groggy messes in the kitchen. Their languid attempts at cooking breakfast were uncoordinated but amusing. Rosalie snickered when Nick burned the sausages.

"You're a professional chef. How do *you* burn sausages?"

Nick's grin spread across his face. "Because *somebody* kept me up all night. I'm exhausted."

"Who kept you up all night, Papa?" Maxie asked nosily.

"Did you have a nightmare?" Remi chimed in.

The two little girls stared up at them like curious puppies with their eyes shiny and heads tilted. Nick and Rosalie shared a small laugh at their expense and humored them. He explained how he was afraid of monsters under the bed just like they were.

"Wow," they gasped.

"Wow is right," agreed Rosalie. She poked him in the side upon passing him in the kitchen. "Maybe we need to buy your papa a night-light."

The girls began bouncing around in an impromptu chant. "Scaredy-cat! Scaredy-cat! Scaredy-cat!"

Nick took the jokes in stride. The large breakfast he cooked for them eventually served as a distraction. The girls nibbled on the sausage patties and crunched on the toast with jam. At one point he caught Maxie smearing jam onto her plate in the shape of a happy face.

"Your food's for eating, Maxie," Remi scolded snootily.

"Says who?"

"Says…says everybody!"

"Nuh-uh!"

The girls launched into a rare bickering match. Nick and Rosalie listened to the back-and-forth with hidden smirks from behind their coffee mugs, and then Nick put the kibosh on the quarrel. Just like that, the girls called a truce and chatted about playing with their hula-hoops.

Nick marveled at their uncanny ability to forget their disagreements at the drop of a hat. His phone vibrating in his pocket interrupted his thoughts. He assumed the caller was a scammer dialing his number to sell him a subscription to something, but the name Zoe was spelled across his screen. She only called when she was going to be a no-show at work. He answered before the next ring.

"Hey, Zoe. Everything okay at the restaurant?"

"Is everything okay at the restaurant?" she repeated against the backdrop of loud voices. The restaurant sounded as busy as it'd been since the festival. "Judging by that stupid question, I'm guessing you haven't seen the Sunday paper?"

Nick's brows creased and he rose out of his chair. "I'd have to read the Sunday paper first. Why, what's going on?"

"*The Tribune* wrote a piece on Ady's!"

"A piece on Ady's? Saying what?"

"You've gotta see for yourself! Google 'em—you can find the article on their website. Was a surprise to me when Mrs. Kettles brought in a copy!"

Nick hung up with Zoe and called up the internet browser on his phone. Rosalie had drunk the last of her coffee and poured a second serving. She hung by his side out of curiosity and asked him if everything was okay. He couldn't answer until he saw the article. The page loaded and the headline jumped out at him:

COMEBACK OF THE YEAR: THE REAL ADY'S CREOLE CAFÉ IS BACK

His mouth hung open and he read the title a second time. Rosalie peered at his phone and gasped. Her fingers gripped his arm and she rocked on the balls of her feet as if unable to contain the sudden excitement wanting to burst free. The article itself was a glowing review of how Ady's was making a full and unexpected comeback.

"I didn't know the *Tribune* was writing a piece on us," he said in a daze.

Rosalie squeezed his arm and shrieked, "Nick, we've done it! The whole town knows it. We've brought Ady's back."

The girls slid off their chairs and crowded around them to celebrate the good news. Though it took them a second longer to realize what that good news was, the instant they figured it out, they erupted in giddy cheers. Soon the entire kitchen exploded in a whole session of rejoicing how far Ady's had come in a few short weeks.

It felt validating to know the rest of the town, from the customers to the attendees at the Autumn Festival to the reporters for the *Tribune* newspaper, recognized this. They had worked their asses off, and it showed. Everybody knew and now it was declared in writing for everyone in St. Aster to see: Ady's was back.

Nick released a disbelieving but enthused laugh and ran his fingers through his wavy hair. Together they had saved Ady's. He had never thought it possible, especially weeks ago as he slouched in his desk chair and snored his afternoons away. The girls broke out into a little dance around the kitchen as Nick turned to Rosalie. She was already smiling at him.

"Thanks," he told her. "This was because of you. You motivated me. You pushed me to get here."

Rosalie slipped her arms around his neck and her mouth hovered over his. "Let's call it even. Thanks to you I no longer cook spaghetti from the jar."

EPILOGUE

One year later...

"**H**appy birthday, Maxie!"

The seven-year-old squeezed her eyes shut and blew out the candles on the purple and green King Cake. The dining room of Ady's Creole Café filled with hoots and hollers from the party guests. Though no one knew what wish she made, it must've been a good one. Maxie beamed and bounced on the spot in her Yoshi dinosaur costume.

She wasn't alone in being dressed up for the occasion. The biggest rule of the day was to come in costume to celebrate the birthday festivities. Half of Remi and Maxie's first grade class showed up with their parents in tow, along with their staff and best regulars. Everybody from Mrs. Kettles to Zoe and Que wore a costume and cheered for Maxie blowing out the candles on her cake. Nick stepped in and began cutting slices. The first and fattest slice he handed to Maxie.

"All yours, kiddo."

He chuckled watching her eyes bulge and face shine with delight.

The rest of the dining area devolved into a noisy frenzy as partygoers queued up along the potluck-style tables and piled food onto their plates. As always, the first thing to go was Rosalie's gumbo. Over the last year it had earned a reputation about town as the best gumbo ever tasted.

Rosalie hung in the background and admired the festivities. Remi and Maxie found seats by Ellie and went to work on their cake. The girls looked adorable, total opposites in their costumes. While Maxie was the green dinosaur Yoshi, Remi opted for the delicate and prim Princess Peach.

It had worked out perfectly. Rosalie smoothed her fake mustache above her lip and hid her smirk behind it. She planned on taking plenty of photos of the four of them in their themed costumes and hanging them up on the walls at home. Maybe even the walls at Ady's. Nick and the girls complained about the pictures she took, but she made them pose anyway. They were memories of the good times.

These days, there were plenty of them.

Ady's Creole Café saw the level of success it experienced decades ago when Adeline Fontaine first opened for business. On a daily basis the tables filled up and the costumers gorged on the items off their delectable menu. Jefferson still handled the kitchen duties, but it was under Nick and Rosalie's supervision. Every once in a while, on days Jefferson was off or out sick, Nick took the reins himself. And sometimes, she did too.

She had come to love cooking, holding an appreciation for the culinary arts. She had learned how to cook every dish and more thanks to Nick's tutelage. He had learned the finer points of running a business thanks to her fiscal savviness. Instead of financial ruin, Ady's was raking in the dough. The equal trade-off only demonstrated how great they were as partners.

When she thought back to a year ago, arriving in St. Aster with five dollars and sixty-two cents in her checking account, she couldn't believe how far she had come. Once the miserable, ashamed divorced single mother struggling to make ends meet, she was an entirely different woman now.

For the first time in her life, Rosalie was standing on her own two feet. She wasn't a failure. She was succeeding. She persevered through the tough times and emerged from the other side better for it. Now her days were filled with running Ady's like clockwork as its manager. In the evenings, she enjoyed life alongside the people who mattered most to her.

The people who were in this room. Her eyes landed on her precious Remi, who swallowed a bite of cake and then beamed across the room at her. Then Maxie, the rambunctious birthday girl already with a mess of her cake frosting on her chin. Ma appeared at both of their sides, dressed in her witch costume, and handed the girls napkins.

In the past, Rosalie's stomach would've twisted in knots at the sight of Ma. These days, she felt like their issues were further and further behind them. Their relationship wasn't perfect by any means, but they both worked toward making it better. Ma frequented the restaurant and Rosalie brought Remi over every week to spend quality time with her grandmommy.

"What's that smirk for?" Zoe asked, sidling up with a plate of food of her own. For the party, she was a pirate wench, complete with leather boots and eyepatch. She followed Rosalie's gaze and nodded. "The girls look cute as hell. But what are y'all supposed to be?"

Rosalie's brow rose and she gestured to her blue overalls and red undershirt. "Are you serious? Didn't you see Nick's costume? Mine? The mustaches?"

"I did, and y'all look ridiculous," teased Zoe. Her dye-job red hair swung with a shake of her head.

"You're hopeless." Rosalie left her teasing coworker-turned-friend and crossed the room. Nick had finished cutting cake slices for everyone at the party and had finally cut his own. He sensed her approaching and looked up with his cheeks dimpling. His matching fake jet-black mustache looked ridiculous on him, in direct contrast with his golden-brown hair. She loved that about him; he wasn't afraid of looking a fool if it made the girls happy.

"Hey, Mario," he greeted. He held up the plate of cake for her to take. "I cut you a slice."

She smiled brightly. "I never knew Luigi was so thoughtful. Thanks."

"I never knew Mario was so hot."

He swooped in and kissed her on the lips. Their fuzzy mustaches made the kiss awkward but funny, and she broke away unable to contain a giggle. Only Nick would call her hot as she wore a thick mustache and baggy overalls. He had been more ecstatic than the girls about their group Halloween costumes.

"We should take a picture," said Rosalie. "I want one of the four of us for the house."

"Stay here. I'll go grab the girls," said Nick.

He walked over to the table where the girls were seated. Rosalie noticed the three conferring with each other, leaning in as if to form an impromptu huddle. She wanted to ask what they needed to discuss if they were taking a picture of their costumes. But the noise in the dining room was too loud. The other partygoers grubbed on their plates of food and chatted away.

Soon Nick returned with Remi and Maxie on either side. The trio looked downright mischievous with expressions that featured little smirks and shiny eyes. Rosalie gave off a confused laugh and tried to figure out what joke she was missing out on. Instead Nick turned to Ma and asked if she could take their picture.

The foursome arranged themselves like they always did when they snapped pictures together. Nick and Rosalie stood side by side with his arm around her waist. The girls in front of them posed with tongues out and bunny ears up for the camera. Rosalie smiled, her top lip hidden by the fuzzy fake mustache, but the way her cheeks curved, she knew it would be obvious how happy was.

"Everybody say cheese!" called Ma, holding up the phone for the photo.

"Cheese!" Remi and Maxie chorused.

Rosalie added her voice too, but noticed Nick's deeper timbre was missing. She glanced to her right to check on him and then noticed he had dropped down to one knee. The shock hit her like a splash of ice-cold water. She stepped back and hit the wall without even thinking about it, her hand on her heart in absolute surprise. Her mouth opened and closed, but no discernible sound came out.

Nick grinned and popped open a tiny box from which inside a diamond ring gleamed. The girls shimmied on the spot as if about to burst with giggles and cheers at any second. From behind the camera phone, Ma was smiling too, and it was then that Rosalie realized it was on record. She glanced around the room and noticed all eyes on her and Nick.

"Rosalie—or should I say Mario?" he teased with soft amusement coloring his tone. "You make me feel like I'm the luckiest guy in town—the luckiest guy on this planet. Since you came to St. Aster, I don't think I've stopped smiling. I know I haven't stopped wanting to make you smile. I'd be honored if you let me keep it up—for the rest of our lives. Will you marry me?"

She was speechless, overcome by the unexpected moment. Still no words came out when she tried, but the tears that brimmed in her eyes spoke for her. The cold shock wore off, replaced by the deep warmth of her love for Nick. The love for him she found when at the lowest low of her life. The love for him that had grown every day since.

"Yes," she finally choked out, nodding.

If the party had been loud earlier, it was deafening now. The entire room erupted in zealous applause for the happy couple. Nick slipped the ring on her shaky hand and rose to full height to pull her into his arms. His grin had gone nowhere, plastered across his face in absolute bliss.

"I'm glad you said yes," he confessed. "I was so nervous I was sweating my mustache off."

It was such a Nick thing to say, Rosalie could only laugh. Fake, fuzzy mustaches be damned, she leaned on tiptoe and kissed him sweetly on the mouth. In celebration of their engagement, and celebration of Maxie's birthday, but most of all, in celebration for the happiness they had found together.

THE END

I would like to thank you from the bottom of my heart for spending time in my fictional world. I hope you enjoyed the read. If you have a free second…

1. Please help others discover *Love's Recipe* by leaving a review on Amazon - .
https://www.amazon.com/dp/B0851P4NGW

2. Check out my website: www.milanickswrites.com

3. Sign up for my newsletter https://www.milanickswrites.com/subscribe so you can find out about my upcoming releases as well as any giveaways and story extras.

4. Follow me on social media:
Twitter: https://twitter.com/mila_nicks
Instagram: https://www.instagram.com/milanickswrites/

Keep reading for an exclusive sneak peek of my upcoming series *Wild, Dark Horses*.

WILD, DARK HORSES

Coming Summer 2020

Exclusive Preview

PROLOGUE

April 1965 - Lutton, Texas

For the fifth time that afternoon, Bucky Ward walked up to the record player and reset the needle on the vinyl. The music started at once, filling up the living room wall to wall. He turned around to find Bunny smiling at him.

He husked out a chuckle. "One more can't hurt, can it?"

"We have time."

"Twenty-three more minutes time. Not that I'm counting. Only that I am."

They met halfway in the living room, right on the spot where the coffee table usually was. Bucky had moved it out of the way along with some of the other furniture. They needed as much room as possible for their afternoon dance party for two.

He loved watching Bunny dance. He had been to nightclubs from the east coast to the west coast in his day; even ones overseas during his time in the Army. But he had never seen anything like Bunny. Nobody danced like she did. Every move, every step was fluid, flowing in perfect sync with the beat. She moved with a sprite energy that was contagious. That had him grinning like an idiot and not giving a single damn about it. How could he when he had the most gorgeous gal in Texas—no, in the world—in his arms?

They danced 'til they were breathless, like always. Bucky reeled her close, hooking an arm around her waist and clasping her hand in his. Her deep-set eyes shone like onyx stones caught in the light as she looked up at him. His heart beat hard against his chest from more than just the dancing. She had that kind of instantaneous effect on him. One look, one smile from her, and he was a goner.

My Girl by the Temptations played. They swayed to the song as if it were the first time. The lyrics were poetry to their ears, bringing them closer together. Her body pressed flush against his and his grip tightened on her waist. She closed her eyes and laid her head on his shoulder, at rest in his embrace as the song's last chords hit. He savored the feel of holding her this close and avoided staring at the grandfather clock in the corner of the room.

Ten more minutes...

The song came to an end and they broke apart. Bunny picked up the TV Guide off the mantle and fanned herself. Her dark brown skin was dewy from all of their dancing. Only she managed to look more radiant when hot and out of breath. He looked a mess, skin flushed pink. He used his sand t-shirt to wipe sweat off his brow. He had a 1500 report time, but what if he bought another thirty minutes? What if he came up with a reason to stay a little bit longer? A stream of different excuses filtered through his head.

"Sweet tea? One last time?" Bunny asked, tossing the TV Guide onto the couch. She might not have realized it, but there was a skip in her voice. There was glass in her eyes, tears that looked ready to fall at any second.

His own throat developed an ache. His ears picked up every tick of that clock. "That'd be nice. We worked up a sweat."

She disappeared from the room and he heaved a difficult sigh. The separation was temporary. Soon he would return from deployment and they'd pick right up where they left off. So long as he kept that in mind, their time apart would be easier. They had already promised to write each other every chance they had.

Bucky didn't know how long Bunny stood in the doorway watching him, but when he felt her eyes on him, he looked over. She stood holding a tray of ice-cold sweet tea and some of her famous chocolate chip cookies. He offered a half-hearted smile, his attempt to cheer her up. He failed and that weighed on him.

"In case you're hungry," she said, setting down the tray. "Listen, Bucky, you should keep this with you. Something to remember me."

The ache in his throat only worsened watching her reach up and unclasp her necklace. The diamond pendant he had bought her to celebrate their relationship. She turned over his hand palm side up and dropped the necklace in it. Her fingers curled over his as she eased his palm into a fist. He tried to swallow but the ache was too much.

"I'm gonna be back."

The corner of her lips twitched as if she wished she could smile. "I know that. I can't wait."

"And we're gonna be together. We'll find somewhere for us—somewhere we can *really* be together."

Bunny didn't get a chance to answer him. The doorbell chimed throughout the house. Their heads snapped in the direction of the front door. For a second as the last chime of the doorbell echoed they considered their next step. They settled on what they usually did. Bucky grabbed his uniform hat and jacket and slipped off down the hall. Bunny fluffed her barrel curls and checked the mirror for any clothing out of place before she answered the door.

It was his sister, Jolene.

Her hello to Bunny was a narrow-eyed glare. "Where is he?"

"Where is who?" Bunny had perfected how to play off cluelessness. She had the knitted brow, soft voice and frown down pat.

"You know who. These are his last moments before he's shipped off to hell, and what's he up to? He's with *you*."

"Jo, I have no—"

"Jolene. You call me Jolene. Let's get that straight right now, *girl*."

Bucky's teeth clenched as he eavesdropped from the hall. Never mind that Jo was only two years older than Bunny, she had no right to disrespect her like she did. He clamped down on the rush of anger overtaking him. He had to or else risk making a scene at the worst possible time. They had done so well keeping things under wraps. He couldn't blow their cover on his last day in town. What about Bunny and the aftermath she'd endure?

The door thudded shut and Bunny returned to him down the hall. If she had looked sullen earlier, she looked flat-out worn-down now. Her blinks were frequent and she kept taking in deeper and deeper breaths. He reached for her, cuddling her to him.

"I'm so sorry," he whispered. "I had no idea she'd turn up. I told 'em I'd be leaving at noon. They must've found out bag drop is really at three."

"It's…It's not that." Bunny buried her face into his chest. The wet moisture of her tears soon dampened the fabric. She inhaled another one of those deep, shuddery breaths. "I don't know how to say goodbye to you."

"Shhh. It's not goodbye." He gently gripped her chin so that she'd look up at him. In her dark brown eyes now glossed over with tears, he saw himself. He was no better, pale skin splotchy and red and heavy brow creased. It dawned on him he wasn't just seeking to comfort her; he was hoping to soothe himself as well. The disquiet in his heart was louder now than ever. "It's never gonna be goodbye between me and you. Understand?"

Tears slid down the swell of her cheeks. She nodded. "I hear Antarctica's warm in the summer time."

His laugh emerged despite the moment's sadness. "Antarctica it is if it means we get to be together."

The pendulum in the grandfather clock struck hard, reverberating as a harsh gong noise throughout the house. It was the top of the hour. It was time to go. Time for them to say goodbye at least for now.

Bucky planted a heartfelt kiss on Bunny's lips. They tasted salty from her tears. He didn't care as he memorized every touch, every scent, every single sight of her. He'd need them for the long, dark road ahead. Bunny was shaking by the time their kiss ended. He wiped away what tears he could with his thumbs and lingered a second longer for a last look at her.

"It's gonna be okay. We're gonna make it through this." he whispered. "I promise."

"Stay safe, Bucky. Please."

He forced himself not to look back once he started walking away. He buttoned on his uniform jacket, tossed on his hat and slid his sunglasses onto his face. He swallowed against the ache of his sore throat and strode for the door.

At the time Bucky didn't know it, but that moment was their last like that. Things were never the same again.

CHAPTER ONE

April 2005 - Lutton, Texas

A week in Lutton tops. Samara Grant leaned against the diner countertop and sighed, dreading the seven days ahead. If she had her way, she would be on a beach somewhere, lying under the hot sun as she sipped a Mai Tai. Instead, she was miles outside the small Texan town doomed to spend the next week sorting out Bunny's affairs.

Her chest tightened thinking about Grandma Bunny. They hadn't talked in years. For no other reason beside Samara always being busy. Always being gone. The last time had been when she was eighteen and freshly out of high school. On the cusp of the freedom adulthood gave her, she had left for college with the intention of never looking back.

Only forward.

For the last seven years, she had succeeded. She was a woman without a past. A woman who came and went as she pleased, hanging around for no one and no thing. She liked it that way. It was simpler that way. Less complicated. Easier to leave without anyone noticing, and most importantly, anyone *caring*.

Samara was the last person who should have been back in Lutton. The absolute worst person to be in charge of handling Bunny's final arrangements. But Mother had insisted. She had pressured until Samara's hand was forced and she gave in. Now, here she was stuck driving cross-country to Lutton, Texas where Bunny lived the bulk of her sixty-eight years.

Her burger and fries were cold, but Samara picked at the food anyway. She dunked a French fry in her chocolate malt shake and stared up at the staticky TV screen mounted to the wall. Originally, the stop at Dot's Diner was only supposed to be for to-go food. Jamari insisted they take a break from the road and dine in. She agreed, if only because deep down she hoped to stall her return to Lutton. Once there, things were real.

There would be no more avoiding Bunny's passing.

Out the corner of her eye, Samara sensed someone staring. She ignored the heavy stare at first, but the more seconds passed by, the more the man's stare persisted. He was old—late sixties to early seventies kind of old—and he had thick bifocals that magnified his hazel eyes to three times their usual size. His gray hair was combed neatly with a side part and he wore the kind of suspenders and button shirt that were dressy for a diner. Was he coming from church? More importantly, *why* was he staring?

Samara's instincts kicked in and she stared back. At first blankly, but that only seemed to encourage him. His sallow-cheeked face lit up and he winked at her. He used his walking cane as a crutch rising out of his booth and trudged over. He had to be coming to talk to someone else. She had no clue who this man was.

"I thought that was you," he tittered in a folksy, guttural tone that even *sounded* old. "How about some sugar?"

Samara leapt off her stool before he was within reach. "I don't know who you are, but if you touch me, grandpa, you'll regret it."

"Oh, c'mon. Don't you recognize me, honey?"

"Honey? What kind of weird game are you playing? Get away from me!"

"Hey!" Jamari exclaimed, emerging from the men's restroom. Never mind that he had toilet paper stuck to the bottom of his sneaker, he slipped into overprotective mode like when they were kids. He cut between Samara and the old man. "You heard her! Why don't you leave my sister alone, creep?"

"Creep? Who's a creep? I was only asking honey for some sugar—"

"My sister's *not* your honey!"

"Folks, everybody calm down," interjected the waitress, joining the fray. She wrapped gentle hands around the old man and guided him back to his booth. "Please disregard him. Ol' Will here gets a little ahead of himself."

Samara put her hands on her hips. "I'll say. He seemed to know exactly what he wanted."

"You two must not be from around here. Will's a regular. Everybody knows he's senile," the waitress whispered once confident he was out of earshot. "Sorry about the hubbub. How about a free slice of pie to make up for it?"

"Pie?" Jamari perked up at once. "Been saving room for some!"

Another thirty minutes later, Samara and Jamari sat in her burnt red Jeep Wrangler stuffed from the free slice of coconut cream pie. Jamari rolled down the window, stuck his head out, and belched. Samara glared and he laughed.

"Sorry, sis. That food was bomb."

"Just make sure *the bomb* doesn't go off in the car, got it?"

"Who pulls over to fart? Seriously?"

"Better than smelling your nuclear gas," she retorted with a snort. They hit the highway again, a mere ten miles outside of Lutton's borders. Minutes of uncertain silence passed. Neither one knew what to say. Samara racked her brain and came up short. She settled on small talk about the weather. "Forgot how hot it gets here. Even in April."

Jamari rolled his eyes. "That's what you're going with?"

"Am I supposed to get what that means?"

"You don't know what else to say, so we're talking about the weather? Like some strangers in an elevator?"

"All I said was it was hot. That's a problem?"

"You know what? Forget it. Forgot we *are* strangers." He slumped in his seat, knees far apart, and stared hard out of the window.

Samara wanted to say something. Explain herself and her absence for what was easily the fifth or sixth time. But she didn't bother. She fell silent and focused on the roads ahead, deciding that if he wanted to be stubborn, she could be stubborn, too.

That only lasted so long. Her Jeep sped down the highway as steadily as ever, along the flat and sunny, dry Texas landscape. She cut him a couple sideways glances before she huffed out a sigh and extended an olive branch.

"Look," she said, eyes still stuck on the road, "how many times do I have to say I'm sorry?"

Jamari didn't answer. She bit the inside of her cheek and held back the urge to lash out.

The next couple of miles flew by. Soon the 'Welcome to Lutton' sign greeted them from the shoulder of the road.

"Can't believe Bunny's gone," mused Jamari suddenly. He couldn't stand the silence any longer than she could. Unlike her, he didn't hold grudges for long. "I thought she'd live to be 100."

Samara slowly smirked. "Me too."

"You know those crazy old ladies who park their boat car sideways and take up like three spots? The same ones who steal forks from Applebee's? I thought that'd be Bunny."

The two of them shared their first real laugh in hours.

"Are you kidding? That was *already* Bunny."

"Remember that time she competed in that hot wings contest and won?"

"Or when she convinced you she was Santa Claus in disguise?"

"I was six."

"You believed her 'til you were *eleven*."

That shut Jamari up. He couldn't think up a rebuttal and his silence was his defeat. Samara snickered spotting the pouty look on his face.

"Cheer up, buttercup," she said, pointing at the quaint buildings lining the streets. "We're here."

It was always hard for Samara to believe Bunny was happy in a town as boring as Lutton. Bunny's personality—*her mere presence*—was larger than life. What was she doing in some rinky-dink no-name town? What in said rinky-dink no-name town could have possibly made her happy?

The Jeep rolled to a halt outside Bunny's Bed & Breakfast. The two-story home with its preened garden and giant bay windows was a childhood staple. The lemon-yellow paint was as fresh and vibrant as when they were kids in the summertime. Bunny's favorite color, she always said yellow could cheer someone up even on the cloudiest day.

On the front stoop were candles and bouquets of flowers. Even framed photographs of Bunny propped against the step. Others in Lutton must have left them to honor her. Samara and Jamari eased around the memorabilia, careful not to knock anything over. The door itself was half-ajar, the din of a dozen voices spilling outside.

"Wait," said Jamari, touching her arm. "Gimme a sec."

"A sec for *what*?"

"Shit just got real. We're here, Sam."

"What did you think was happening when we drove the nineteen hours to get here?"

"I know, just didn't expect it to feel like this." Jamari trailed off in a mumble and dipped his eyes to the pavement, where Bunny's photographs lay.

Samara frowned. She was the worst at consoling people. Even her little bro. "Jam, it's going to be okay. We'll get through this together, alright? Me and you just like before."

"And no mom?"

"*No* mom," she said, scrunching her nose.

"That makes me feel better. She's still pissed with me."

"Don't worry about that now. You know mom—pissed is the only mood she knows."

Their laugh eased the heaviness anchored in their stomachs. Samara prodded the door all the way open and took in the sight of the foyer. No wonder the mishmash of voices had been so loud. A brigade of Bunny's friends lingered in the foyer, mourning and chatting together. Everyone was at least sixty and over.

The second they spotted Samara and Jamari in the doorway, the old folks dropped whatever the topic of conversation was. They formed a strategic circle around the siblings like an elderly street gang. Fawning ensued as they poked, prodded and pinched Bunny's two grandkids they hadn't seen since childhood.

It didn't matter that Samara was twenty-five and Jamari was twenty-one. In their squinting, blind as a bat eyes, the two were still younging's. Samara politely played along. Jamari not so much.

"Bunny was right. You are a spitting image of her!" Ms. Klum sobbed into her handkerchief. "Last time I saw you, you couldn't've been more than fifteen. My, how the time passes by. You're a woman now. Your hair…it's so…so…interesting…"

Samara cringed at her clueless ignorance. Ms. Klum's baffled stare was like being under a microscope.

Elsewhere, Jamari suffered through an awkward exchange with a woman named Janice Sorensen. She eyed him from top to bottom, sizing him up. "How tall are you? You're so handsome. Now, my granddaughter, she's a bit on the thicker side, but she's a total sweetheart…"

It was with relief that Samara and Jamari bid farewell to the crew several minutes later. Jamari strode up to the front door and twisted the lock.

"So they can't get back in," he murmured.

"Oh, c'mon," Samara said, a hand on her waist, "they weren't that bad. Especially Mr. McKenzie."

"If you like the stench of Bengay…"

"Shut up and be nice." She shoved him as she gave off a small laugh.

"But Ms. Klum though. Pretty funny hearing her describe your hair."

"She's probably never seen a box braid in her life."

"It wouldn't surprise me if Bunny's the only black person she's ever met," said Jamari with a hapless shrug.

"You Samara and Jamari?"

Samara turned around to face the B&B's front desk. The door behind it was now wide open. A woman had emerged from the back office. She shook her shaggy brown fringe out of her eyes and extended her hand for a shake.

"I'm Lea. I always hide in the office when the oldies come around. They love coming by to drop off flowers."

"Hi, Lea…" Samara made little effort to hide her confusion. Her brows pushed together and her blinks at Lea were slow and dragged out. "Sorry, but what are you doing here?"

"I'm the head receptionist—well, the *only* receptionist. Bunny gave me the title anyway."

"Sounds like Bunny. I'm Jamari." Jamari jutted his chin as a substitute for a wave hello.

Lea grinned switching her gaze from brother to sister and back again. "So y'all are the famous Sam and Jam. I've heard all about you from Bunny. She loved bragging about her grandbabies. How's law school?"

Samara's smile faltered. "Law school is on hold right now. Indefinitely."

"Ah, gotcha. Sorry for bringing it up. Well, welcome!" said Lea with a full-steam ahead speed to her words. "You're probably already tired of this place—some say it smells too much like shit with all the farms and ranches—but I'm happy to have you either way. How long you staying for? Funeral's next Sunday, right?"

"Sunday," Samara and Jamari answered as a unit.

Lea laughed. "Don't blame you one bit. But you're a whole week early?"

"We're here early to handle Bunny's private affairs," explained Samara. "Our mother is a workaholic and couldn't spare more time off work."

"Gotcha. Need me to show you around?"

Jamari piped up. "We got it. Spent one too many summers here."

"Course you did. Bunny mentioned that too. Said she loved those summers. The place isn't the same without her. She was my boss, but sometimes she felt like my granny too."

"I'm willing to bet a lot of people feel that way about Bunny," said Samara reminiscently. Lea's comment warmed her heart.

"Too true. Anyway, I'm off shift in another couple hours. We've only got 2 guests checked in right now. Y'all up for a night out later?"

Samara and Jamari glanced at one another. Jamari mumbled something about the luggage in the Jeep and excused himself from the conversation. Lea quirked a brow in obvious question.

"We're both pretty exhausted from the drive. We're probably going to hang out in our rooms," said Samara. "But thanks for the offer."

"Here's my number." Lea scribbled her info on a notepad and tore off the sheet. "In case."

"Right. In case."

"There's plenty of food in the kitchen if you're hungry."

Jamari returned hauling a suitcase under each arm. He dropped them at his feet and wiped sweat off his brow. Samara teased him a small smile.

"Looks like we're cooking dinner for ourselves."

His jaw dropped. "Sam, stop playing. Your cooking *sucks*."

⁂

That night after a generously long and hot shower, Samara shut the door to Bunny's bedroom. The decor was like traveling a couple decades backward in time. The furniture was burly oak and the floral patterns on the bedspread and on the walls were eyesores. Samara chalked it up to Bunny's age and plopped down in the armchair in the corner. Outside the second-story window, the town was startlingly dark. Few lights lit up the black landscape. She checked the time. It wasn't even 9 p.m.

For the second time that day, Samara wondered how Bunny had possibly been happy here. Some streets were missing stoplights and they only had one grocery store. The internet connection loaded at a pace that made a turtle look fast. A quarter of the town was over fifty-five and they drove large boats for cars. She wouldn't be caught dead living in a place like Lutton.

It might have held a novelty during her childhood summers, but now? No amount of sprinkler-running and ice cream trucks could mask the cold, hard truth: Lutton was a bummy town that nobody would miss if it suddenly fell off the map.

Samara opened her journal to a fresh page and scribbled the date on the top corner.

April 18th, 2005

So today was interesting. Drove the last leg to Bunny's. We made it, but Jamari started being an ass again toward the end. I know it's my fault. I have to find a way to make things up to him. Just wish he would try to see my side more. At least we decided to work together handling Bunny's affairs. We don't need mom.

As for Lutton, it's...different. Same place as before, but as a grown ass woman, it's torture. I already feel suffocated. I'm already plotting the next time I can hop on a plane to ANYWHERE but here. I don't know how Bunny spent decades trapped in this town.

At least everybody's been welcoming. Except there was this old man at a din

Samara drug her pen on the paper several times but no ink came out. She sighed and tossed the useless pen into the wastebasket. Her search for another turned up less results than anticipated. The one in her purse was missing. She checked the drawers, uncovering things like medication, sewing kits, socks—lots and lots of socks—and photo albums.

But no pen. The photo albums at least distracted her. She smiled, splaying one open in her lap. The next few minutes passed with her flipping through the pages and reliving classic family moments. It had been so long since she had fondly thought back on the good times they shared, however few and far between.

She was about to return the album to its rightful place in the drawer when she noticed another book in the corner. It was leather-bound, a rich cognac in shade, with a yellow ribbon poking out between the pages. She connected the dots almost immediately.

Bunny kept a journal too. For some inexplicable reason that revelation surprised her. She clutched the cognac book in both hands, studying its glossy logo and wondered what sort of things would Bunny have written about. Though curiosity cloaked over her, it felt wrong to invade Bunny's privacy in that manner.

Samara eased the book open at the same second a sharp knock sounded on the door. The abrupt noise startled her, causing her to jump and drop the journal. She scooped it up and stuffed it under pillows on the bed. The door fell open and none other than Lea poked her head inside.

"Hey, sorry to disturb you."

"I thought you were already off shift?" Samara was breathless, feeling like she had been caught with her hand in the cookie jar.

"I'm off now. I was about to go, but just couldn't bring myself to."

"Lea, what are you talking about?"

"Put your best denim on," said the overtalkative receptionist. She grinned, fringy bangs in her eyes. "I don't care what you say—I'm gonna show you a night out in Lutton. You ready to go have some fun?"

Printed in Great Britain
by Amazon

LOVE'S RECIPE

MILA NICKS

First paperback edition May 2020

Book cover design by Red Leaf Design
Formatting by Polgarus Studio